X

By the Author

Punk Like Me

Punk and Zen

Red Light

American Goth

X

Sakura Gun (London)

Sakura Gun

Visit us at www.boldstrokesbooks.com

What Reviewers Say About the Author

X

"As always, JD Glass delivers an irresistible gem. *X* is a provocative thriller with all the right ingredients: chilling suspense, adventure, high tech conspiracy, madness, surfing, and love. The plot effortlessly zips along. Amidst it all, JD deftly weaves a poignant love story that drives straight to the heart of the reader. Do not deny yourself *X*! It guarantees a riveting ride." —JLee Meyer, author of *Forever Found, First Instinct, Rising Storm*, and *Hotel Liaison*

"JD Glass has done it again! *X* is not a book for the fainthearted or intellectually lazy. While the sex is hot, the characters are multi-dimensional and complex. What is fascinating about *X* is its implications in the broader context of gender and power within queer culture and deserves serious attention. It is complicated, intense, and a chilling schema of where the soul of America has gone to. Hold on to your dreams, because *X* is one hell of a nightmare ride." —Merry Gangemi, Host of *Woman-Stirred Radio*

"A *Brave New World* for the cyberpunk generation, J.D. Glass's smart and forward-thinking new novel, *X*, has all the hallmarks of a modern-day classic. Skillfully weaving together spellbinding suspense, romance, political intrigue, and the intricacies of our technological society, *X* is smart, thought-provoking, and a cautionary tale for the 21st century." —Rick R. Reed, author of *IM, Deadly Vision*, and *Orientation*

American Goth

"*American Goth* is…an alchemical reaction of ink, paper and intent, forged in the mind of a writer to tell a tale of a quest, of a destiny, of the life of a woman….J.D. Glass combines the tension of a young woman grasping at her chance to make a life after tragedy and to rebuild herself and her emotional stability with unfamiliar (to her) surroundings, people and rites. Glass's blend of music, ritual and sex forms a bond of its own, as we find ourselves drawn into Samantha's life, her quest and her growth….Less hard-edged than Glass's previous novel, *Red Light*, this novel is no less edgy. Like a piece of Celtic knotwork, the reader will be following multiple threads through many connections, until the whole resolves itself into a powerful and exquisitely detailed pattern." — Erica Friedman, author of *Shoujoai ni Bouken: The Adventures of Yuriko*

"…Fast-paced and unapologetic, Glass's novel is equal parts esoteric thriller, coming of age story, and expertly crafted, gender-bending queer erotica. Its protagonist is refreshingly unconflicted about her sexuality, and even gender exploration is treated with a frankness that belies the author's unstated assumption that her readers are sophisticated enough to have moved beyond the need for "coming out" angst…devoted Glass fans will no doubt read into the mystery surrounding the disappearance of Sam's lost love. Could she be the same Nina that appears in Glass's other novels, *Punk Like Me* and *Punk and Zen*? Glass isn't telling. At least, not yet." — Courtney Arnold, *Foreword Magazine*

Punk Like Me

"*Punk Like Me*...is different. It is engaging. It is life-affirming. Frankly, it is genius....This is our future standing tall and, most of the time, alone, and this is the impact of this story. At a minimum it compels us to listen and to remember. Glass wants us to take notice...This is a rare book in that it has a soul; one that is laid bare for all to see. We owe it to ourselves to read this book, but more importantly, we owe it to our future." — *Just About Write*

"Powerfully written by a gifted author in the first person point of view, *Punk Like Me* is an intimate glimpse inside a cool 'dude's' head....Glass makes it fresh, makes it real, and gets to the heart of the matter where there is nothing left but truth....Speaks to lesbians of any age but straights will love Nina too. This important novel should be required reading in high schools across the country, especially religious schools, since teaching tolerance should be part of every curriculum. Although adolescents will love it, this is not a young adult novel, but rather a mature account of an admirable woman who stands up for herself. It is truly inspiring." — *Midwest Book Review*

Punk and Zen

"Glass has done a nice job exploring Nina's 'coming of age' story with a timeless quality that will hit a chord with most readers...This is not a lighthearted story but one told with soul that has the right combination of angst and spirit to engage the reader." — *Lambda Book Report*

Red Light

"...Glass constructs a well-researched world around the fierce desires of her damsels....Emotional thrills, medical chills, erotic interludes, and sweet romance: this page-turner has spirit to spare." — *QSyndicate*

"...Glass has created her own formula as a storyteller that is in your face gutsy and down to earth....She knows what she is writing about, and better than that, she communicates it beautifully in novel form....She tells it to us straight from the gut and heart....Glass continually does what few authors can do well—write in the first person and still let us know what all of the characters are thinking and feeling....Red Light is definitely a must read." — *Just About Write*

"Whether you're looking for a sexy book with a plot that holds together, or a good book about a good character, with some romance and passion, then this book will definitely be worth adding to your 'to read' pile." — Erica Friedman, President, ALC Publishing

X

by

JD Glass

2009

ISBN 10: 1-60282-048-1
ISBN 13: 978-1-60282-048-7

This Trade Paperback Original Is Published By
Bold Strokes Books, Inc.
P.O. Box 249
Valley Falls, NY 12185

First Edition: February 2009

Credits

Editors: Ruth Sternglantz and Stacia Seaman
Production Design: Stacia Seaman
Cover Design By Sheri (graphicartist2020@hotmail.com)

Acknowledgments

Beta Readers: Cheryl Craig; Dr. Cait Cody, MD; Eva; Jeanine Hoffman; Jenny; Paula Tighe, Esquire; Dawn Vincent, Sys Op Manager. Thank you for your tremendous patience and careful feedback during the creation of this book.

Special thanks to Commander DJ Glass, USN, and to Erica Friedman.

To the publisher and editorial staff of Bold Strokes Books, my gratitude always for the opportunities and the lessons learned.

And Ruth? I love your mind.

Dedication

For everyone, always.

Dave the Rave…I love you. Thank you. Can we go surfing
now? And no hammerheads this time, 'kay? That kinda sucked.
Shane…nothing would happen without you. *Te adoro*.

In the councils of government, we must guard against the acquisition of unwarranted influence, whether sought or unsought, by the military-industrial complex. The potential for the disastrous rise of misplaced power exists and will persist.
                              —Dwight D. Eisenhower, 1961

DRAFT

SECRET

SENSITIVE

To:	The Secretary
From:	CLASSIFIED
Date:	XX/XX/XX
Topic:	ROMELLO

Jason:
Please have the
following checked for
accuracy—fill in any
minor points or missing
facts. Michelle wants
to assure the Secretary
that the memo has your
full concurrence.
Sandy

The following is an excerpt from the first direct communication (apart from the manifesto that arrived four weeks ago). Herein he has made references to specific operations:

A Letter to the Wolves:
    Let me begin, as many things should, with a quote by no less a personage than Isaac Asimov: "The advance of genetic engineering makes it quite conceivable that we will begin to design our own evolutionary progress."
    You know what I'm talking about; I know what you've done. Because I'm an honorable, ethical man despite your best attempts, I give fair notice: I will use them—quite deservedly—against you. This is inevitable. Survival of the fittest means survival of the best. You are most assuredly not that. Darwinism has come to eat you. Call it EuGenX, if you like.

There is in fact more (addendum to follow), but it is obvious that the situation is no longer quite as contained as originally hoped. Responses now include fighting fire with fire: the assembled outer field operatives will include agents with the strongest "I" designation. This team will be on a need-to-know footing and are being given the strict text of the manifesto, with a breakdown of the rogue agent's history. His letters, however, are eyes only and will remain so for the duration of the op.

There is currently no need to deploy Gate Team. Standard declassification timeline—fifty years, and then only after appropriate redaction—will be maintained; Delta protocol plausible deniability options (disseminated through usual channels) still in effect.

SECRET/SENSITIVE

 # ping –c 1 –w 1 xxx.xxx.x.x

OPEN SESSION

Consortium Chat   Month/Day   00:00:03

Open Session

```
00:00:03 haze:     is it set?
00:00:04
00:00:05
00:00:06 Lex:      ha ha - you don't know?
00:00:07
00:00:08 Drgn0:    work hard - party harder!
00:00:09
00:00:10 critter:  check your text messages in ...5
00:00:11 critter:  ......4
00:00:12 critter:  .........3
00:00:13 critter:  ............2
00:00:14 nyrdmstr: got it!
```

00:00:15

00:00:16 IMcre8tor: I'm so there!

<MODERATOR> more of the usual suspects, we see <g>

<MODERATOR> CharliX sends regards

00:00:20 haze: X is coming?!?!?

00:00:21

00:00:22 Drgn0: stunned…

00:00:23 webmnkee: yo X!!!

00:00:24 hac10: let's go let's go let's go

<MODERATOR> Hackers and crackers only – no script kiddies!

00:00:27 CharliX: Everyone's got to start somewhere <g>.

<MODERATOR> yeah, but not stay there!

00:00:29 Stealth: hey X!

00:00:30 nemesis: yo!

00:00:31 IMcre8tor: surprised you're stepping away

00:00:32 IMcre8tor: from keyboard!

00:00:33 CharliX: lol! It happens sometimes ☺

00:00:34 CharliX: back to work for me – see ya!

00:00:35

Session terminated

❖

Anna knew even before the location was texted to her PDA that she was going, had known it even before, or perhaps at the same time as, the board—or the Consortium, as this elite online group of coders, hackers, crackers, and technical creatives somewhat officiously called themselves—had learned X would be there.

Of course she had to go; she needed to network, to touch base with the members of this highly skilled and scattered community, both the white and the black hats. Things were happening all the time— new groups, new alliances, new technology and applications—and this was the best way to find both those and the people that led and created them. And this particular gathering, composed by invitation only of the best of the best (and every member knew it) had ties to them all.

For any of them, herself included, it was not enough to be cutting edge. She found herself mentally repeating the credo her group worked under: *Wanna lead? Gotta bleed.* That, she reflected, applied to so much more than just the technology.

All the research, all of the painstakingly slowly collected scarce evidence told her change was coming, events were almost right on top of them. This particular gathering would be a good opportunity to maybe, just maybe, find some of the people—or at least connections to the ones—who were leading the charge. And there was *definitely* someone at its head.

Anna knew who, not only because of the directives she'd been given but also deep in her gut, that nebulous place where information was gathered, sorted, analyzed, and concatenated into new configurations, new probabilities and solutions at such speed the calculations themselves could only be discerned after the fact, via reverse engineering.

It was these analytic and accurate flights that had initially made her valuable in the field. But it was after a second op, where the same explainable-after-the-fact solution had been employed, that she had been temporarily pulled from the field. The official explanation she'd been given was that her skills would be put to even better use in another, more challenging setting. So, after two months of tests and training, her file was given an "I" designation and she herself given a dual mission.

One was intended to serve the other, and did, with even better results than initially expected, since she was now in the right place to find the proof, the definitive link between the mastermind and the minions, and from there hopefully learn whatever she could of their ultimate plan. This social cyber celebration was one of the places to seek the information she needed, and— She mentally shook her head. Even with all of that, Anna also knew there was one more very personal and very compelling reason to attend, and as she nodded hello to everyone she passed, she couldn't help but remember not only the reason she actually wanted to be there, but also the reason she would behave the way she would when she saw *her*.

It had been a great surfing weekend, one of the last ones before the season ended, and before it had even really started, they'd slept together.

It really shouldn't have been a surprise; after all, they were both single and attractive, they worked together and got along well. In fact, there had been on that day the sense of a certain inevitability about the whole thing. And so there had been the first time, after an amazing wave set and a great barbecue back at the house the company—in its new-breed high tech and higher energy enthusiasm—had rented for the second summer in a row for any and all of its employees' free-time use.

The second time between them, with its subtle shift in power, the evolution from mutual seduction to…well, it had been different, anyway, sweet and savage and had held a "we definitely should do this again" feel.

But it was the third time, the third time that something had… what had been a little casual with a deeper sort of friendly thrown in had suddenly become more. She couldn't name it precisely, but she remembered exactly what had happened.

Anna woke up suddenly, fully, not really sure why and glanced over her shoulder as she sat up to find the bed next to her empty. The fact that the sheets under her hand were cool but not cold meant it had not been too long, and the clock on the nightstand revealed it to be an hour before sunrise, just in time for dawn patrol, as the die-hard surfers called it. Not a bad time to hit the beach, considering the forecast, she mused, but still too dark to be something safely done alone. It would be their last day there, and probably the last ride for a few months. More than likely, she decided, her companion had gone foraging—the term *she* preferred for excursions from the office for food or caffeine.

Well, she mused with a grin, between the surfing and the after-hours activities, a snack wasn't a bad idea, and she pulled on a T-shirt and the board shorts she'd discarded earlier, before she headed out the door and down the hallway, work, research, and her investigations far from her mind.

The several other coworkers who'd joined the excursion had either only come out for a day or were sleeping soundly in one of the other shared rooms, filling the house with deep-sleep quiet. She could hear the roar of the ocean only a few dozen yards away—the surf was pounding—and a quick glance out the window into the predawn gloom showed the faintest hint of exactly how hard those waves were hitting.

Hope it lasts a few more hours, she thought as she flipped on the low light over the stove, then poured herself a glass of water. She heard the back door slide open and the sound of bare feet across tile as she peeked into the fridge.

"Hey." The voice was low, raw, and when Anna glanced up in the half-shadows of the room, all she could see was the damp silhouette, the tear in the right shoulder of the rash guard, and the dark gleam on the exposed skin, changing the warm friendliness of welcome she originally felt to the beginnings of concern, mixed with alarm. She took a hurried step over and reached for her friend.

"Are you all right? What ha—"

The face that pressed against hers was damp, cold, but the kiss she received was hot, hungry, and ignited an answering burn. "Baby...please." The words whispered into her ear in the same low and aching tone. The soaked rash guard transmitted the heat and the beat of the heart it protected. "Make me come."

The fingers were gentle even as they demanded, pulled on her, framed her length, drew her tee along skin as they moved through the hallway, and the pulse under her lips was jagged and wild. Palms fit and pressed over curves, over points they raised and hardened, teased until she caught her breath, desire a cool burn that crashed through her with the sound of the surf outside. She allowed herself to be drawn back to the room they'd both left and once more through the door. Those same fingers tugged at her shorts until they fell unheeded before the bed.

They tumbled on it together, a tangle of arms, legs, skin. "What happen—" She tried again through the building haze of desire, of sheer physical need that had muted the initial alarm she'd felt in the tone she'd heard, in the tear she'd seen, an alarm that rang again at the not-quite-silent "mmph" of pain that escaped the lips she kissed when they peeled the body-hugging shirt off. But she was shushed once more by another kiss, the delicately sensual tongue play, and the warming hands that guided hers.

"Make me come." It was a breath against her neck under the sensitive spot of her jaw even as those hands touched her again, touched her with knowledge and need.

Anna willingly moved to comply and discovered this was not the body of a woman ready with want, with desire, despite the urgency of her words or the insistent touch of her lips, the sure slide of now-heated fingers exactly where they'd be most effective.

Low gray light seeped under the windowshades, too low and too dark yet to know if the sun would shine, and something stirred in her, a feeling she couldn't name as she carefully took those hands in hers, then shifted the thawing woman beneath her.

Any other woman who'd asked her, asked her in the way she'd been asked, there would have been no problem, no question, no doubt. She would have already been happily buried within her, moving along the same path and stroking out her request. But not this time, and not this woman—somewhere along the path, there was a complete disconnect from the words, to the heartbeat, to the body, and she was too well trained not to notice.

Yes, the breathing was hard and fast, the way she was held desperate, close, too close to mistake the throb against her chest for anything other than what it was—and she recognized it: fear. In that instant, she knew something more. She had watched her surf, the way she attacked the waves, how she threw her body into them, almost daring them to knock or drag her down. The risks seemed outrageous, but they were carefully calculated; she'd worked with that mind too long not to know how it operated. *Wanna lead? Gotta bleed.*

She added that information to the early hour, the hammer of the foam she had seen and heard outside the window, to the tear in the rash guard that prevented a deeper one on the skin it had protected. Something had happened, something strong enough to take this woman, to take her and drive her to need, to ask for, a closeness that she craved through a contact she didn't really want.

This woman, she realized quite clearly, the woman she worked with, surfed with, had just spent two nights with, was testing her, testing her and testing herself.

And so Anna did something she never had done before as she smoothed her hands along silken strong legs and guided them around her, rocked carefully against her, and pulled her into her arms even as she wondered why.

"Easy, baby," she murmured into her ear, then gingerly pressed her lips to the very edge of the forming bruise that surrounded the scrapes along her shoulder. "Ease down." Anna raised her head and carefully stroked away the long, damp strand that fell across her face to land against her chin, brushed against a finely boned cheek that hadn't fully lost the chill of the Atlantic. "All right? You're all right."

What she saw as she gazed through the early gloom into the face below her made her throat hurt, because it resonated through her whole body—the deep, shuddering breath her coworker, her surf buddy, her *friend* took as she closed her eyes. The momentary tightening, the stiffening of her entire being, before she let it out, and let her body relax. "Okay," her friend breathed and nodded slightly, opening eyes that held a hint of amber glow even in the low light. They focused on her. "Okay."

In that moment, Anna forgot who she was, who she was supposed to be, forgot everything she was supposed to know and remember as the naked truth stared up at her. They had touched before, had enjoyed sharing their bodies, but if she wanted to really touch *her*, and right then and there she knew that's what she wanted, to touch *all* of her, this wasn't the way. A child stared up at her, a trusting, scared child, nakedly vulnerable, waiting to see if the trust she offered would be broken.

She had already lied to her, not intentionally, not cruelly, just part of the job. Perfectly logical, understandable, necessary, even, but she was being offered something that, if she took it, she knew no amount of logical explanation would erase the hurt she was suddenly very certain her nondisclosure would cause. It shouldn't have mattered, they were friends, they had jobs to do, and even this could be a part of it, but suddenly it did matter—a lot.

And so instead of fucking her, and instead of letting her friend and whatever more she might be make her come again, Anna held her, smoothed her hands in gentle lines and circles along her arms and back. She kissed her gently, and even though she no longer tasted tears in some of those kisses, the easy motion between them continued, soft, smooth, and somehow profoundly satiating, until at last they both fell back to sleep.

She woke alone again.

That had been a few months ago, and situations had drastically altered since then. There was a sense of expectation, a dramatic alteration in timeline. The excitement filled the air and the Internet, was a buzz that sang under every interaction, made—

She had a job to do, she reminded herself firmly as she lifted her chin and scanned the crowd with a studied casualness.

Despite the still near-winter cold outside, there was a dress code the ravers observed: a mix of shiny metal and bare muscle, the savage and the sage united in one body that pounded itself in precise formations sequenced to a techno beat.

Even had it not been required of her to fit in, she would have anyway, because she understood—in a way that ran through her blood, lifted her to a state both primitive and purely intellectual, heightened and sharpened both, simultaneously—the dichotomy these people embraced. And she *was* one of them, part of the techno tribe.

The synthetic fabric, a liquid red that shimmered as it poured over her, skimmed against her thighs as she walked with a lithe purpose through the converted warehouse, the stabbing colored strobes of light and heavy bass pulse that shook the floor making thought almost impossible, which, given the environment, was of course the point.

She'd been given this assignment because of her work, her discoveries so far. Because she had been able to balance fact and fiction, never a misstep in where her loyalties, her primary allegiance lay. She knew who she was and who she was supposed to be, and she had to remember that, she told herself. She had to do whatever was necessary, because if she was right, and she was gut-level certain she was, then she—

Anna spotted *her* through the crowd, and the genuine smile that flashed her way when their eyes met made her mind go blank even as her mouth went dry.

As usual, her teammate was surrounded but subtly in charge as she always was at these events; there were those who wanted to learn from her, the ones that respectfully admired her work, and those who simply…wanted. That was an expression she recognized on a few of those faces that glanced over then made way for her, even as they exchanged greetings—she was better known here than she'd thought, she realized, and filed that away for future reference.

"Chilled Stoli—straight up," she asked the bartender. Her peripheral awareness told her it was a young man, perhaps mid-twenties, who pulled and poured behind the black glass bar, but her smile and gaze were focused on her target. She smiled again when she was handed the cool glass cylinder that held exactly what she'd asked for, but not by him—by *her*.

"Cheers," she saluted and lifted her glass. The smart clink of a drink against her own brought them closer together, and she saw it flash quickly through her eyes, the borderline reached between welcome and flight.

"I knew you'd...come...tonight," murmured against her ear during a welcoming embrace, those silky lips so very close they brushed against her skin.

"Did you?" she asked as matter-of-factly as she could manage, knowing how well her counterpart *could* make her come. She downed her shot before facing the dark gold gleam of her eyes and the sensual half-smile that accompanied it.

Anna knew the game well by now—let her lead, but take some initiative as well. Pure followers were despised, treated with a coldly polite contempt, but a certain type of dynamism—that got respect, and that Anna knew she had. And she already had her attention and interest. "What about *you*?" she countered, returning the almost-touch while the Stoli burned the rest of the way through, warming her limbs even as it loosened her tongue. Fine hair brushed against her lips. "Think you'll...come...tonight?"

"Are you offering?" The words were spoken in her ear again in the face of the heavy beat that suffused everything, and she was certain she didn't mistake the slightest touch of hesitancy she heard in them.

She gazed into smoky amber eyes, the expression almost, *almost*, unreadable. Except... "Yes," she mouthed and nodded once.

She watched as her eyes changed, the quirk of her lips shifted, opened, just about to speak, when someone jostled into them.

When that jostle turned into an invitation to dance, she caught the slight shrug of apology and the quickest glimpse of—was it regret?—before the mask slammed down, became the smile turned upon the young man who didn't know what he'd interrupted.

She watched them, watched them dance, watched him fall

completely under her spell, and she knew she couldn't force it, couldn't bring herself to do it. To push and break those walls so carefully placed—it wouldn't take much, all she had to do was walk over, claim what she wanted. And that was the problem: it *was* what she wanted, job be damned.

Anna already knew all about the former live-in girlfriend, even without the help of the dossier that sat on her hard drive. Knew exact age, height, blood type, every vaccination, allergy, school attended, had complete files on family and friends, even had a theory as to why there where no records for two years of her adolescent life, the relentless drive that marked every accomplishment after that, the drive to prove *something*.

She'd also learned for herself how well their bodies fit together, the way her mouth tasted. But what she *really* wanted to touch, wanted to know…Anna knew this wasn't the way to find out.

And besides, there were rules. They were, perhaps, subtle, unwritten and unspoken, but they were still rules, a code for engagement to be followed. If she did that, broke the strictures of engagement, used the personal knowledge she did have to her own advantage, Anna knew she would have to offer something in exchange, maintain a special sort of balance, make promises she didn't think she could keep because of the same job that demanded she *not* do that. And because of what she did know, the thing she instinctively understood, she also understood the damage she could, she *would*, cause. Much more than the temporary sting Anna felt, watching the flirtation with a man she knew wasn't really wanted, not in any true way.

Dammit. She couldn't do her job, she couldn't do what she wanted, and she didn't want to hurt her.

In the end, Anna did the only thing she could, which was to finally turn away even as she silently asked her, "God, baby. What in the world *are* you trying to prove? And *who* the hell are you trying to prove it to?"

Starting program: /hacking/$ ./exploit

THE ART OF EXPLOITATION

BB84 Secure Session - - Loss 0 Month/Day 03:25:03

```
03:25:04 ChknMan: you've got the receiver set up?
03:25:05 DsrtFx:  hitting the system
03:25:06 DsrtFx:  it's in
03:25:07
03:25:08
03:25:09 ChknMan: connected. Sending now
03:25:10 DsrtFx:  transferring
03:25:11
03:25:12 ChknMan: nervous, man - someone's gonna
03:25:13 ChknMan: find something sooner or later
03:25:14 ChknMan: she's no dummy - wants to
03:25:15 ChknMan: restructure
03:25:16 ChknMan: She'll look at everything,
03:25:17 ChknMan: she'll find this, she'll know
03:25:18 DsrtFx:  we'll be long gone.
```

```
03:25:19 DsrtFx:  Dude, you're helping people,

03:25:20 DsrtFx:  healing the fucked up gov't!

03:25:21 ChknMan: fuck the man!

03:25:22 DsrtFx:  lol - exactly.

03:25:23 DsrtFx:  Only 2 more and it's done -

03:25:24 DsrtFx:  first one was fine - this'll be

03:25:25 DsrtFx:  too.  You lay the trail?

03:25:26

03:25:27 ChknMan: Right to the door.

03:25:28 DsrtFx:  Fine.

03:25:29 DsrtFx:  I've got the other one handled.

03:25:30 ChknMan: You better
```

BB84 Secure Session Unsecure

WARNING - DATA LOSS DETECTED

Session terminated

BB84 Secure Session - - Loss 0 Month/Day 03:25:30

    Kevin tested his bonds. She'd tied him firmly, as firmly as she'd promised she would the second time he'd tried to touch her.

    He breathed it in, the fizz that seemed to pour over him as he forced the tension from his arms. The tang of it was an alternating sharp and soft just under his skin as he lay back on his own bed. It made the familiar and known heady and strange, and the low light of the room heightened the electric expectant mystery as she hovered over him.

"If you can't restrain yourself, I'll do it for you," she'd murmured into his ear, then pulled the scarf from around her neck. He'd felt the sheer material wisp across his chest, then his neck, when she took first one hand from her waist, then the other. Her touch had been gentle but sure as she bound his wrists to the headboard over his head.

He'd seen her for the first time, what was it, four, maybe six months ago, at one of the better raves, an underground party/ electronica gathering that the Consortium—the online hacker forum he belonged to—had put together. She'd very obviously been with one of the most beautiful redheads he'd ever seen.

"Digerati," his friend, Lex, had leaned over and said into his ear when he'd caught the direction of his stare. "*True* digerati—that entire crowd."

Kevin eyed Lex doubtfully. "No," Lex said finally to Kevin's questioning glance, "Not that 'I'm a magazine article writer' crap. I mean, they don't just know the shit, they *are* the shit—they invent it. Just sip your drink and try not to drool too much, little code monkey. Even her PDA's got more testosterone than you'll ever have." Then Lex had knocked his shoulder, right in the spot where he'd gotten the barcode for "Bawls," his favorite caffeinated drink, tattooed just two days before, and made him spill his…what was it he'd been drinking, anyway?

In the end, it had been good advice, because the next time he'd seen her, maybe a month, maybe two, later, there'd been another girl, and another, and by then… Well, it didn't matter. For whatever reason, this night he'd finally screwed up enough bravado after downing enough whatever those blue shots were that Lex had shoved at him, and asked her to dance. So, okay, maybe he could have been a little smoother, and he probably should have skipped that last shot instead of tripping over whoever it was she'd been speaking with, but it hadn't mattered because now, right *now*, she was *here*, with him, on *top* of him. He was afraid to pinch himself in case he *did* wake up.

"I…I thought you liked girls," he managed to splutter anyway through the sensual haze that clouded and filled him within and without as she slid down him to rest on his thighs. The light flickered over her, turned the silver she wore to shifting hues of flame, darkened the shadow of the valley that dove between her breasts before it disappeared beneath the flowing fabric.

Kevin had so wanted to touch that place, to explore and discover it, feel her mold under his hands and so he'd reached once, twice— but she simply wouldn't allow it. The restraint and the frustration only expanded the desire; it made him want her more.

"I don't 'like' them," she corrected him, then drew her tongue along the edge of his ear. "I *love* them…love to touch them…to fuck them…to let them fuck me."

She licked and nipped at the skin of his neck "How do you want me to fuck you?" she purred. "Do you want it like a boy?" She ran her hands, hard, strong, across his chest, her thumbs digging into his pecs as her lower body pressed harder against his. Her tongue flicked delicately across his nipple and he felt his breath catch, amazed at how sensitive that was. He was hard, so hard beneath her his skin hurt.

"Do you want me to fuck you like a man? Or…" she said as she gripped him, then pressed just…oh…beneath that…intense… so… "do you want me to fuck you like a girl? Do you want to know what that's like?" she whispered throaty and low, pressing again into that spot, that place he hadn't even known existed. "Imagine my tongue inside you," and she slid her tongue between his lips, delicate strokes, hard strokes, a slide against the roof of his mouth and those fingers a rhythm against him, a pace that matched her mouth.

"You'd be so wet, so fucking wet," she said, "but maybe you'd like my hands better. Can you feel that?" she asked as her hand wrapped around him, her thumb playing along the shaft to the head and the pressure, the pressure built, kept building, a burn, an inferno that licked at his thighs and singed under his navel and he saw fire play along her skin, shifting and gold and molten and… He felt like he was going to burst, and he shifted his hips beneath her, urging her on.

"Don't move," she whispered, releasing his throat from her teeth and stilling her hands. He instantly understood what she meant but couldn't suppress the shudder that ran through him anyway, as he once more tensed his muscles in an attempt to stop the motion instinct drove. The curve of her lips as he quietly fought for breath did something to him even as he wanted to beg her to continue.

"Good," she said, her breath a touch against his sensitized lips as she moved him again. "You're gonna come soon, real soon," she whispered into his ear. Her teeth played against the lobe. "And if you were a girl, if you were *my* girl, you'd be *so* tight, so fucking *tight* with me inside you."

His body…God…the muscles, tendons, taut, hard, straining, pulling… He could no more stop what was happening in his body than he could stop the words, the words she spoke that drew him on, that fired his mind and his blood. Suddenly, her hand wrapped, hard, so fucking hard—

"And you'd come like a girl," she told him as his hips pressed against her and he fought to breathe against the pulse that pounded out of him because he would, he was, and there—"deep and hard, inside."

❖

The red icon that flashed in the lower right hand corner of his screen brought Franko out of the torpor that babysitting activity across the network inevitably brought with it.

Instantly alert, he toggled to another screen. Nothing. Well, that figured. Momentary glitch, that was all. Ah, he knew it would be, he thought as he yawned heartily, stretched his arms over his head then laced his fingers behind his neck. Riven was fucking paranoid, that's all, he decided. He yawned again and reached down next to his chair where he'd dropped his latest F/X mag.

Franko kicked his feet up on the desk and shook his head as he flipped through the pages to find his place. One little bump a few months ago, and she wanted actual eyes on server traffic when major transactions went through the system. What a joke—nothing, but absolutely *nothing* had happened, and even the last time, the recovery had been almost instant.

But no, he continued, the word sarcastically drawn out in his mental monologue as he spotted his article, *she* insisted they watch, *he* watch, until the new systems she wanted were in place. "These systems are patched together, they're all being integrated too fast," she'd said. "We have no backup."

Backup, he snorted as he carefully thumbed over to the next page, who needed that? He considered his booted feet. They weren't the same comfortable and beat-up work boots he'd worn at the dot-com, but they *were* a nice, corporate black. Fuck the rest of it, *and fuck backup, too*, he mentally added. She had him and she had Chickenman Coop, while she herself was—

He found the page he'd wanted, an old joke he wanted to tape to his monitor: The Unix Guru's View of Sex. He forgot about work for a moment as he copied the command lines into a new document he would print, then decorate with.

```
#!/bin/sh
#The Unix Guru's View of Sex
unzip;
strip;
touch;
grep;
finger;
mount;
fsck;
more;
yes;
umount;
sleep;
```

Franko chuckled to himself as he sent the page to the printer, the engaging click and hum of it the only sound above the whir of the cooling fans in their tower cases. Another click sounded through the room, the disengage of the paper tray, and as he reached for the new printout, the red light went off again. Instantly all sense of play left him. He whirled in his seat and straightened, banging his knee against the desk when he brought his legs down. "Fuck!" he muttered, annoyed with himself as he automatically rubbed the incipient bruise with one hand and reached for his keyboard with the other.

This time when he toggled screens, he found it. It blinked in, then blinked out—and there! He quickly popped up another screen, the printout dropped and the pain in his knee forgotten as he viewed the incoming and outbound chatter. An unknown origin source was hitting into the heart of the system and there was no way to stop it, short of pulling the plug, literally. Fuck. Fuck. *Fuck!*

Oh goddammit—the calling tree, where the fuck is the calling tree? he asked himself desperately as he searched through the papers on his desk and his e-mails. He found it buried in a folder labeled "Shit You Really Need—DON'T DELETE" on his hard drive. *Which one first?* he asked himself, panicked again as he scrolled through names. There were *two* VP-Ops. Fuck again. *Riven—it's* got *to be Riven,* he decided. She had asked *him* directly and this was her baby, that meant she had to know *now.* He picked up the phone and dialed with one hand while he texted one word over and over.

BREACH BREACH BREACH BREACH BREACH BREACH BREACH

❖

He was very, very, pretty, she thought, even more so now, his shirt hanging off him, the deep blue with its metallic shine puddled like water beneath him, his silver pants open wide and framing what had turned out to be a rather nice package.

She could see his dark eyes were barely focused as he stared over his head, at the wrists she'd tied with her scarf when he wouldn't listen, couldn't control the reach of his hands. She was pretty sure she'd just fucking blown his mind, was certain that had been the first time he'd ever come like that, body choked, the sensation bursting backward.

The momentary high of watching him struggle for control over himself even as she took it from him, the sharp burst of an almost grim satisfaction, was already fast fading into the familiar dullness, mingled with a faint—

She turned her mind from it.

Maybe… She considered it as dispassionately as she would choose a fork or open a soda; it was simple analysis, it carried no emotion and therefore meant absolutely nothing. Maybe she'd make him come again.

She could see it so clearly, the way to play it, the way to play him. Such a nice body had to have a nice back and if she flipped him, hands spread and tied, she'd get to see it, maybe she'd even enjoy watching those muscles *really* work and flex as first she took away his reservations, then leaned along his spine while she pressed against his boundaries, eased past them—then took him for a ride he'd *never* forget, probably spend years dreaming about. It would be *so* easy, *he* would be so easy to—

It was the chiming that brought her away from her contemplation of Kevin as he lay breathing hard beneath her.

She leaned back to reach for and into her bag, fingers unerringly closing around her PDA. *Dammit!* she thought as she read the screen. *Franko*. She knew if her second shift admin was calling, no, *paging*, it meant nothing good, and the one word that scrolled repeatedly across her LCD confirmed that. "Shift your right hand to the left and you can untie yourself," she told Kevin, dismissing him to the periphery as she snapped on the earpiece. "Go."

She got off the bed and then slung her bag over her shoulder as she listened to Franko's terse report. Panic. She could hear the panic behind his words as she straightened the skirt of the silver halter dress she wore, the material deceptively light despite its metallic mix weave. She hadn't even bothered to undress; she looked almost exactly as she had not quite an hour ago. The only difference was in her eyes. A honeyed calm contemplation had been cleared to a fiery amber that snapped with focus as her feet easily found one shoe, then another. Her body was on autopilot as she slipped a finger between the upper and her heel to make sure it fit properly, her complete focus on the data she received. She absorbed it, her mind racing with plans.

"So what do you want done?" Franko asked.

"Isolate the LANs and freeze every remote ID—if they shot off a packet maybe we can contain it. Snapshot IDs on every LAN to WAN—no, all of them, all the remote ones, too—and I want that list by the time I get there in…" She did a quick calculation. "Twenty minutes. I want to catch the—"

The second chime that rang through her PDA made her skin go cold, and the muttered expletive under her breath matched the one the sys admin shouted in her ear. The system, the network that carried sensitive data, information that made or broke fortunes in numbers seemingly fantastical, that transferred currency in the same outrageous amounts, in numbers that were larger than the gross domestic product of some nations, had shut down—internally, and equally important, externally. "Go through the entire calling tree. I want heads and hands and I want them in forty-five minutes."

Another chime cut through. The system was back up. "Yes," she spoke over Franko's squawk of protest, "I *know* we're up again, and I know it's three fucking thirty. You're up, I'm up. *Get* them— tell 'em to call a car if they have to, jobs are riding."

She spoke into his silence. "Franko, consider it job grooming— you want my post, I want to head Ops, you need to get used to this. Besides," she reminded him, "it's the second time. I'll make the call to Pendleton."

"Aw, fuck—you're right," he conceded, and cursed lightly under his breath.

"Of course," Charli answered lightly, even while anger, pure and simple, rode down her spine in cold waves. "Make the calls— I'll see you soon."

Fury warred with frustration as she cut their connection. Not only had she warned about the real threat of total system failure in repeated meetings and reports, she'd also just turned down an offer for what would have been potentially unpredictable, probably mind-blowing, and definitely mutually damned good sex from her counterpart, the other Second VP-Ops, about two hours ago. And now she had to call her in for an all-hands fucking fire drill.

Oh man, this is so gonna suck! Charli thought while she took firm strides through the apartment and scrolled through the information on her screen for the next number she needed. She plucked her coat from the back of the sofa and shrugged the fine black wool over her shoulders.

"Hey, problem?" Kevin asked as he followed her to the door.

She hit a key that would dial the corporate car service her company used. "This is account TX-427," she told the receptionist. "I need an immediate pickup. We're making two stops." She glanced up at Kevin as she waited for confirmation.

"Got to head into the office," she explained, then gave the pickup address to the operator. She'd stop at her apartment to quickly shower and change first.

"Firewall breach?" he hazarded. He folded the scarf nervously in his hands.

"Something like that," she answered, quirking her lips in what might have been a smile before she returned her attention to her PDA. She brought up her itinerary for the next day and the file she'd finally been sent for the interview she'd have at nine. She wanted to bring in new systems, and that required new blood. She'd had her admin hound Human Resources to get the information they held on the candidate. As for the rest, well, she'd hired Laura for her resourcefulness, and Laura knew exactly how much Charli hated to walk into a meeting or an interview without as much intel as possible. She'd even included a graphic with a note that said she'd sent the rest of the info to her space on the server. *Laura*, she decided as she opened the file, *deserves a raise*.

Hmph. She smirked to herself when she saw the picture that accompanied the file, then glanced back at Kevin. *Oh, perfect. Just bloody motherfucking perfect.* His shirt still hung open and loose, displaying a nicely toned upper body and defined abs, and while he'd zipped his pants, he hadn't buttoned them.

She hit another key and in the nanosecond it took for the wireless link to engage, she typed in a quick query. Bingo. Everything.

"Yeah...I hate those," he said and held out the gauzy material to her.

"Keep it," she said with a slight wave as she put her other hand on the door latch. The door swung wide. "Good luck with your interview tomorrow."

"Oh man, thanks. It's the last of four fucking interviews. I'm meeting with Charlie Riven, the lead architect for the team, a VP-Ops or something like that. Everyone says get by Charlie and... Wait a minute." He eyed her a bit warily as she stepped into the hallway. "How'd you—"

On second thought, she took the scarf from his hands. He wasn't quite as bright as she'd hoped, and besides, she rather liked that one. It had a pretty silver shimmer that had been hard to find, and she'd lost too many of them the same way. "Kevin Nguyen, top three MIT, aka Dragon Zero and master of the Holidaze worm?" she asked with a smile.

This, she thought, *is so very lose-lose for you, guy.* He hadn't hooked up with her because he knew who she was business-wise, which was much to his credit, but then again, as an applicant and potential employee, he should have read the company's Web site, should have known. Her photo, along with the ones of the rest of the IT heads, was on it.

She now knew everything about him, from his birthplace to his blood type, including—she mentally shook her head—that he dressed left.

"Yeah," he said finally, "but how, I mean, when...?"

She stared at him for a long moment, surprised at what she read. Kind. His eyes were kind. Well, she considered, perhaps he simply didn't know how to play the game. His coding and administration skills were supposedly superb or he would have never made it through the screening process to her office, but she'd find out in a few hours for certain. "You're a nice guy, Kevin," she said with a little sigh, surprised again at what she found herself about to say. "Here's a hint. Nine a.m. is considered late for Whitestone in general, and in *my* book particularly. Show up for eight forty-five if you want to impress me." She kissed his cheek. "You probably should have asked me earlier, I would have told you." The sheer ridiculousness of the entire situation hit her. Considering that she knew exactly how he'd spent the night, his early arrival might not truly impress her, but she would certainly respect the feat if he could accomplish it. She couldn't help grinning at him as he walked with her to the elevator.

"It's Charli with an *i*, and not an *ie* or a *y*," she told him and pressed the call button. The number of shocks he could take for the night had probably been reached, she thought, as he shook his head and gave her a questioning look. "Charlotte Riven."

Two taps brought up the contact for her counterpart, the Second VP-Ops, and knowing that she too kept her electronic leash on and nearby at all times, Charli text-paged a breakdown of what she knew as she rode down to the waiting car.

```
Tell her to take a number, stud—need you now—
complete breach and failure (we're up). Calling
tree activated (thank Franko). Headed in—see you
in 20.
C
```

The program is running. Exit anyway? (y or n)

CHASING RABBITS

"If a packet hits a pocket on a socket on a port..."

The singsong light words and the rich tone they were delivered in made Charli glance up from her desk to mark the entrance of Anna Pendleton, her counterpart and co-lead. Anna had already been part of the team, another employee at the now-defunct dot-com Charli herself and many of their subordinates had worked for, back in the days before the group had gained the contract, then been bought outright to be absorbed into Whitestone's corporate entity.

Glancing up from the reports that spilled before her and across her desk, Charli arched a sculpted eyebrow at her, took in and appreciated the lovely shape of the body that leaned against her office doorway, the teasing twist to the curve of her mouth. She knew quite well both the angle and the smile were for her benefit.

"...and the bus is interrupted as a very last resort?" she returned sardonically as she returned her focus to her work.

Anna laughed as she entered, and her hair, a skim-above-the-shoulder light brown, with golden highlights strung through it, waved about her face.

Charli knew she came by that color honestly, a lasting kiss from the sun, and she also didn't have to watch Anna walk to know her hips would sway just so, or that the finely cut black slacks covered an *almost* perfect pair of legs, legs sculpted from years of surfing every American shore and quite a few foreign ones. Changing *almost* to *definitely* meant legs that could have been wrapped around Charli's waist, or better yet, her neck, the night before.

Not that it couldn't happen, not that it hadn't already, and not that it wouldn't have been better, Charli admitted to herself, it was simply that there was an acuteness, a connect, and it left Charli distinctly uncomfortable. The last time it had been that intense had been right before the company buyout, the last good surfing weekend in October. She and Raven had finally parted ways several weeks earlier after nearly two years together, two years that started out nicely enough and ended with an unnamable and therefore unspoken mutual frustration. The dissolution had been amicable enough, and they even ran into each other from time to time, but still…

Charli had finally begun to feel free, the imprint of the ring she'd worn fading, no longer the faint noose that ringed her neck, the vague guilt of feeling like she was with someone when she wasn't.

What a weekend it had been, though. The water had begun to truly chill, the waves had been perfect, and between the bonfire and the beers it had been so easy to continue what had already started on the sand back at the shore house the company had rented for the crew. It had been easier still, muscles sore, body achingly alive from the total saltwater immersion, the skimming liquid high from riding the waves, to dive the same way into what had happened between them, already familiar with each other from weeks spent working together into the early morning hours, the only two in the office, hundreds of hours spent intent on work, on play, and the "I really like you" physical focus of the night before.

Away from work and the silent reminders at home or in the local and not-so-local social places she occasionally frequented, loosened by water and heightened by the flame on the sand, knowing they felt mutual respect and admiration and followed the blazed trail of an already acknowledged if heretofore unspoken attraction, Charli hadn't been too surprised that the first time had been good—*really* good. No. What stunned her, had really thrown her off guard was the second time—not that it happened, but *what* had happened. The second time had been even better.

She was jolted awake afterward by impulses she could barely understand; snatches of images and shadows of emotions kicked through her mind, punched a frantic quick start to hammering in her chest with frightening and wakeful demand. Charli sat up and opened her eyes as she caught and controlled her breath, forced her body down from its fight-or-flight status. As she breathed, she listened to the surf beat its siren song outside the window. It sang with a soul-cleansing clarity.

The elemental melody soothed her, called her—she had to answer. Charli dressed with rapid quiet, her fingers certain and sure in the dark, and as she passed the boards that leaned up against the wall off the deck, she hesitated. *Fuck it*, she decided, *I'm going for the pure body rush*. She headed straight for the shore.

She watched. She waited. The first set had been perfect. Just barely able to see the darker loom of the rises and troughs, she grabbed a few in just the right spot, caught, directed, cutting and steering through the pure power that sluiced her toward the shore. The second set had been even better, the low, low light of the coming day a distant gleam in her eyes as she stroked out, casting even deeper shadows on the shore.

It was the third set. The third set had started out nice and clean, straight-up lines to the horizon and almost double overhang, or approximately twice human height. Beautiful. She'd already decided it would be the last go for now—there'd hopefully be more nice rides later. Apparently the ocean had agreed because as Charli hooked to angle into the wave, there was the moment of catch and then—just as she caught her breath—it let her go.

She fell through, no longer buoyant, as heavy as the silent weight in her head and the water as insubstantial as air for an eternal panic-inducing half-second before she was caught again, trapped now by the dreaded "washing machine," the powerful cycling churn that propelled the wave above it, gave it both its speed and strength.

It had happened before, a hazard of the sport, and she usually pulled through just fine, but this time—she mentally shook herself, she didn't want to think about, or remember, *that*, the places her mind had gone, events that still haunted in its darkened corners only to be fully relived when all she could do was force herself not to panic.

It was a double overhang, not a triple—no one as far as she'd known had *ever* survived a pin-down by a triple, but a double… *Every wave flows to the shore*, Charli reminded herself, the mantra forcing her brain to calm, to remember that no matter what happened during the churn, as soon as the force that slammed her into the rocks and sand hidden below the double overhang was done working her over, she'd float up, that much closer to the shoreline.

Battered by the surf, shaken by the way she'd been tossed, body and mind, by the ocean, she took measured steps back to the house. She spat out the sand between her teeth, felt the coarse, chill wet sand give way to dry. She was cold, so damned cold, and she was aching in ways she didn't want, aching to forget—everything. *She ran into Anna in the kitchen.*

She'd had to leave almost as soon as she'd woken up, half an hour, maybe even a full one, later. They'd been too close, it was all too much: the gentle rock between them that had gone from soothing to deeply satisfying, the instinctive response Anna had had to her, every right move, every right word, as if she *knew* her. But Charli knew Anna didn't, not really, and that she'd come so close, too close, to believing that maybe, just maybe, just this *once* she could trust herself, trust what she felt and what she knew.

She fell asleep on the train, knowing that would have been a grave mistake.

Anna had been her normal self, the Anna that Charli knew, when they'd seen each other at work the following day, nothing different in her tone or touch, no allusions whatsoever to the weekend other than to agree with the general office commentary that the surf had been "happening." The fact was that it was Charli who had been wary, leery even, that Anna would ask her something, anything from why she'd left (and admittedly, Charli acknowledged, a bit more than rather abruptly) to asking her out, but none of that had happened.

It had never even come up, not in word, gesture, or tone, leaving Charli enormously relieved, and while she and Anna still occasionally spent social time together outside of work, she'd never allowed it—correction: she'd never allowed *herself*—to go there again. She wasn't certain if there was the slightest hint of regret under the relief she felt that Anna had never questioned or pursued it beyond what it had been: a couple of great nights after some really good surfing days.

What they had together was a good mix of workplace respect and camaraderie joined to a mutual admiration, as well as acknowledged attraction. There was that, Charli concluded, and probably one more reason why they got along so well: Anna always seemed to know when to leave something alone and, Charli admitted grudgingly to herself, when not to, as well.

Still, though, there had been a moment last night when she'd seriously considered—well, it didn't matter. Kevin and his unwitting interruption had provided the perfect opportunity for Charli to discover a few things for herself. She'd examine it further, later. Right now, it was time to leave those questions alone.

"You look great for a sleepless cyber savage," Anna laughed again, an appraising gleam in her eyes as she sat on the corner of the desk. "Bad interview today? You should have come home with me last night," she said casually as she picked up a sheaf of printouts and leafed through them. She gave Charli the slightest of glances, a glint of hazy green filled with promise, over the pages. "Franko could have had two minutes of wild fantasy in his brain before he melted down—three thirty, Charli! Do you know the *damage* we could have done to each other in that time?"

"Between one and three thirty?" Charli grinned at her and let her honest admiration and enjoyment of how well they had already implemented and could further deploy their more carnal skill sets on each other show in her smile. "Not as much as we could have between one and five." She was relatively certain Anna didn't know what had happened after she'd left the club. She'd made sure to leave a few minutes after Kevin had gone ahead to hail a cab.

Charli sighed to herself, frustrated and tired from the dissatisfaction of the night, and the breach—no, it was the total collapse—of the system, the system she was responsible for. She checked over her shoulder, the dark strand of hair that normally fell to her chin safely tucked behind her ear, and reassured herself with the sight of the well-carved long-board she'd brought from their former offices in the Puck building farther downtown Manhattan, right on the edge of the East Village.

Now they were firmly ensconced in midtown, on Fifty-first Street and Park Avenue, the literal heart of some of the most expensive real estate globally. The dot-commers might have gone corporate, but Whitestone had promised to let them maintain their internal culture, or at least some of it, Charli mentally amended. They used to wear jeans and T-shirts—no slogan too outrageous or taboo so long as they didn't display hate speech of any sort—have late-night pizza and Chinese food with the team, summer Friday cocktail hours that started at three p.m., and company-wide surfing trips. Now they had suites and suits, although khakis and chinos were the uniform for late-night and holiday hours. They were allowed to play whatever music they preferred on quiet, polite headphones, instead of blasting the latest find of someone's favorite band over the PA system. Oh, and they were encouraged to decorate their offices and cubicles comfortably.

Charli had gained an office, a new wardrobe, a staff of approximately fifty, and an assistant. She'd lost the ability to sit late at night, in her favorite sweatshirt and jeans, music pumping and the ideas flowing, everything a puzzle to be solved, whether it was a snippet of code or designing an entire technical infrastructure.

Gone too was the easy give and take between her and her team, the open door that meant she had a desk in the middle of the floor, easily visible and available. Instead, she now had functional groups that worked under a strict hierarchy, and everyone made appointments.

There were two things Charli hadn't given up: her friendship with Anna Pendleton and their mutual wave addiction. That board, the one that leaned on the wall behind her, the board that was now a beautiful wood sculpture since it had been cracked after a nasty run-in with a rude surfer who'd dropped in on her wave, had been custom made by a local Long Island crafter. It had been her first such purchase for herself, and though she preferred body surfing to board, she loved the totem that it was. It had been a long enough winter, and a new season was upon them. "We still on for tomorrow?" Charli asked, even though she knew the answer.

"Oh, please." Anna rolled her eyes and put the stack of papers down. "Like anything could stop that. Although"—she pointed to a line on the top sheet before her as she picked the stack up again—"I could see where this might cause a delay."

Charli didn't even glance at the page. "You caught that, too?" She watched as Anna studied the ID. There were times Anna surprised her. She'd been brought into the group when they'd first landed the contract with Whitestone to integrate Whitestone's system to the Fed system, make it functional internally for corporate needs, externally for clients. And what they needed for their team, they got: Anna Pendleton, the graphical user interface—GUI—guru. Most GUI designers were just that, designers who knew nothing about code, but Anna was different. She knew the code, understood the concepts that drove it so well, she'd pitch in with the team in emergencies and during crunch times. Added to that, her ability to translate from geek to normalspeak with clients was so fluid that it had seemed natural for her to be promoted to co-architect, then design team lead, on par with Charli. But because Charli's focus was purely technical and structural, while Anna's was all about interface, both technical and client-wise, she found that she sometimes forgot that Anna actually had superb coding skills.

There were moments Charli wondered what the real deal was with Anna, for there were a few other things, too, things about the way she stood sometimes, or the way she held her hands, that reminded Charli of her brother, a marine engineer and career Navy officer. That occasional glimpse in and of itself made her wonder on occasion, because it was rare in her experience that someone had those mannerisms without that background—and nothing like that was revealed in the background search.

Anna's records had been thoroughly investigated by every means available before she'd joined. Professionally, it was standard operating procedure, both for security and research reasons, but personally and individually there was curiosity, too.

While not officially encouraged, it was unofficially expected. After all, their group was essentially made up of hackers, and finding information was what they did for fun. They surfed as much electronically, digitally, as they did the ocean, perhaps even more, searching for and finding intelligence and news that floated through the electric ether like so much flotsam and jetsam. They were capable of and enjoyed performing investigations that were thorough and rigorous despite their apparent informality, and generally speaking, discovered much more information than those who investigated through more traditional channels.

Anna had turned out to be almost surprisingly clean, though; no military history, no high school jock shots, no college club pix, just one mention of a white paper written a few years ago, *Communications as Metrics*, but otherwise, nothing out of the ordinary—at all.

On the one hand, for people who worked in the field, that was normal: most tried like hell to ensure none of their personal information could be found, but on the other, it was almost as if—

"It *does* look like a normal call to the host," Anna said, interrupting Charli's thoughts, "but the address looks like a host change—do you think it was a scramble, or a scrub?"

Charli stretched as she stood and considered her response. A scramble meant that the sending IDs had merely been disguised, scrambled to read as something else, either misdirection or utter nonsense, as a way to hide the sender and the source. But a scrub…a scrub indicated an executable piece of code had been injected to the system that would do whatever it had to do, then erase its tracks and itself.

That the entire system had collapsed told her. "Both, I think. Whoever did it was super sharp—knew the system well enough to tunnel in, then collapse behind. I think they dropped in an executable with a self-erase. Had we not frozen and isolated systems, we wouldn't even have found it."

She walked over and ran a hand over the outline of her board, reassured by the wood under her hand and the faint smell of salt and wax that still clung to it. The truth was that had an active and live pair of eyes *not* been watching, the whole event would have simply become a blip, an incident automatically noted on the server log only as a momentary failure.

It had been instinct, a hunch she'd played when she'd asked Franko to do it. She'd told no one else, not wanting to tip her hand on the off chance that it had been an inside job. And if it had been Franko, she reasoned, the event might not have happened at all. As it was, her gamble had so far paid off, for both of them. She had evidence of an event and so long as Franko told no one she had ordered his night watch, it looked good for him, too, added to his cred as capable. *Job grooming*, she mentally repeated, *it's all about job grooming*.

"Something came in, Anna, and it looks like something went out, because there are calls at the gate, and thanks to the dinosaur servers from this"—and she waved to indicate the building they were in—"this *acquisition*, there's no telling where they hit in the system, or what they went out with."

She didn't notice the sharp look Anna gave her or that she'd crossed the carpet to stand behind her.

"What about destination addresses?"

"Unknown—the collapse wiped them," Charli answered. It was funny, she thought as she straightened and turned to face the voice that had sounded almost on her neck, how Anna always managed to move so silently. "And again, no redundancy along those routes, so between that and the system reset, without that"—she pointed at the pages Anna held—"I've got nothing. I'm waiting for Cooper to bring the snapshot for the server feeding the Fedwire, and I sent Franko home—he'd already put in twelve hours before the clusterfuck."

The rest of the team, or rather the three separate groups ranging from five to fifteen members, each performing a separate yet distinctly important function, Charli had fine-tooth combing through their codes, checking for compromises, for the tiniest of mistakes in syntax, for the insertion of code snippets or even just degrades over time that might possibly become larger issues.

Anna nodded in agreement. "I've got my team checking their end of it," she told her as she handed the pages she'd examined back. "They're checking for loopholes in the interface. Oh hey," she continued, her tone lightening considerably, "is Coop *still* holed up in the server room by himself?"

Charli laughed and nodded. "Yeah. It's the scented soap and deodorant thing—he *still* won't use any."

"Yeah, Coop's a real high-tech hippie," Anna agreed. "The only thing that's missing is—"

"The only thing that's missing is taking the farm *completely* off the grid," a laconic voice said behind them, "and I'm having a self-contained solar-powered electrical unit installed."

Both women turned and faced the lanky frame that stood in the doorway, a folder undoubtedly containing the activity readout Charli had asked for with a still-steaming cup of coffee in his left hand—and everyone knew he took it black. A bit over six feet and reed thin, Ben Cooper with his dark ponytail and thick beard still had the appearance of a man who could talk or fight, though both Anna and Charli knew well it was the verbal, political arguments, delivered with defiant and defensive vehemence that he preferred, and the ones everyone else preferred to steer clear of. He was a self-admitted misanthrope; his skill set made his job perfect for him. It left him alone.

"Well, lucky for us that you're still building your cabin out." Charli grinned at him. The entire original crew had been treated to tales, specs, and pictures of the property Cooper had bought in celebration of the bonuses they'd all received during the takeover, the market-share value of the stock they'd all been gifted with by the original dot-com. "You're the only one besides me capable of handling these dinosaur servers."

"What about the pretty-boy interview this morning, Zero Boy or whatever?" Ben asked with a slight lift of his brow and a disparaging twist to his mouth.

"Yeah, what about him?" Anna turned and asked her brightly, and Charli caught the quickest of hidden smirks.

Charlie rewarded it with a brief sidelong glance, although she didn't blame Anna for tweaking her just the slightest bit. And she knew it wouldn't be taken any further than that.

She settled the papers back on her desk with one hand as she reached for the new readout she wanted to review with the other. "Nguyen's got skills, but he's not a server admin. So no worries, dude, you've got your chicken coop all to yourself for now," she answered. "He'll join the new script team in two weeks."

She opened the folder and began to flip through the pages, the readouts all in seeming order at first glance. "Did you catch a look at—holy shit! Look at that encryption!" she said almost to herself. "Contained *in* the firewall and looking too—ah fuck!" She jumped away just in time to avoid the splash of coffee that missed her but managed to soak the report she'd just put down.

"Dude—so sorry!" Cooper apologized as he tried to snatch back what remained of the cup, managing to instead dump the rest of it on the new report, and on Charli.

"Shit!" she exclaimed again as the fluid continued to find its lowest level and she leapt to quickly rescue her hard drive.

"Can you reproduce those?" Anna asked quietly as they mopped up the mess.

Charli shook her head with disgust as she dumped what was left of the illegible mess in the metal mesh waste basket. "Can't," she answered shortly. "The kick-over wiped everything." They were screen shots done as IDs and IPs hit in and out, and they couldn't be duplicated. Fuck. This was a mess, and it was her responsibility. If she couldn't find out where things had gone or where they'd come from, she could at least find out what they did or didn't do, to a degree. *Inside*, she thought, *that encryption call was from the inside. The timing is too right...fuck.*

There were only a handful of ways that could happen, some perhaps innocuous, but it was the timing, that was what alarmed her, *that* pointed to only one motive. She needed to know. Charli strode to the door and stuck her head past the frame. What she was about to do would override the chain of command, but there was no help for it. She'd been stymied the last time, she wouldn't be this time.

"Laura?" she called to the redheaded young woman who was

managing a conversation while compiling the presentation Charli would give next Tuesday, the one that again called for the remodel of their more important gateways. "Get me Eric."

Laura put her call on hold and swiveled around, shock writ large in her slate blue eyes. "Are you *serious*?"

Eric Lundenman was the CFO, the driving force behind Whitestone's climb from small but aggressive boutique hedge fund manager, with an office in New York and another in San Francisco, to financial baby giant with a corporate presence in every major financial city including London, Singapore, and Tokyo. The company was the largest manager of its kind, handling assets of over thirty billion thanks, in no small part, to the rapid acquisition of other smaller, well-heeled firms.

Tall, charismatic, and sporting a thick white shock of hair, Eric was also the most influential man on the board of directors, and prone to occasional flares of temper that were already the stuff of legend. In fact, the office workers had a saying about him: when Eric gets mad, get out of the way.

Fits and flair aside, his management style meant he generally preferred to let divisions run themselves so he could maintain his focus on Whitestone's continued growth, leaving him free to direct and develop the future heading of the company he nurtured.

It had been Eric's idea to bring the dot-commers in as a full division once technical needs had outgrown the feasibility of having outside contractors. It made pragmatic sense: the tech group knew their systems, how to run them, how to integrate them, better than any new group could be trained to do, since they had created them. Besides, it had been their innovative technology that had given Whitestone the earning edge over the competition, drawing new clients and investors, and it was the continued efforts of the now-absorbed group that kept Whitestone ahead of the game.

As one of the heads of that group, and, most critically, as the person responsible for creating the program that kept Whitestone so much more than solvent, Charli knew she had a special leverage. Even with a failure of the system, even if it had been complete and irreparable, Charli herself was an asset. She could walk out of

Whitestone at any point she chose and any other corporation would be happy to have her, and pay a premium for her services as well.

Eric knew that. Let the rest of the teams be as afraid of Eric as they wanted to be, Charli frankly didn't care. Hell, if he fired her, she'd spend a week or two surfing—she could take a month, more if she wanted, then walk into a new position anywhere. That was if she didn't decide to go mercenary as a consultant, selling her skills to the highest bidder or the project she found most intriguing, or just simply run her own operation. There were days she wondered why she didn't do just that.

But she wasn't doing any of that at the moment, and she wasn't one to shirk her responsibilities. If Charli could present her concerns to Eric before the presentation on Tuesday, she'd have a valuable ally. She didn't consider it possible that he might not listen or take her concerns seriously; after all, she *was* a VP-Ops for a very good reason. What she wasn't certain of was whether or not he'd authorize the expansion of her investigation, beyond merely a review of code, to the activities of each and every single account Whitestone held. If, as she suspected she would, she found *something*, she'd walk into the meeting with his backing and gain the rest of the Board's as well.

"Yes. I want the first meeting Monday morning. Thanks, Laura," Charli answered and ducked back into her office.

"Christ, Charli, what are you *doing*?" Cooper asked in an unmistakably anxious tone as she crossed the office and began to pack her things.

"Don't you think that it's beyond coincidental that both times we're hit it's when quarterly dividends are being distributed?" she said finally, the question rhetorical as she straightened and gazed first at Anna, who nodded in agreement, then at Cooper, who stared at the fresh coffee stain on the rug as he shook his head.

She surveyed her desk one final time—all clear for the moment, and nothing left to be done until she met with Eric on Monday. With all the extra hours she'd already put in, her team scrambling to find details, and now, the fresh stain of coffee —she mentally winced at the imagined reaction she would receive when she presented the cream suit to her favorite dry-cleaners, she'd have to stop there—she could leave early, take the small bit of time necessary to recharge and resharpen, especially since next week promised to be brutal.

"What do you have in mind?" Anna asked from behind Ben.

Charlie slung her case with her laptop over her shoulder. "I'm calling for an audit of all the sends and receives on accounts active within the last twenty-four hours. But right now?" She grinned at Anna. "Charli's gonna surf."

CODE CALLING

SECURE ENCRYPTION – SECURE ENCRYPTION – SECURE ENCRYPTION

15:10:04 Austin: Four days for you to wrap up.

15:10:05

15:10:06 Pendleton: It's not her.

15:10:07 Austin: Can you prove it?

15:10:08 Austin: She wrote the code.

15:10:09 Austin: Do you have a drop source yet?

15:10:10

15:10:11 Pendleton: Not exactly.

15:10:12 Pendleton: she called for audit.

15:10:13 Austin: She's covering. Prove it –

15:10:14 Austin: or get out of the way.

15:10:15 Austin: We move in Tuesday –

15:10:16 Austin: she's going down.

15:10:17

15:10:18 Pendleton: Need more time.

```
15:10:19

15:10:20 Austin:   You're done.

15:10:21 Austin:   You have until Tuesday at

15:10:22 Austin:   0900 hours. Clean house.

15:10:23

15:10:24 Pendleton: Done.
```

Session Terminated

SECURE ENCRYPTION – SECURE ENCRYPTION – SECURE ENCRYPTION

Once upon a time, the settlement of interbank payment obligations often involved the physical delivery of cash or gold to counterparties, which was both risky and costly. Theft took place at gunpoint, on horseback, at remote train stations and lonely wayside stretches of highway by outlaw gangs and desperadoes that were the stuff of American legend. But technology changed that. The advent of Morse code created a system that connected the twelve Reserve Banks, the Federal Reserve Board, and the United States Department of the Treasury and gave them the ability to transfer balances held at the Reserve Banks using a secure communications network. This was the foundation of Fedwire operations.

Of course, this improvement in exchange was not done out of a simple goodhearted and generous desire to protect the hard-won gains of laborers, orphans, and pensioners; protection had its price, and the Fed made sure they got paid.

As men with saddlebags, armored trains, and trucks were replaced with higher and more complex levels of technology, criminals got smarter, too, and although many aspects of the Reserve Bank's payment services had been centralized, individual Reserve Banks remained responsible for maintaining relationships with institutions and for limited operational processes such as updating account profiles. This meant that organizations with ties to the Reserve—such as fund, income, and asset management companies—were on their own when it came to their equipment as well.

It was super-criminals, the most elite of thieves, who attempted to crack into that, looked for the loopholes, the systems without redundancy, older operations, cracks in the hastily patched and connected network that would allow for hacks, malware, viruses, and worms that would redirect funds.

Clearly the Treasury was in an uproar on the rare occasions something affected them, incoming or outbound; not only was it theft, but each transaction that went through the wire earned interest for the Fed and its investors every moment it sat in their system, and the high number of transactions per day generated enormous revenue—average daily volume ran into the trillions of dollars, and the percentages on that alone resulted in income to the federal government almost staggering to contemplate.

Anna understood all of that. What she failed to grasp was why the Treas didn't really examine the destinations. Theft from the wire—despite the short-sighted assurances from her superiors within that agency—required more than just someone having written a code that took non-transactable denominations, a third of a cent, or a thousandth, dumped them into an interest-bearing account, then redistributed funds again once numbers were again transactable for each and every client. This was the code Charli had originally conceived of, the one she had written to show it could be done, the reason why she was considered a person of interest to Anna's supervisors.

She shook her head and breathed out the frustration she felt over their lack of cooperation as she slipped the disc into the slot that would deliver new data and allow for a new, one-time encrypted session to open.

```
ONE-TIME-PAD  -  DESTROY  SOURCE  DISC  AFTER  USE
```

```
15:11:03 field-op3: Treas. moving Tues. at 0900

15:11:04 field-op3: we're gonna lose him.

15:11:05 field-op3: 90% certain on inside guy

15:11:06 field-op3: Have soft evidence,

15:11:07 field-op3: getting hard data

15:11:08 field-op3: Treas. has wrong target

15:11:09 field-op3: Orders?
```

```
ONE-TIME-PAD  -  DESTROY  SOURCE  DISC  AFTER  USE
```

She closed the session. The Treasury Department couldn't see past its own navel, she thought with a resigned sigh as she removed the disc; as a government agency—a subdivision of which was the Secret Service—the Treasury focused on financial crimes, but not the motivators behind them, which was why Central Intelligence had moved its own operatives in there. Of course what the Treas did *was* important, she reminded herself as she magnetically wiped the disc, then fed it through a shredder. But they were wrong about the who, and they were wrong about the why.

No. Someone had to be inside and on the network to know when the exchanges happened, and someone had to be outside to receive it, to make use of it. She reviewed what she knew, the puzzle and its missing pieces as she mentally built its frame. A person or persons had gone through the trouble of hitting one of the largest, if not *the* largest, funds transfer systems globally. This revealed things in and of itself: it spoke not only of hubris, and of contempt for the government that supported this particular system, it also plainly showed a need for cash on a level that implied still more possibilities for motivation. Of those, only a very few were highly likely: a greed so hungry that it had no boundaries, or, more importantly and probably more accurately, a need for liquid *cash*—easily accessed funds in large amounts.

Her mind continued to follow the trail. The need to move cash that rapidly signified a quick exchange and in the world she operated in, those exchanges—usually clandestine and pre-arranged—involved something difficult to acquire through normal channels at best, and at worst illegal, either under U.S. law or international treaty.

This made whatever the acquisition was something those in the Company euphemistically referred to as "exotic," and that covered a short and lethal list. This included smart, high-tech bombs, deadly toxic gasses, and fighter jets, when thinking large and more visible as well as violent scales of destruction. But there were also small nuclear containments, exclusive hacks, viruses both virtual and real, toxins, radically redesigned and malignant bacteria. These small, hidden killers were easy to transport, simple to deploy and—unless someone had inside information, claimed responsibility, or left a traceable chain of evidence—provided the perpetrators with a level of invisibility.

She suppressed the shudder that naturally arose when she made a quick estimation of how much damage any of those things could do, globally or locally. Quite a few had no defense, and worse yet, others had no cure.

The Treas had no clue of what was truly going on, she concluded, no knowledge whatsoever of what their moving in would mean to the real operation behind what they thought was merely a matter of theft—they thought they had a smoking gun in hand, they thought it was Charli, when all they really had was smoke and Charli was the screen. She was close, knew it, could feel it, closer than she'd ever been to her true objective.

Why Tuesday, why not Monday, or even now? she wondered, but the answer came almost immediately: they needed the system up and running—because money had merely been temporarily diverted, not stolen outright.

The crime itself was elegantly simple: the invested money earned interest. That interest would be temporarily redirected back to the wire to earn even more interest, and then the original earnings were sent where they belonged, while the new earnings went… somewhere.

The Treas, not wanting to lose even the tiniest fraction of the fees that would have been generated by that exchange, was going to attempt to back the funds back in, recoup what they considered to be their lost interest. The rest was simple: once they'd recovered their perceived loss, they'd move against the person they thought had done it.

Well, doesn't that just figure, she chuckled sarcastically under her breath. When a corporation took money and invested it, keeping the profits before giving the initial investment back, it was called banking, and they collected a fee for the privilege of making money on customers' money. If and when an individual did the same thing, it was a crime. Of course, that was an oversimplification. For a person to do that, they needed access to all sorts of information and equipment, proprietary things owned by the financial institution they more than likely worked for. And of course, they needed access to the funds to make it all work.

But it was clever as all hell. Romello, she thought. Her handlers had known exactly what they were doing when she'd been sent into the Treas, known what he'd need. It had been no accident that she'd found him.

When the Treas had put her into the dot-com, it had been routine. The contract the group of engineers were under required they hook up the then-small Whitestone to the Fedwire. Because the financial services company was an unknown entity at the time—it had been less than a year ago, she realized with a touch of surprise—the plant of an agent and the surveillance from the Treasury was standard operating procedure, especially given the current national and global situation.

As Whitestone continued to grow and absorbed the dot-com as their technical lynchpin, there was no need to pull her. She was in the perfect place to observe—that was part of her job, or at least the surface of it: to observe and report. She was considered a researcher, an analyst, and of a medium level at that, able to receive and pass on potentially critical intelligence. There were no expectations that she would play any sort of role in the actual arrests or confrontations, and in fact it was quite discouraged, since it would blow the cover the Treasury wanted her to maintain.

But there was so much more going on beneath that seeming-secret surface, because there was quite literally a higher power that pulled her strings. She was one of the new breed of agents, younger, savvy in the new technology, the blend of operative and technician, and while she didn't know it, one of a very few to receive the "I" designation.

And so she was to perform her role for the Treasury, using a name that was familiar and comfortable for her, with a cover history close enough to her own that she couldn't be startled into unexpected revelations or inconsistencies. Not that the potential for that really concerned her; she'd never blown an op either as a run-of-the-mill field agent or as a team lead.

From this vantage point, she was able to pay attention to the flow of the new cyber frontier that was led by geniuses and madmen, idealists and demagogues, the perfect place for someone to hide, to grow, to create a very valid, new threat, the parameters of which finally now, several years after its birth, were first being evaluated.

Only two government agencies even ventured to guess what the nature and scope of those threats might be and had taken steps to attempt to discover and prevent the now-here future: the National Security Agency and the Central Intelligence Agency.

And the CIA knew that Romello was smart. The Fox was one of the best operatives the Company had ever had.

He'd gone from inside to outside, was the first to point out the potential of the new technology, had been an enthusiastic adaptor, or so said the files her group had been given to read.

She didn't know what had changed for him, and she didn't care. What she did know and care about was that he'd gone from loyal soldier to sworn enemy, espousing an ideation that she found chilling. She had, along with the other agents similarly deployed, read his philosophy, if one could accurately call it that, his prose ringing with pronouncements such as,"You the inferior, with your ability to breed like rats, have held sway over the world for too long, due only to your strength in numbers, and the misplaced charity of your betters—but no longer…"

The rest of the manifesto that Romello had sent to his former supervisor—copies of which had been made available to the team—had contained further details of his plans for what he called "the *true* people."

She knew, because she'd already been told that they were all to operate on a need-to-know basis, that what she'd read had only been one part of it, but the part she'd studied she found repugnant.

Romello, among other things, believed in eugenics—not the sort based on the vagaries of culture, of ethnicity, of physical appearance, but one based on intellect. It seemed that his true aim was to create a society wherein those under certain threshold IQs were either eliminated or subservient to what he referred to as "real humans," at least until those "superior intellects" created enough machines to completely replace those he considered undesirable.

She wasn't entirely certain why she'd been selected for this particular assignment. But as an operative who was both a qualified engineer as well as a communications specialist, she was, her superiors informed her, "a natural fit," even before the testing and the new training. And when she was advised of the scope of the position, she'd been told that this was the perfect place for her true specialty: the forecasting of trends and behavior based on presented information, the source of her explainable-after-the-fact decisions. Communications as metric, indeed.

"True analytics are wasted in the field," her new handler had said. "Anyone can dodge detection, throw in a couple of incendiaries, and shoot straight, but not everyone can do what *you* do—paint an accurate picture of tomorrow based on today's data."

Her new assignment and designation appealed to her on many fronts, despite her initial misgivings. On one level, it allowed her and her peers within the Company to truly demonstrate the value of the new frontier and their skills within it. But on a personal level, it had brought her to Charli.

All the intel they'd begun with had very directly indicated that Romello was using the electronic medium for recruitment, and with her ideals, skill set, and enthusiastic use of it, she threw herself into the investigation.

That was both metaphorically and literally true. She'd jumped into the ocean, surfed the Internet and chat rooms, raves and beaches, all with one single-minded intent: find something—anything—that would put her on Romello's direct trail.

Millions, perhaps billions, would suffer if even part of his plan came to fruition, and through no fault of their own other than having been judged unworthy by one man who had decided that intellect was the only true God.

He could not be allowed to slip away, to even begin to put his machinations into motion. She debated her options. She could let the Treas move in, with every single point of circumstantial evidence leading in one direction—a false one—and maintain her cover. There were lies, she reminded herself, and there were nested lies. She knew, because she lived one.

Beneath her role at Whitestone, she was a Treasury agent, but beneath that, she was Central Intelligence, and she balanced them all perfectly. But even with the outer deceptions, she couldn't lie to herself. It was integral to her ability to maintain her cover, a cover she knew she'd risk blowing sky-high come Tuesday morning.

If she even hinted to the Treas another agency was running an operation within theirs, there would be hell itself to pay when this thing blew up in all their faces and traveled up to the executive branch. And, she reminded herself, while all the territorial pissing went on and internal investigations and committees blustered at one another, Romello would slip away with the money, and that much closer to whatever he thought he needed to gain his ultimate objective.

❖

To: APendleton@zoomail.com

Hey Gorgeous,

Just home. Mushy at Plum, but better than nada, right? Check the LOLA report—looks like it's rippin' for the next few days Jersey or LI. Shame I'll pass, though. Ping me when you're free—we'll talk.

Hey, if you're going bring your rubbers—the 8 mm ones—the water's still way cold.

C

Charli reviewed the options before her while she showered after her late afternoon spent off the Brooklyn shore, not far from Plum Beach. It was early in the season yet, and definitely cold, but definitely worth it, if only to get out into the water, let the issues that weighed on her head be beaten away by the pound of the surf, the green-glass glide, the occasional swallow of seaweed, she joked to herself as she removed a bit that had managed to get under her hood of her wet suit—military issue 8 mm "rubbers"—and into her hair.

Still, her concerns hadn't disappeared entirely. Laura had paged her confirming her eight a.m. on Monday with Eric, and except for reviewing any possible exceptions her team might have found, there was "Nothing—not a bloody thing so far," Eunae, her section lead reported, when Charli pinged her for an update.

There was nothing else to be done until Charli got the okay to perform a full audit of every account and every transaction in and out of the wire. She could have performed it anyway, but the information involved was ostensibly private and to be read only by the account manager and the client. Without permission from on high, that meant breaking both the terms of her employment—the bonding they'd all been required to take—and the law. That she wouldn't do—unlike whoever it had been who'd tapped into her system. And that brought her thoughts full circle. Something about the whole scenario with the server up and downs really irked her. Suddenly, Charli realized what she was contemplating. Was she really going to blow off what could be a great weekend to review and search for what she already had her team doing?

Let me check LOLA again, she told herself and quickly belted on a robe, then toweled her head. If she was still going, she had to pick up the car she'd reserved and tomorrow they'd drive out to…Long Island, she decided. It faced south, easily picking up windswells, which became more common in spring. Besides, late March into April meant some dramatic weather changes.

```
LOLA SURF SPOT FORECAST

Time Zone XXX Period XXX

Chart Center: Lat XXX Long XXX

Forecast Center: Lat XXX Long XXX
```

She leaned over her keyboard and replaced the placeholder *X*'s on screen with the coordinates of the location she wanted to investigate. LOLA. Variously nicknamed by its users as "lots of lip action" and supposedly by its makers as "lots of linux activity," LOLA was a proprietary, Web-based program that allowed surfers and seafarers to plug in coordinates and view the specific forecast for that region.

Charli sat before the forecast she had running. *If Plum Beach was anything to go by,* she mused as she quickly opened another window to cross-reference and query a few other possible locations. A quick check of the local surf reports and Web cams and…it seemed there was another possibility. She zeroed in on it.

The Jersey shore, with its variable swell, wind, and weather— fifty-degree water in July but seventy-five degree air in January— showed some promise. There were eighty known surf spots in New Jersey, one hundred and nine known ones on Long Island and… she enlarged the weather tracker to get a better look. No. There was a system collecting farther north and that system was tracking toward…she scanned through. Fire Island. Kismet. If they left early in the morning and took the ferry over, they could get a full day in, and if the day ended up as ripping as the forecast promised it would, they could decide if they'd stay overnight either on the drive, or at the end of the day.

She popped open another window to query available locations, then hesitated a moment over the keyboard. What was she *doing*? She'd just e-mailed Anna to tell her she wasn't going and besides, the last time they'd actually stayed together—

Charli dismissed the thought and forced away the visceral wash of memory. They'd be all right, just fine, she assured herself. They worked together, they still hung out together, there were no hard feelings about last night, right?

That caught her short: Should there be? Did she herself, Charli, really wish it had gone differently? She'd already keyed the query and she bit her lip as she thought about it, really thought about it for the first time.

For whatever reason, the image and memory of Raven, beautiful, talented, and driven with vision, an artist with a hard-core business sense, a feel for how the world worked in her field, rose in her mind. *Raven*, she smiled ruefully to herself, *was a glorious mistake.*

Charli had met the visual artist in the dot-com next door, where Raven worked in graphics, when they'd run into each other several times in the halls, then again at one of the parties thrown by a client their companies shared.

The relationship itself had started out nicely, just enough friendly, just enough heat, and Raven, with her long fall of dark, dark hair and sharp blue eyes that seemed to glow when she spoke about her work, enjoyed Charli's approach to everything. But that had been the problem too, eventually. Everything, from food to fucking and so many of the little things in between, had ended up becoming Charli's decision, and Charli didn't have the time, the energy, or the desire to run anyone's life besides her own.

She and Raven had never argued, nor had they ever disagreed, about anything, and that was what had ultimately made it end. There was no spark, no *anything*. Nothing. That's what had come between them, a growing nothing. Raven didn't challenge her, didn't contest her, had never noticed, not once, not even in their closest moments, that there were times that Charli wanted, *needed*—Christ!

The crawling discomfort that flooded her skin made her slam her hand down on the desktop as she stood, then walked away from it. She strode with deliberate, measured steps through the apartment into her bedroom in an attempt to force one physical sensation to replace another. *I've* got *to get this out of my system*, she told herself firmly as she reached into her closet.

Charli thought as objectively as she could about Anna as she dressed. She liked her, they got along, and there was no denying she found her very attractive as a person, as a woman. They worked well together, they surfed well together, and she couldn't—nor did she want to—deny how much she'd enjoyed the taste and touch of Anna's tawny skin, smooth, slick, soaked in salt and sweat as they moved together. Then there had been that time, the "almost" that Charli knew was the *real* reason she'd headed out for the train back to NYC.

It wasn't because Anna couldn't affect her, but because she could, she did, enough to make a voice from the buried past echo through her head, a voice that made her question what her real motives were. She put that thought with its unwelcome memory and voice away so she could continue to think clearly, without a distracting overlay of emotion. Her hands moved automatically as she drew up her slacks, the dark wool and viscose mix cool and fluid, a comfortable flow against her legs.

Okay, so Anna was different, Charli could admit that. She enjoyed her company, her mind, and, as she tucked her blouse below her waistband, silk smooth beneath her fingertips, she smiled to herself at the memory that played for her.

Her hands closed the zipper and set the flat-fit hooks as she checked the drape in the mirror, but what she saw was the way Anna's body leaned and curved and twisted on her board to master the wave. That same fluid grace that had moved under and with her those nights they'd spent together.

All right, too. She wanted. She could admit that as well, and had Kevin not—she huffed one long sigh as she moved through the hallway back toward her desk. It wasn't Kevin's fault, she acknowledged with a twinge of something deeper than regret, it was someone else's, it was her own, and honestly, what she really needed to do was—

The soft ping that sounded as she neared her laptop told her the results had been tabulated and she read through them. *Nice, very nice*, she considered when she found a location she thought would suit, not more than fifty yards from the beach she figured they'd hit. Charli hesitated, fingers over the keyboard and ready to plug in her credit card numbers as she debated her options.

No one, no company officer, member of the board, not a single member of the accounting team, no client, had complained officially or unofficially to the company or to her team, as far as she could tell.

There had been no hue and cry about theft, of funds or identities, and with the exception of the single crash, there were no residual issues, not even a hiccup. No malware had infected the system, there were no operational delays or information drops—except for the kickover that had wiped the record of inbound and outbound chatter.

"Something's *very* wrong," she said to her screen as she toggled to another program and opened the window that would allow her to watch traffic flow along the main branch of the network. "This doesn't make sense."

Charli reviewed what she knew. Everything *seemed* fine, but why select such specific, quarterly transfer dates? If the intent was to in effect say "knock-knock—can't keep me out," then why was there no calling card, no signature of some sort?

Charli knew how hackers worked and thought, since she was in essence one herself. Hackers were the good guys, they did nothing bad, just had some logical fun, puzzles really, but it was the crackers that gave them all a bad name.

A few idiot journalists who knew nothing about technology but were rushed with deadlines to report about "the cyber frontier" couldn't be bothered to differentiate, and now everyone was tarred with the same brush of bad intent.

Thing was, Charli considered, white or black hat, when hackers and crackers invaded systems for good or for ill, they wanted bragging rights. It was electronic bravado, machismo, who had the biggest brain and the baddest code. And there was none of that here, at least not in terms of signatures, which meant, as far as she was concerned, that this wasn't ordinary hacking.

Criminal activity left its own mark. Stolen money was almost always immediately obvious, and identity theft became apparent in very short order—but if that had been part of the purpose, then why had nothing shown up in that arena within the last three months since the system had first been hit?

No. She could see what it obviously wasn't, and quite clearly what it was: planned, purposeful, directed. She simply didn't know at what—yet.

What she did know was that she'd never run before, not from anything, especially things that puzzled or challenged her. Everything she did was about tackling things that seemed impossible, insurmountable, from pushing the technology envelope, to challenging the ocean.

When Anna called, maybe she'd have her come over, maybe they'd go out and grab a bite, but either way, Charli decided, she was going into the office in the morning.

Satisfied, she closed the now nonessential windows and pulled out a set of disks: she had a burned copy of every code that ran on her system, and she'd start there.

The program is running. Exit anyway? (y or n)

FAIL-SAFE

BB84 Secure Session - - Loss 0

18:12:02 DsrtFx: you do it?

18:12:03 ChknMan: yes.

18:12:04 DsrtFx: they'll move soon - don't worry

18:12:05 DsrtFx: we'll get her out.

18:12:06

18:12:07 DsrtFx: she'll go. The other one's done.

18:12:08

18:12:09 ChknMan: you sure?

18:12:10

18:12:11 DsrtFx: you got your end, I got mine

18:12:12

18:12:13 DsrtFx: 41°10'59"N, 72°11'25"W

18:12:14 DsrtFx: 13:00 Sunday. Get to Greenpoint

18:13:15 DsrtFx: I'll escort the rest of way

18:13:16

18:13:17 ChknMan: ok

BB84 Secure Session TERMINATED

❖

Ben Cooper's hands shook. They shook so badly that it took him a few seconds to realize the vibration came from somewhere behind his navel and spread downward through his thighs as well as upward to his chest before it branched out to his hands as he stared at the closed connection through the numbness that pressed against his temples.

He'd done it, he'd actually done it. Ben had been couriered a key, and that key he'd been told would fit a locker at Port Authority terminal. After he gave the junkie with his well-maintained bicycle a few bucks for his next fix, he followed instructions.

It took him fifteen minutes to get from his apartment to Port Authority, and once there, he found the locker he'd been directed to, then took the cell phone out from within it. Ben dialed the number he'd been told to and spoke the script he'd been given, the one he'd rehearsed over and over in his mind on the subway ride over. Afterward, he threw the phone into the nearest trash can.

It was possible for Ben to be honest with himself to a degree, and for the moment, he was. He felt horrible about seeing Charli blamed for something she didn't do, and he simply couldn't take it, the crawling guilt that tunneled under his skin, anymore. He'd called John, aka Desert Fox, to warn him about the audit she had requested and was almost positive she'd receive a go-ahead on— if, he reminded himself, she wasn't already doing it on her own, manually.

He certainly didn't put it past her; Charli truly did bleed to lead and was more than likely to apologize later—smile shining in her eyes because she knew she was right, she always was—than to ask for permission.

Still, though, it was a move neither he nor John had anticipated. Ben wasn't entirely certain how he'd accomplished it; he'd never been a great speaker, had always found it easier to work with code and systems, to communicate his ideas through his actions, but somehow, he'd found a way. This morning, he'd managed to convince the man he'd met online through a chat group over a year ago that Charli was vital, could be, *would* be, a valuable asset to them.

Within half an hour of that conversation, John with his inside contacts and his rapid-fire planning had scripted Ben's phone call, had changed the fall guy from Charli to someone else. Their last exchange confirmed this and of course, Ben knew exactly who it was: he'd suggested the substitute.

He drew a still-shaky breath. He felt as if he'd somehow always known it would come down to this, known it since the first time Anna Pendleton had been brought into the original dot-com group.

Most tech jobs were what were commonly referred to as sausage fests: all dicks, no tits, as the guys said. Ben had assumed that after the initial "it's-great-to-see-another-female-'round-here-besides-the-receptionist" novelty had worn off, Anna would—very much like Charli had—become one of the guys. Not that all of the guys, especially the ones in graphics, he amended with a little snort, were "manly men." Heck, almost none of them were by the stupid cultural standard, the one that rewarded brawn over brains, but still, there was that *thing*, a bonding of sorts, a core similarity they all shared.

Charli had proven she was one of them and Ben knew, perhaps better than most in some ways, that it had been pure ability and skill that had landed her in the positions she'd occupied. Any grumbling or resentment from the coder troops in those first few days was quickly silenced by the evidence—Charli worked hard, played harder, and took care of her team; she was great to work with, and even better to work for.

Still, even though she showed no favoritism once she'd become team lead, there was an indefinable something different in how Charli related to Anna as opposed to everyone else, and while

Anna had indeed become one of the guys, there was still something different in the way Anna behaved around Charli. Ben didn't know at all how to describe it, but he certainly knew it when he saw it.

This morning, after he'd finally delayed as long as he'd been able to—after all, there was quite a bit of his own work to do—and brought the printouts to Charli's office, he'd frozen, then forced himself to calm when he'd seen the way Anna gazed at and stood so close to Charli.

They'd been talking about him and he'd been grateful for it because it gave him a few moments to choke back, to choke down the rage, the sense of invasion that mixed with the fiery pulse he'd felt thud in his neck and the heated punch to his groin when he'd seen it, their bodily proximity, the way they seemed to align, fit to each other, even with the slight space between them.

If he'd been better at self-examination, he'd have caught himself and understood the true reason that led his reaction, and if he didn't proudly carry the aura of the perpetually persecuted, he might have perhaps even taken a moment to respond to their conversation, perhaps explain his ideas about the importance of natural treatment of the body, the toxin buildup and the resulting damage from what people considered to be routine parts of their day. Not that he hadn't held forth on that subject before, when they'd all worked in the Puck building.

Instead, something about Anna's smile, smirk really, when she'd glanced up at him—so damned arrogant and somehow so damned smug—*he* knew what she was saying, what she meant. She might as well have yelled it at him, with her "I'm here, right here next to her, and *you're* all the way over there. What are you gonna do about it?" damned look. It made him *so* mad…He could barely breathe, never mind speak.

To make matters even worse for him, it had thrown him back to the days before they'd worn collars and suits, to one of the last peer code reviews the group held before the company had been bought out, and it had been his project chosen for the weekly highlight and discussion.

They needed a new way of allowing customers to view their

accounts and their recent activity that was secure, but still end-user friendly, and without compromising their existing security and log-on requirements, he'd told the assembled group as he prepared the laptop to send its display. *This is what I gave 'em.* A quick keystroke put the code—exactly as he'd written it—on screen before them, and Ben remembered pinching his lips in the hollow of his fist, mouth tucked and tight in the circle of his thumb and forefinger, holding back the smile that so wanted to escape. It was a great joke, and he'd known the team would get it.

There'd been silence for a few seconds, as his audience read, and took the time to understand and then...

While the crew had hooted and hollered and there had been all-over admiration for the functional elegance of his code and even Charli had laughed at first, every smile had disappeared with hers when she was the first to ask, then answer as she realized, "Holy shit...this code is *live*? Coop—my office—*now!*"

The cool stare Anna had thrown his way as the meeting broke up posthaste, amid a rush of pushed chairs that scraped against the floor and muttered excuses from his fellows as they beat a hasty retreat, had made a blush of shame, then a flare of defiant anger blaze under his skin even as he followed Charli out of the conference room and back to her office. Anna's cold jade glance, though, the superior "you're such a loser and I am so much better than you—*she* likes me better than *you*" shine of it, had stayed embedded in his mind, had kept him mute while he rehearsed silent rebuttals and didn't really listen, even while Charli explained that although she agreed in principle that some clients really were a pain in the ass, it was not only completely improper to call the program "FuckDaMan," it was also equally wrong to create a live code that read such as he'd displayed it.

```
<QUERY NAME= "WORLDFUCK" DATASOURCE=
"WORLD-FUCKERS"
    SELECT D.IDIOT_ID, D.IDIOT_NAME,
        B.BULLSHIT_ID,
        M.MORESHIT_ID
```

```
           A.ASSHOLE_REALNAME
FROM D.IDIOT A, B.BULLSHIT O, Y.WE_R_FUKD,
N.U_R_FUKD
           and D.IDIOT_ID = L.ASSHOLE_REALNAME
           and B.BULLSHIT_ID and M.MORESHIT_ID
order by D.IDIOT_ID, B. BULLSHIT_ID, Y.WE_R_FUKD
</QUERY>
<FORM ACTION= "TAKE-THIS-SHIT.XML">
    <GRID NAME= "GUILTYLIST1" QUERY=
"GETTHISSHIT"
           SELECTMODE= "TROUBLESOURCE"
           HEIGHT= "300" WIDTH = "400"
<GRIDCOLUMN NAME = "Account_No.">
<GRIDCOLUMN NAME = "Client_Name">
<GRIDCOLUMN NAME = "Recent_Activity">
<GRIDCOLUMN NAME = "Current_Balance">
</GRID>
</FORM>
```

She'd shut him down. She could have, and maybe she should have, fired him on the spot—but Charli was more than just one of the guys, she was one of *them*, soul surfer and techno tribe, not a mere corporate drone.

Ben knew in a way that he couldn't explain that she thought the way he did, felt the way he did. There was something in the way she'd laugh at things he thought were funny, the sharp glances, the glimpses of fury quickly hidden. He even liked the way she moved, though he was careful, or so he thought, not to get caught watching. There was a fluidity in even her most economical motions, a flow that coupled with the curves of her body made her represent—to him anyway—something essentially feminine, despite the dark hair that angled short in the back and gradually lengthened to her chin in the front.

Of course he found her attractive—all the guys did, though they were careful not to talk too much about the boss. But what had cemented it for him was the day he cracked her code, the code he now knew for dead certain had won them the corporate position they had and her role as Second VP-Ops. Well, all right, he admitted, he hadn't actually *cracked* her code, per se, but he had administrator rights on the server, so he'd merely bypassed the securities and read it outright.

She was damned brilliant, that's all there was to it. Charli took a process—aggregating non-transactable dividends across thousands of accounts, dipping them into, and then back out of, the Fedwire for interest purposes, and then distributing the funds back to the source accounts—that would have taken more time and money in man-hours to accomplish than was worth actually doing, then automated it so that the only cost involved was the actual coding of it in the first place. Then she'd made it scalable, portable, and secure. It was sheer technical poetry.

He and John had been discussing via IM how to obtain the funds necessary to build the school, the *army*, that would save the nation, maybe even the world, from its excesses. Ben had mentioned in passing their then-new contract with Whitestone, and their connection to the massive exchange of currency on the Fedwire.

What had started out as speculation became a plan, then had become an accomplishment: using his permissions as server admin, Ben had taken Charli's code, and thanks to the many systems that had to dump data into the one main one that connected to the Fed, he was able to insert his own bit of code at the gate itself. It took a percentage of the returning interest, sent it back into the wire where it would once again gain interest, then took the new earnings and funneled them to an account John had set up with his own contacts.

No muss, no fuss, and in essence, no loss. The investors got all the money they'd earned, he and John simply piggybacked off it. The only one who lost anything was the Treas, and that loss was more theoretical than real, since they wouldn't know that he and John had transferred funds to and from the wire without paying the mandated fees.

It was a beautiful irony, Ben thought: they were using the

earnings of the greedy rich who were destroying the planet and the tools of the government that was aiding the process to fund their liberation effort.

They weren't some crazy right-wing militia, they weren't terrorists, they were informed, concerned citizens who'd had their country stolen from them—and now they had a way to get it back.

Ben Cooper knew things. He knew he wasn't some creep who wanted to go back to the stone age, or live a feudal life. He respected the planet, he was multicultural, he ate Thai food for chrissakes, and he respected individuals, men and women. He was pro-technology, pro-choice, and pro-equality.

Shit, he figured, while he couldn't fully understand what in the world one guy could see in another, it didn't really bother him, and he was certain he could at least understand dykes, and the occasional threesome featuring girl-on-girl bisexuality. After all, some girls were just *so* pretty, so soft and perfect—how could anyone really resist that completely?

And Charli, to his mind, was like that: too pretty to really be a total dyke. Yeah, sure, she'd lived with that Raven chick for what, one year? Not quite two? What did that prove? What it showed, he was certain, was that one woman couldn't hold her interest for that long. But a man like him—he was smart, he was conscientious about the things that mattered, like the environment, the economy, third-world nations, he was *sensitive*, or so his last two girlfriends had told him before they'd left him because, as they said, he was "just too good" for them, what with his political causes and all.

And he wasn't all *that* bad looking, either. Since the acquisition, he'd taken to tying his hair back, trimmed his beard—Charli had even noticed, commented on it. All right, he considered, maybe he wasn't as pretty as that boy who had walked past his door that morning to interview, but Cooper was a man, not a boy, and he knew that Charli could tell the difference.

She was smart, different. She was perfect, and while he felt guilty for the way the plans he'd set in motion with John had been originally laid, everything was going to be fine. John had been convinced of Charli's value, and he promised they'd get her out.

Ben knew he could count on that, count on John's word. John was a good man, a man like his father, or what his father could have been if Vietnam hadn't left him with a piece of itself in his spine, leaving him able to only do odd jobs here and there when the pain and the memories didn't overwhelm him, a man who'd loved and served his country, and then been left with nothing but the scars in his body and the jungle in his head. And on the day Ben left for college, his father finally took it out by the roots, just one shot nice and clean—sniper perfect, he would have called it—through his skull.

Ben shook his head. His father would have liked Charli. Charli had that spark his father had told him his mother had had, before the war, before the Veterans Administation, the VA bullshit and the medications, before they'd moved and he'd been too small to remember, but it was then, his father told him, then that the world, the government, and big business and their lies, they'd stolen his mom from them.

He couldn't let that happen to Charli.

They'd save her, him and John, they would. Once they did, got her out of the corporate hell that was destroying the soul of their once-great nation, of the world, all they had to do was explain: about the violations of the sacred privacy guaranteed by their betrayed constitution, the economic and ecological damage being perpetuated on a mass scale, the creeping global enslavement. She'd understand, she'd willingly join them.

When she did, Ben thought, she'd not only be free, eyes wide open, she'd also see that he was right and had been right all along. Charli would then see, would finally know he was a real man, a true hero and, well, the math from there as he figured it was pretty easy.

That, he concluded with a grim satisfaction that settled and then erased the buzz that had grabbed his very bones, made—the word *betrayal* whizzed through his mind, but he quickly shut it out—getting rid of Anna Pendleton completely worthwhile.

❖

To: CRiven@zenchat.com

Babe:

Step. Away. From. The. Keyboard. Coming over now
with bribes: Brazilian fusion, a venti caramel
macchiato, and enough double shots to keep us both
up all night—not that you need it ☺ (!!!)

Yes, let's talk. Have some thoughts. See you in
about 15.

A

She blew her breath out in frustration as she got into the cab.
She'd played this badly, because the perfect alibi, the almost ironclad
proof of innocence could have been had, and she herself could have
backed it, guaranteeing her the further time she needed to draw the
delicate net around the rogue agent. But she'd failed to push the
opportunity.

Dammit. Charli, with her façade of openness and sudden
withdrawals, a depth that she had only briefly glimpsed that could
become a remote freeze that brought down entire room temperatures,
would have been a great agent. Certainly better than she herself
was.

Logically, she knew that she could explain to the Company
that what she was doing made sense, that it would protect her cover

in the Treas and prevent an injustice. It made objective sense, it made ethical sense in a larger, abstract way, but had she really been concerned about those things, she would have put herself aside, her personal knowledge and concerns away, and made it happen. With an unshakeable alibi in place, none of this would be necessary.

Wrapped in her red-white-and-blue lie to the world, she told herself the truth. She *could* say she'd been objective, keeping a neutral distance, but that wasn't reality, not her reality. She hadn't been objective at all. And where Charli was concerned, she hadn't been for a while.

She grimaced to herself as she tipped the driver. She was an agent, and if she was a stupid one, she'd let them take Charli, which in turn would tip off both the inside guy and Romello that their days of free-feeding were over, just as they were sniffing at the surface, a search for sustenance as it were. And like other nocturnal, hidden creatures, revelation of any sort would force them further underground once more, to plot and plan in darkness until they were ready to move again. From there, there was no knowing where anything would surface, or what form it would take.

She shook her head as she walked to the elevator in the Chelsea apartment building. She absolutely could not let Charli go back to the office, hands-on with the server codes, or to even hit them remotely from home. The Treas would use that as evidence confirming Charli was erasing her own tracks, and she needed any shred of evidence she could get to prove it wasn't her. She needed to be allowed to continue the surface investigation while she got that last bit of proof on Cooper, that final thread connecting him to the inside job and Romello. Let them remain complacent.

But first things first: she'd allowed personal considerations, personal knowledge, to get in the way last night. This time, no matter what she thought the consequences might be—

Something twisted under her skin, tensing the muscles in her neck. Duty and desire, lies and loyalty. What she wanted and what she had to do ran across lines that were crossing, blurring, disappearing, and she had to keep a grip. Okay, they intersected, there was nothing really wrong with that, and if the investigation went the way it should, if she maintained her cover and assignment, there was no reason why—she resolutely stopped herself there.

The Treas tracked her, she knew that. No matter what else they might think, after tonight she would be able to at least prove, beyond any shadow of a doubt, that at the very least, Charli had been nowhere near—physically or electronically—the Fedwire. It would at the very least remove some of the suspicion from Charli, if not completely remove her from their crosshairs.

If there was fallout, she'd handle it after—if there was an "after" to even discuss. What had she been *thinking*? That somehow, after all was said and done, she could breach those walls, take her to a safe house and explain everything, then make it all better? And then, what, they'd date? Have something even resembling an actual relationship?

Yes, that was *exactly* what she'd been half daydreaming in some unsanctioned-by-the-Company way. She would have smacked some sense into herself if she thought it would really help, but none of that mattered at the moment, she reasoned as she balanced her packages and entered the elevator. Her mission right now was to keep Charli out of the office and off the system.

❖

"I need to do this more often," Charli said as she took her focus away from the screen and glanced about the living room from her spot next to Anna on the sofa. "You really know how to deliver a bribe," she added, friendly admiration in her voice as she observed the profile focused on one of three screens—one from the tower system, and two laptops.

Between the latte, the food, and the cans of chilled espresso, they had wine, and together they'd run through not only Charli's code, but Anna's as well.

"And we're done." Anna grinned at the screen, then faced Charli as the last testing window was shut.

"I need to check what's going on with the server itself," Charli told her as she reached for the system to key the connection. "See what the differences might be."

"Franko's there right now, you know he's working on that," Anna reminded her, "and you've got that thing"—she pointed to the PDA on the coffee table—"programmed to buzz you with alerts." She gently but forcibly took Charlie's hands away from the keyboard. "Leave it for now, babe. You know you've got a great team," Anna told her and smiled, still holding her hands. "Take a break."

Anna's hazy green eyes stared intently back at Charli's, telling her something more than what was spoken. She dropped her gaze to her mouth, to lips that had stopped moving, a sensuous curve that lifted lightly, lips she knew were tender, soft, devourable really, and suddenly she realized just how much she'd wanted to all along.

There was nothing to stop her, to stop them, really. It was one of those funny things, Charli observed, that she could literally feel Anna's intent through her touch. She could do that with a lot of people, actually. It wasn't something she could explain, it was simply that while she knew—it was obvious to her in that same inexpressible way—that there was something Anna wasn't saying, her hands, her skin, the way her fingers gripped, sent her an easily decoded message: Anna cared.

Certainly, too, there was desire in that touch, but it was different somehow, warmer, giving almost, in a way she didn't know how to fully describe. There was no sense of...*avarice* was the only word she could think of, as memories flew through her mind, of people she'd—

She shook her head and carefully withdrew her hands. She stared and wondered at the strange feeling of them, the surprise and shocking emptiness of her skin.

"Anna. I owe you an apology," Charli began quietly. She raised her eyes to Anna's and searched them.

"Why? I mean, what for?" she asked in return, her voice almost equally low.

That gaze seemed closer and Charli felt the sudden start in her chest, the sharp painful lump that traveled up, became a pulse in her neck. She had, she realized, a choice. She could tell the complete truth, or a partial one. There was a sense of something—maybe it was the expression Anna wore, or maybe it was as simple as that touch, the one that had held her hands, the fingertip that now brushed her hair off her cheek, tucked it carefully behind an ear.

"Last night…" Charli hesitated. She wasn't ready to explain, wasn't sure if she could, if she really understood or had the words for herself. "The breach and all…definitely no fun. And tonight," she gave Anna a smile, "tonight you could be getting all sorts of laid and ready to rip this weekend, and you're here, reviewing code with me instead. Not that I don't appreciate it," Charli added, still smiling as she waved to indicate the detritus of their meal. "I mean, it's been great and all, but—"

Charli was surprised only after it happened. "And who says I won't?" Anna murmured against her lips, a breath away from where they'd just been. "Make it up to me. Fuck the job tonight, Char." Once again green eyes bored into hers, a message she couldn't fully comprehend, but the touch, the sincerity that flowed from it, the emotion that rode beneath it… It was nice, no, it was more than that, Charli thought, to have someone be simply honest. Tone and touch matched, and that she understood. Completely.

She'd already wanted, had admitted that to herself, was aware of the mutually acknowledged attraction that still flowed between them, but it was Anna's honest and blatant declaration that took want to need, a need that flew with an almost dizzying rush to her head, a thrill of power and arousal that sent sparks tingling under her skin, each one a rein, a string, a thread she could collect, gather, control. She knew what to do with that, too.

Charli let her wait while she studied her, the high rise of her cheeks, the curve of her lips, the exquisite line of her neck, the pulse in it a revelation of the emotions that drove it under her fingertips as she traced what she saw until her finger rested just above the V of Anna's blouse. "Fine, then," she answered, the words almost a purr as she thumbed the shell button through the silk and traced the warm skin beneath it, across the edge of the curve that silk still covered, along the fine defined lines of muscle and bone, the jut of her collar, and up the line of the neck she'd just admired, until she curled her fingers through gold and satin strands and around Anna's neck, her thumb outlining her jaw. The kiss she gave began as something delicate, sensual, and quickly evolved into a primal demonstration of intent as Charli covered Anna's body with hers. "I can do that."

Starting program: /hacking/$ ./vuln-test:execute

THE WALRUS

```
Consortium Chat - Member Email


To CharliX - - Private Chat Request - - From DsrtFx
```

Although she hadn't answered his private chat request yet, he wasn't concerned; she was a bona fide technophile, and even with the plans Ben Cooper had told him she might have, it was almost outside the realm of probability that she'd leave in the morning without checking her e-mail, her PDA, or her cell phone—and he had all night. Besides, he had a complete dossier on Charli, or "X" as she'd been nicknamed on the board, and he knew her, had even met her several times, though he was certain she wouldn't remember it. Then again, she wasn't meant to, and he was good—perhaps one of the best, if he thought about it—at remaining or becoming anonymous. He had based an entire career on it. Besides, why would she remember the man who came to water the plants at the new office, the elevator repairman from the Puck building, or any of the many people who populated the occasional raves and parties the Consortium she belonged to threw?

He shifted in his seat and swiveled away from the screen that would alert him when her response came, back to the detailed schematic spread across the desk.

CharliX, he thought as he traced different routes with a fingertip, memorizing hallways and ducts, a vast but ordered maze of old structure, new construction, and hidden connections that might prove useful. Charli for her own first name, for the boy on *Star Trek* who had made things happen by merely thinking them, which was exactly what Charli herself did, create things from her mind, and X, the Roman numeral for ten. Of course, there was also X for the unknown, and that's exactly what she was, to everyone but him. There was yet another reason, of course, an ironic one to be sure, he chuckled to himself as he stared at the lines before him, selecting then memorizing two routes, one easily accessible, the other hidden by a new wall, but he doubted very highly that any besides himself, a few upper-echelon players within the Company, and a select group of scientists and government officials knew the true reason why an entire generation had been tagged with that specific moniker.

But those reasons weren't the center of his focus for now—Charli was. Twirling his seat back to his screen, he clicked on the icon he'd parked on his desktop. He drummed his fingers, an old marching cadence he liked, as he waited for the file to open. When it finally did, he reviewed the information he already had and searched for anything he might have missed, any new connections that could be made.

Charlotte Audrey Riven. One of two VP-Ops for one of the most stellar financial performers globally, had been the one to come up with the concept, then written the code that gave her company the earning edge on every level. Previously team lead at a now-defunct dot-com after paying her dues as a member of the code team. Bachelor of science from Hunter College in computer science; two parents: father Aaron Cole Riven, a school psychologist, mother Helen Renee Riven, née Daughtry, a high school principal, both were alive, still married, and living part-time during the summer in Ulster County, New York, the colder rest of the year as snowbirds in Florida. They were in many ways typical Boomers, but with no history of the usual diseases such as diabetes or blood-pressure ailments, indicating good genetic stock. And the larger hallmark he'd been looking for: both paternal and maternal grandfathers had served in the U.S. Army during World War II. Each grandmother had visited Army doctors, each one had borne a child within the right time frame.

People, John repeated to himself another countless time with a little snort of black humor as he toggled from one screen to another, were genuinely stupid. Most who thought at all seemed to think that genetic manipulation began with Watson and Crick; they didn't realize that Watson and Crick had discovered the double helix *structure* of DNA, not DNA itself, had forgotten that it was in fact an Austrian monk, Gregor Mendel, who had discovered what would eventually come to be known as genes through his research with humble garden peas. The rest seemed to think it had been only the Nazis who had engaged in genetic research.

He puffed out a laugh even as he shook his head in bemusement, eyes flowing over the colored lines on the graph before him. It had been almost gestalt at the time, and the United States had devoted substantial resources to the field.

The products of those experiments were spread among the Boomer generation, the results of that phase examined in cultural and formal laboratory testing. A nested lie had been created, the truth partially revealed to the guinea pig public by the cryptonym MK Ultra, the designation MK stating directly that the project had been run by the Company's Technical Service Division.

But among the many things the public didn't know after all the forced hearings and apologies was that neither the experiment nor the testing were over: it was the next resulting generation—the *X* generation—that was to be the true subject of the experiment.

It was by deliberate design and not by accident that Generation X was the most tested generation yet in American history, tested in grade school, at routine medical and dental appointments, in every way, manner, and form that could be conceived of, intellectually, psychologically, and physically.

The results they received were all on record, both academic and medical. For those who hit certain criteria, their identities and dossiers were forwarded to a division within the Company. Taken together, the collected data on *X* painted a picture. John pursed his lips and traced the blue line that angled up sharply to the right with a fingertip held just barely above the electric discharge of the screen, before he minimized the window and returned to the original file.

That picture, he believed, that picture looked *exactly* like Charli. John continued to review the things he already knew about her. One brother, twenty months younger, Cole Alan Riven, a marine engineer and career officer with the Navy and recently stationed in Angola—which was good leverage, he considered, and probably more good genetics, too. His accomplishments on record very much seemed to back that; he was one of the youngest officers to be promoted to commander who had not come out of Annapolis, the service academy. His early records matched Charli's as well.

She'd had a more than decent GPA in high school, all relatively uneventful except she'd been out of school for a two-year stint, and digging there revealed very little. She'd dropped the art classes she'd focused on as well as the soccer she'd played when she finally returned as a senior, still able to graduate with her class without losing any time, and had managed to be in the top five.

Good IQ scores all along, much better than average, the same with aptitude testing. The usual childhood illnesses, though perhaps fewer of them and generally faster-than-average recovery times. Everything was normal, as to be expected, if it was a world that expected excellence. In a world that worshipped mediocrity, though, it made Charli exceptional, and Charli was definitely the sort of person he wanted to see grow strong, thrive, in the new order he had in mind. He more than strongly suspected Charli was part of the generation that had been specifically bred to lead exactly such a world.

There was one thing he didn't know, the final proof that the experiment had succeeded, had bred *true*, the one thing he kept searching for in all the information he had available. Those records were the only ones he'd not been able to access—yet. In the end, he suspected it would require personal interaction to verify, and then it wouldn't matter.

And to facilitate that verifying moment, finding Ben had been fortuitous indeed. Ah, Ben… He'd needed to test Ben, see where his loyalties lay, what sort of man he really was—what in the hell was a username like *Chickenman* supposed to mean? John decided it belonged to someone who saw himself as a victim, as something to be eaten—or something being eaten—by the world. Not a man like he himself was, older, clever, cunning, the tricky survivor and hunter, the fox.

He had never intended to let Charli take the fall—but he'd never let Ben know that, either. Ben had been the route to cash and to Charli.

Ben was, in John's estimation, brilliant. He was brilliant but delusional. He couldn't hide his true intentions or feelings about her from him, and John Romello understood what Ben quite obviously did not want to: Charli was a lesbian, she would never fall in love with him. Which was too bad, only in the sense that she had good genetics; it would be a shame not to pass them to a future generation if she chose not to. Well, that and she had a classic sort of beauty John himself found attractive, but her sexual orientation neither bothered him nor offended his sense of pride.

But still, with her intelligence, he was certain the logic of improving human stock would overcome any reservations she might have over the issue of issue—John chuckled at his own joke—and that was even assuming she had any; there was no reason to think she did. And in this respect, the fact that she was a lesbian was actually a tremendous advantage, since it increased the probability that pure genetics rather than random lust or chance would play a strong role in actual procreation.

Of course John had studied and watched her closely over the last year, the way he'd watched a few others he thought would be worthy of joining him. He wanted to find as many of the *X* children as he could. It had been an almost lucky accident that he'd found out about them at all.

He himself shared the particular marker so typical of the test generation: his own father had been barely more than an infant in the early 1920s when his family emigrated to the United States.

But the part of family history that stood out for John was not the fact that his father had been an officer during World War II, but, rather, the story of his birth, as imparted by his mother. His parents had tried desperately to conceive, but luck and timing were against them. When his father returned home from the Pacific Theater in 1947 at all of thirty years old, they tried again and this time, John Senior, who by then had completely rejected his Italian first name, insisted they visit one of the military medical specialists.

"I just went to the doctor one day, and the next thing you know, there was you," his mother would tell him with a loving smile. "The doctor did it."

He'd simply accepted that until he began his own career in the military and there heard similar statements from certain men he'd worked with, men who wondered during serious and reflective moments, moments that hovered on the knife edge between an uneasy safety and certain mortal peril, if they, too, should they be lucky enough to survive, possibly have similar difficulties one day; and in these random yet frank conversations, a pattern seemed to form. It teased at his mind, as did many other things.

It was his performance on a recon job in Laos as a member of the Special Forces that had given John the opportunity to join the CIA, or the Company as it was referred to, and on a hunch, he'd begun investigating. It had been a whim, a slight fancy, and as he made the right connections and began to ask the right questions, he discovered that what had seemed a peculiar coincidence was in fact a marker, a hallmark, even, and that what seemed wild speculation was actually part of a long-range plan.

The investigation at the time had been something that kept him distracted from the constant slippery shift of who were the friends and who were the foes in the global arena, even as he learned—the hard way—that the old saying that it mattered not to peasants whose ass sat on the throne was nothing but brutal truth. They all suffered and died anyway. Democracy, such as he not only saw it practiced but helped to enforce, was a failure and a farce. Friends and allies who had aided and sacrificed in one conflict became nothing more than collateral damage in the next, and he learned that loyalty, true loyalty, was not something one pledged to the vagaries of politics, but to individuals who shared ideation, who'd proven themselves.

Loyalty took blood to prove, and blood to break. Or perhaps it was simply blood that had opened his eyes...

So even before he'd thought they'd be useful to him, before he was even certain of what they were, never mind who, he'd started searching for answers to the half-formed questions his life, his men, and the stray little bits of information that came his way combined and raised in his mind.

He'd had nothing terribly in depth to go on, or at least not yet, not at the time, but the puzzle of all the Army-made babies distracted him during his dissolution of faith, or rather, *disillusion*, a process that had begun where he had—in Laos. Laos: the country that first they'd been ordered to secretly help, then only a few years later would drop over twenty thousand pounds of ordinance on. Dropped on the same people whose lives they'd saved, who had aided the Americans at great risk to themselves. Dropped and the results called collateral damage. That had been their reward for helping democracy. The price of freedom to sell Coca-Cola and McDonald's, to wear jeans and listen to rock 'n roll. Not that they could then, not that they were able to, now, not really. But it *had* been the promise held out to them, the false carrot of capitalism and free enterprise incentive.

And it wasn't that they'd been merely blown up, which was horrible enough in and of itself. An old weapon from World War II had been upgraded, reengineered, and reincarnated. A new Death had been deployed. In its first incarnation, it stuck to walls and ceilings, it stuck to metal and to moving targets and it burned, burned at more than three times the melting point of steel.

In its new incarnation, it stuck to skin and continued to burn, burn through muscle, through bone, while those not struck directly died of asphyxiation and heat stroke from the ambient air. But that was not the worst of it. The true horror of napalm was that the majority of its victims tended *not* to die immediately. It was slow death by a weapon that tortured those it killed and indelibly marked the living it left behind, left them with diseases that, too, slaughtered in increments and inches, cell by cell, left them with the inability to produce healthy offspring. It was indiscriminate, affecting the enemy, the volunteers, the armies that deployed. His men. His friends. And all of it collateral damage.

It was avarice, greed for money and greed for power, one backing the other, greed for *more more more* that drove the policy and the treatment and the lies about the long-term effects of the poison. And that knowledge, the what and the why and the how… it made him sick—physically ill—was a part of the burning mix of pain and shame and loss that over time had cooled to become the sharp and glacial power that carved and shaped his mind even as it drove him.

He'd hoped for some time that he was wrong, that perhaps the cover-up was merely temporary, an act of expedience by an administration that would do right by its patriots and the people it claimed to protect; and to distract himself, to give his mind something else to focus on, he'd started doing some research on the seemingly random facts he'd accumulated.

In the end, what he discovered both fascinated and proved to him once and for all that one single administration, one single person or generation, was not the source of the lies he'd uncovered.

It was so much more than merely an interesting experiment: it involved multiple agencies, all branches of the military, and select areas of private industry, all working together. And there was a list, a master list that named many who'd ranked highly in the military and other services; they had been knowing and willing participants in the project during its initial phase.

The facts he could uncover revealed that as the project had expanded its scope, its need for appropriate subjects had expanded as well. Initial selection had been based more on individual merit rather than political connection, but when more guinea pigs were required…the more easily accessible records and much more transparent revelations of personal ability made the servicemen who had sworn their lives to their country both a logical and an expedient solution.

Now that he was armed with information, knew what to look

for, he began his search, all the while honing his network, developing his plans. For the longest time technology, as was publicly available, was thirty years behind what the government and the military had at their disposal, but finally, the people and the times had caught up to the curve. And that meant everything had finally fallen perfectly into place.

He searched for the *X*s, guided by the hallmarks and the test results gathered over time by other agencies. He had no definitive proof, only an outline of searched-for final outcomes—*markers*—because ironically enough, the generation that had been so looked forward to and tested was the most distrusting of everything.

He found about fifteen hundred known test subjects, each with a varying number of offspring in a wide range of ages, the youngest barely in their teens, the oldest tending to run into their later forties. Not all of them, in fact, not many of them, fit the complete spec for the end-result criteria, though most seemed to have some. A handful of the ones who seemed to have all of them had committed suicide.

But if others continued to monitor the experiment, the silence around it was for the time being absolute. John could track the disappearances of a few who had seemed to completely conform to spec, but could find no overt links to the Company in the circumstances surrounding their seeming vaporization. What he could find, what they did all have in common, were some final civilian medical reports that claimed various forms of mental instability—which John immediately recognized as part of Delta protocol discreditation process. And then—nothing. They were simply gone.

John knew the Company, John knew the government. Those disappearances were neither accidental nor voluntary. He was certain that even now, those *X*s that were in what he considered captivity were being trained, tested, possibly tortured, and turned from the ideals and ethics that were their natural domain.

John considered it part of his mission to find them, to help them, and to turn them into a force to be reckoned with, before the Company, before the cabal that truly ruled the world, did.

He had discovered perhaps a few over a hundred of them, and thanks to the Internet and the ideations, the gestalt produced by this generation, had managed to contact thirty of them directly, and another thirty or so indirectly.

But it was Charli who intrigued him most, the one who seemed to fit every last criterion, and so he did what he did best: he gathered intelligence that would be used to form an action plan. He knew about her lovers, kept tabs on her assignations, was aware that they had on occasion included men.

It was not in the least bit unexpected; this group had a higher statistical propensity toward bisexuality, and even homosexuality.

In Charli's case, while the men almost never repeated, the women sometimes did, and in fact her longer-term relationships had been with women. That by itself proved, to him at least, where Charli's primary emotional energy and attractions lay.

The one thing he had no intelligence about, the event that made him wonder and search the most, that he was certain held the last bit of important information about her, was that blank spot, the two missing years. He kept searching.

This, he thought with a smile, *is the glory of the information age*. Anything and everything was available, one just had to know where to look, and he knew he was the best at finding it all. If it had been encoded somewhere, it could be borrowed, stolen, looked at, copied, repeated, and kept available eternally. It was what had brought Charli to his attention, made his plans possible. It was also, and he scowled to himself as he briefly checked his screen for any changes, what had set the CIA and their supposed Treasury agent on his trail. Hell, he considered, she was probably part of a special detail created by picking select Company agents.

He supposed he should be flattered, but instead, he spat eloquently. Fuck the CIA—they violated civil rights, they violated human rights. He thought about the casual legislative disregard of the Constitution, the disemboweled Bill of Rights—the protection of American privacy—what a joke that was!

John had stopped believing in the Company a long time ago, a belief stripped bit by idealistic bit until only the horrifying truth remained. He knew exactly the sort of agent the supposed Anna Pendleton was; he'd been her, once upon a time. So many more, like her, like he used to be. Still idealistic, still *deluded*, and their intelligence and idealism being used against them—against *everyone*—to maintain a ravenous system that cared for nothing about the ideals its loyal supporters stood for.

But careful screening, planning, and most especially, *timing*, meant that some of those agents were now loyal to him—and not half an hour before supplying Ben with the information and the wherewithal to accurately blame-point away from Charli, his CIA informant, an agent undercover within the Treasury, had contacted him. And revealed Anna as another agent under similar assignment.

All John had to do was ensure that Charli and Anna didn't meet before the sweep went down. That had been a nice piece of subterfuge, he thought, using the gov's own phones to call the Treas and tip that their undercover operative was not just at the center of the crisis, but its source.

While the agencies stumbled about each other and the agent cooled overnight in a government holding cell until the CIA straightened everything out—if they did, if they actually admitted she was one of them and didn't instead do what he thought more likely, leave her to rot in jail for what in the end would be considered treason—he'd already have Charli, the money, and his exchange ready to be made.

It was a shame about the agent, but she needed to wake up. She would learn the hard way, the way he had, that the government she served wasn't out for anything other than the interests of those in power, and making certain they kept it. If the Company didn't step in to straighten out their mess, she'd more than likely be left to find her own way out, which she would, eventually. And her CIA handler would tell her it was part of her training or testing, *if* she survived, *if* she returned to the Company—and if they didn't again betray her and claim no knowledge of her. Experience would teach her, like it had taught him.

The quick dossier he'd managed to assemble told him that the agent herself, like Ben, like Charli, like the group he'd begun to gather and groom, also had quite a few of the requisite markers, if not in her family background, which he'd ascertain at a later date when he could verify her identity, then at least in her own personal history, such as he'd managed to collect and observe it. Besides, she and Charli were quite obviously drawn to one another, and John was certain that with this particular group, given their propensities, their attraction had much more than the usual, obvious meaning. Like called to like.

He'd find the agent again, and when he did, with that betrayal under her belt, she'd more than likely want to join him, too. Besides, by then his plans would not only be underway, he'd have long had Charli aboard, and if Ben's reports were even half as true as what he occasionally let slip about Anna and the way she behaved around Charli, coupled with the photographs he had...

They weren't anything too revealing, just some good long-range shots taken during the last group surfing expedition the dot-commers had gone on. A not-so-casual embrace by the bonfire, the exchange of a more than friendly kiss when they'd been the only two left on the sand, and another, minutes later, by the front door to the beach house. This one had showed something else, something written clearly and plainly to the lens in the way they held each other, exposed on film in the splay of fingers, the grip of hands.

As the memory of the moment and the image played through his head, he idly wondered if either of them knew they seemed like a couple in the very beginnings of the fantasy called love. John himself didn't believe that particular fairy tale; he was a man of realities, and he'd experienced many of them. Romantic love, such as it was popularly construed and media propagated, hadn't been one of them, and therefore, in his world view, it didn't really exist. But he'd stopped taking pictures then. The moment was meant to be private and after all, he wasn't a voyeur. And perhaps, if X *had* bred true, if Charli had inherited one of the final markers, any of the traits he'd been searching for, and if the agent had as well, then it was just possible that maybe, for once, there could exist between them something that poets and artists had praised through the ages.

Ben, he was certain, had inherited it to a degree, or he would never have the response to the agent that he did. But even if Ben hadn't, still, the pictures John had were damning enough to be used as leverage over both Anna and Ben.

It was funny, John mused, what sex and attraction could do to otherwise rational minds. John had pictures—absolute proof—of something they both wanted. That would more than likely prove to be incentive enough.

The program is running. Exit anyway? (y or n)

DEEPER THAN SKIN

BB84 Secure Session - - Loss 0

21:12:02 DsrtFx: bit of news for you.

21:12:03 DsrtFx: change of plans

21:12:04

21:12:05 ChknMan: ???

21:12:06

21:12:07 DsrtFx: your pigeon's a stool

21:12:08

21:12:09 ChknMan: what do you mean?

21:12:10

21:12:11 DsrtFx: Anna—she's undercover.

21:12:12

21:12:13 ChknMan: are you sure? Now what?

21:12:14

21:12:15 DsrtFx: dead certain. I'll meet you

21:12:16 DsrtFx: on the usual corner

```
21:12:17 DsrtFx:  You have 20 minutes

21:12:18 DsrtFx:  to get ready

21:12:19 DsrtFx:  —we're getting Charli

21:12:20

21:12:21 ChknMan: How?

21:12:22 DsrtFx:  Any means necessary

21:12:23 DsrtFx:  Do you understand?

21:12:24

21:12:25

21:12:26 ChknMan: Yes. I'm there.

21:12:27
```

BB84 Secure Session TERMINATED

"No safe words," Charli said into her ear, between nips and licks that made the race in her chest become a thud that bordered on painful. Charli had stopped for one moment, just a single moment, to gently cup her face and gaze into her eyes. "Say 'stop,' or 'no'—that's enough for me, okay?"

"All right." Anna nodded in agreement and Charli smiled, a sultry twist that transformed her further.

"Are you at all…accessory averse?"

She barely had time to answer by threading her fingers through the hair at the base of Charli's head, then gripping her about the waist, pulling their bodies closer. "Not at all," she said to the eyes that shone with a honeyed glow on hers.

"Good," Charli told her, "because I've something new I might like to...*share* sometime," and then she was already naked, moving under heated soft skin, until finally they were locked in the full body embrace, Charli in her arms and wrapped around her, a gliding sync of breath and beat and muscle and—

"Baby..." The word was a choked groan whispered against her temple even as fingers clutched at her shoulder, tangled in her hair, pulled her even closer, and the body that pushed against hers ground with greater urgency. "You...you're gonna...God-I'm-gonna-come."

"Oh yeah...please. Do," Anna managed to gasp back. She gripped at Charli's hip, deepening the connect, the slick of the body on body, the drive within. This she already knew from previous experience was rare, and knowing that it was going to happen, that she was a *part* of it, amplified everything she felt, kicked the answering throb within her that much higher.

God, she'd lied about who she was, her name, her job, even her reasons for being there in the first place, but what she felt, felt in her body, in her mind, *that* was something very real, very true, and she so hoped that no matter what came next it came across, that no matter what, Charli clearly and absolutely *knew* it, because she herself knew—could actually *feel*—just how much Charli did trust her. Knowing that she was very likely to betray that in the next few days...it didn't bear thinking about in the here and now. She wanted to simply be in this moment, this very real exchange, focused solely on this private and oh-so-ephemeral world they had created.

She held Charli even tighter, stretched her fingers under the fine dark hairs that skimmed her neck, kissed her, lips and tongue begging for the warm reaches of her mouth. God, she so wanted this, *needed* this, had known that this was what had hid beyond the surface, below the job, beneath everything.

To get to this level, to earn Charli's trust, she'd had to first give her own. "I trust *you*, Char," she'd told her and meant it, completely. Anna had already decided she'd lay it on the line, convince her somehow to accompany her to one of several designated safe extraction points where they could stay until the issues with

Whitestone blew over, and then tell her—everything. She gently stroked the face above hers. "I...before this goes any...I want to tell you—"

Her name, she was about to start with her name, when Charli silenced her confession with another kiss.

"Everyone has their secrets, Anna. Forget them and just feel," Charli told her as she nibbled a line along the column of her throat, "what I'm doing to you. Be here, now," Charli told her and laid a teasing line of wet fire just under her ear. "You have a choice, and"—Charli ran her fingers up Anna's arms until she held her hands—"your decision will lead to more choices. I can restrain you," she said as one silken thigh brushed against her hip, then another. Charli's body was the lightest skim against her own, placing the beginning of what would be an exquisite pressure where it was needed most. "Or you can restrain yourself. I'd rather not have to," she added softly.

Tawny eyes searched through hers even while that beautiful body hovered above, fingers interlaced with hers. "I want to trust you," Charli said. "You can trust me to hear you—*nothing* happens you don't want. Can I trust *you*? I want to trust you, Anna."

This was not the first test Charli had made of her, and something in Anna's expression, or perhaps it was communicated by the way she'd curled her fingers through Charli's, answered in the right way and passed.

Charli took Anna's hands and placed them on her shoulders. "If you get uncomfortable, tell me. Otherwise," and she smiled as she let go, "not another sound—for now."

And that was exactly where it had started, an adventure in mind, in body, that left Anna alternately breathless and powerful, wondering or flattened by the sheer intensity of the physical, at the woman who stretched her definition of body and disregarded the boundaries of physical gender. It wasn't that there weren't differences, merely that to Charli, they didn't matter, and everything was a test: what Anna enjoyed, what she enjoyed more, how she responded, the way she responded. Every bit of that she could see Charli note, then act and react to, a system of gates and switches, like binary code, ones and zeroes, on and off, if this, then that.

At one point she took Anna's hand and asked her to touch herself.

"I want you to feel what I'm feeling—how fuckin' hard, how fuckin' *beautiful* you are," Charli said, then caught Anna's lower lip between her teeth.

"Feel that, baby? That's right...just like that," she encouraged, the soft growl sexy and low in her ear when Anna shifted her hips in response to the combined stroke, and together they pressed down—*hard*. Oh...that was— "Push it out, push against me...Let me feel you. You..." Charli said, her voice even lower, hoarse with feeling, even as she licked along the delicate pulse point in Anna's neck, modified just slightly what she did with her hands, "you're so *fuckin'* big. I *love* the way you feel."

There was something so very deeply erotic in the way Charli spoke about her body, her arousal, the taboo phrasing that disregarded gender norms. It changed Anna's view of her body, of what they were doing and how they could do it, set loose something primal she hadn't known had been chained all this time.

Her fingers dug into the nape of Charli's neck, needing, frantic, aching to— "Charli...let me touch you," she groaned out, unable to keep silent any longer, not knowing the right words nor how to describe or ask for what she really wanted.

Charli laughed lightly in response, took the tip of her tongue away from the now so hypersensitive and hardened point she'd bathed on Anna's breast.

"You *really* want to touch me, baby?" she drawled, her mouth once more a breath away from Anna's while her hands— "I think you want to *fuck* me...put that hard-on where it wants to go."

God—Anna had no clear idea of exactly what Charli's hands were doing, only that they moved with and around hers, set a fire that seemed to focus on the— Christ, had she ever truly been that hard or that wet before? "I want to make you come. Don't you just want to come? You're *so* close..."

Charli was going to push her there, had already put her there, maybe moments, maybe hours before. Anna felt the very welcome pressure of a fingertip as it stroked beneath her slick and hardened shaft before it eased inside her, Charli's own heat just above their joined hands, and even as Anna couldn't help but respond, she knew this was yet another of Charli's tests.

Charli pushed the boundaries of code, of what one human being could do to another, of what she would let happen to her. And Anna wanted to touch her, wanted to come *this* time with Charli hard and wet on her hands, her mouth, the taste of her skin more than just a memory. Anna wanted so much, much more than to merely fuck her, wanted to sink beyond blood and bone, wanted to feel Charli come, too, for her, with her, in so deep they shared breath and beat and body riding the wave until they were the same and—

"I want…I need to touch *you*, Charli," she said, the submerged truth finally gasped against the rising tide, the pulsing flood that filled her from the most sensitive spot of her body to her chest, her arms, her head, and she dared to reach careful fingertips to the face above hers. The skin was warm, smooth, and when Charli didn't pull away, she dared further, held her cheek, kissed her with all she felt and all she wanted riding the tip of her tongue. "*Let* me…please."

"We need to take care of this, first," Charli answered even as Anna felt the closing in of her body, hot and wet, and…that…was… so…*good*… A sound of air—of breath, short, sharp, shocked at the infuckingtensity—escaped her as Charli took her hand, licked at her fingertips, ground against her. And then the sensation heightened.

"Now," Charli breathed against her lips, "*now* you're touching me." She was. She did. As the movement evolved from languid to urgent, became the liquid heat that melded them, Anna's hands were now free to roam, to visit and explore the places she remembered, the places she still wanted to know, to memorize with her fingers, palms, lips, and tongue the curve of the breasts that were just below her chin, the strain of the muscles that met and marked the channel of her spine, the slight curve and flare of Charli's hips as Anna finally gripped and held them while Charli rode her body with the same power as when she cut through the ocean, the same fluid wave surrounding them, rising tide and blood filling all the empty spaces, and in the moment she beheld Charli's face, the full expression of her mouth, the shock and wonder in the glow of her eyes, something so much deeper than awe claimed her as the wave crested and took her with it.

❖

It was time, John decided as he cut the session, to find out exactly what sort of man, what sort of *soldier*, Ben Cooper really was. John's own chat request to Charli remained unanswered—that didn't trouble him. What did bother him, though, and had set his hand to motion was the urgent text message he'd received from one of his own inside: the CIA wasn't about to blow their operation in the Treas, so despite their own inside knowledge, they had not revealed their agent. But the Treas itself was in an uproar. It would take them almost five hours to get themselves together to organize the strike team to gather their supposed rogue, but they already knew where she was—the tracker placed in her laptop told them—and now he knew, too. She was at Charli's apartment.

Taking into account what he could piece together from Ben's commentary and the pictures he himself had taken, the situation as he saw it was now unacceptably volatile. An agent wouldn't normally give up their cover, but an agent with a vested personal interest such as the one he was certain the so-called Pendleton had, that could very well be another story. And someone who thought or felt like they were in love… More than one agent had been ruined and even outright killed because of it. It made Ben transparent and manipulable, it made "Agent Pendleton"—who could probably not even put a name to what it seemed she felt if John remembered the training right, and he knew he did—a dangerous unknown. That he simply could not allow.

It took him nanoseconds to change course to his already designed plan B. This, he reminded himself, was why there was *always* a plan B, and why it always paid to be doubly secure, belt and suspenders, as it were.

Reviewed from a different angle, the situation could play out to his ultimate advantage, and the slight modification would allow him to exploit both Ben and Pendleton's feelings, not only for Charli, but also for one another or, at the very least, Ben's toward the agent. And it would also allow him to leave another unmistakable message to the Company he had once been loyal to.

He was no rearguard officer, he was a front-line leader. And if Ben Cooper needed to see what that actually meant, John mused as he checked first one gun then another, tonight he would.

This one—he hefted it, enjoying the solid feel of it—was the one he'd give Ben. Ben had once said he'd wanted to be a cowboy; tonight he'd get his chance. It was a traditional Colt .357 bored out to .45, and the rounds—John smiled at the blue tips and brass casings as he loaded the chamber—he'd made them himself. They'd hold velocity and accuracy for about twenty feet, which was more than necessary, he was certain.

He carefully packed the spares into a case and, satisfied that the rest of his equipment was in order, he checked himself once more before he put on his coat. The forecast that had predicted a storm now called for snow. It would not do well, he thought with a small chuckle and pulled on his gloves, if the man who was leading the charge to create a new world let himself get frostbite. He hummed a tuneless song deep in his throat.

Everything he needed was within easy reach, and he didn't bother to lock the door behind him after he hefted his case and let himself out.

❖

"You did well, son," John told him with a friendly pat as they settled into the car for the long drive to their originally planned meeting point. "Get some rest, you'll need it. Not every day you start a revolution," he said and grinned as he turned the key in the ignition.

As warm as the regard in John's tone and expression made him feel, his heart pleased in the same way it had been when he was a young boy, when he'd done something that earned a compliment from his father, try as he might, Ben couldn't return the grin. He stopped trying as he felt the painful rictus that stretched his face, while the crunch of the engaged ignition rang loud in his ears. Charli was—at least he *hoped* she was—comfortably stretched across the backseat. "She'll be fine, a little nauseous later maybe, perhaps a bit off balance here and there at worst, but fine," John assured him, correctly guessing his concern when he craned his head to peer back over the rear bench seat.

Ben felt rather nauseous himself, and it wasn't just the sight of Charli's seemingly asleep form—though knowing how it happened was enough on its own. It was adrenaline, it was fear, it was shock, he admitted to himself, shock over what they'd done, over what *he'd* done.

He'd been surprised when John had shown up in the slightly weathered Chevy Caprice as opposed to on foot as was usual, and even more so when he'd been handed the gun. "You know how to use it, right?" John asked.

Ben forced himself to raise a casual-seeming brow at the man he so admired. "Single action Colt revolver? Of course," he answered as he felt the grip, then quickly examined its construction, a flare of childhood excitement thrilling through him. ".357, looks like it's been bored out to .45 and..." He briefly spun the barrel. "Loaded."

The enjoyment quelled almost instantly when the reality of when and where he was, they were, returned. He tried to act as naturally as if he'd been handed a cup of coffee when he took off his coat to don the holster, then safely nestled the gun within it. But this was something much hotter—a gun he had no license to carry in this state, the model he'd talked about with John, the one he'd shot as a young man, out with his father. They'd shot small game, deer. But the one in his hands now...he hoped he was meant to use it as a deterrent. "When you've got a gun, son, you better be prepared to mean it," his father used to tell him repeatedly, "or it'll mean it for you."

Ben thought he'd heard, that he'd understood, every part of the plan as they parked around the corner and he paged Charli with the urgent request that she speak with him, now, privately, away from work, because he had an idea about the breach and failure.

It had taken three pages to her emergency contact number before she'd answered.

"Charli—go."

"Charli, it's Coop." He took a breath, knowing everything depended on what he said next. "I've been doing some work—I think I know exactly what happened to the network. It's got to be bits of code at the different gates, buried lines that each do a step, then concatenate at the main gate," he said, forgoing apologies for the hour or any of the other social niceties. It would have wasted time and besides, it wasn't something he did naturally, not unless he was achingly hyperaware that a situation required it and forced himself to go through the motions. That was too much work. Besides, that sort of behavior had gotten him into trouble once upon a time and he'd learned his lesson well.

Ben added the conclusion he knew Charli had probably already come to herself. "It's…it can only be an inside job." That was it. That was the bait he had—a partial confession. He didn't know he held his breath while he waited for her answer.

"Can you prove it?" He heard the sharp interest in her voice through the phone.

"I've got a copy of the server codes burned to a disc—I can get it and be at your place in ten. We'll hit the servers from your home system, print it out before we put in the corrections. You can go with that to Lundenman before you even run the audits."

Charli was a leader who gave full credit to the coders when things went well, and took full responsibility for the failures when it didn't; she wouldn't rest, *couldn't* rest, until the problem was solved—and he knew that, had worked with her, then under her, for too long not to know that.

"All right. Give me twenty. You remember the address?"

Ben chuckled with relief. It had been that simple, it had worked. "Yeah, from the party before the takeover."

"Good," Charli answered crisply. "Twenty, then."

Ben folded his phone and put it in the front pocket of his pants. "We're set," he said to John. "She said to give her twenty minutes."

"Good man, good job," John had answered him with obvious

approval and a warm clap on the shoulder. It made Ben feel very good.

All set up, with him and John on their way, Ben couldn't help but think of this in his mind as an actual, honest-to-goodness rescue, a mission like the ones his father had gone on in *his* jungle. It made him feel useful, directed and purposeful, powerful and just plain good. He felt better than fine, filled with an almost surreal calm as he and John rode the elevator to the sixth floor, even more so when they knocked on the door. Fact was, he could never remember ever feeling quite so clear.

That had all shattered to pieces when he'd seen Anna, not more than five feet behind Charli, and before he'd even fully registered that she was wearing the Hunter College sweatshirt he'd seen Charli wear what seemed like a hundred years ago on a hundred different days, back when they worked at the Puck building, before he found the chat group, before he'd met John, before—they'd slept together. He *knew* it, could see it, could actually *feel* it even as he felt the heat tear through him when he realized it was probably not the first time. The fury of the confirming knowledge was a ravening blaze that took away reason, blinded him. He peripherally saw Charli sway when John entered the apartment, heard him say "Take the agent," before he reached into his coat and...

Their eyes met, hers wide cool jade on him as he burned.

The cool peace, the logical calm he'd felt, shattered by the dizzy flushing rage from reading the block letters that spelled "Hunter" emblazoned across Anna's chest, returned as he drew.

He realized neither that he mouthed a quick apology nor that he'd closed his eyes as he pulled the trigger.

THE FEW THAT REMAIN

She couldn't decide which annoyed her more, the tickle against her temple or the incessant electronic chirping that sounded in the near distance, but both brought her out of the comfortable sleep state she'd been snug within—Anna could ignore one, but not both. She finally gave up and as she sat up to scratch the incessant itch, memory flooded back with a strength that made her retch.

Cooper, she remembered vividly as she took stock of herself and wiped at what she realized was a nice gash along her temple. It was bruise-sensitive and stung under her fingertips. Ben Cooper had drawn, leveled, and shot her. There had been a single moment where she had thought maybe, just maybe, he wouldn't, and she'd known the way everyone knows there would be no way to dodge a bullet, but she couldn't overcome the human reaction to try anyway. The movement that had saved her from receiving the blast in her eye, and at the very least permanently blinding her, had tripped her over the low table instead and—she waited for the next wave of nausea to pass—she'd apparently knocked herself out on the table.

Well, at least the worst of the concussion has passed, she decided as the queasiness abated. She examined the detritus between her fingers: blood, her own, and something not quite granular, though small, translucent. It felt, of all things, waxy. She combed her fingers through the rug in an attempt to find what she'd been hit with. He'd drawn what looked like a .357, and at under fifteen feet, she was surprised she was still able to breathe, never mind sit up and look for anything at all.

She reached for the phone she'd reattached to her waist when she and Charli had made themselves presentable for Ben's unexpected and urgent visit. It still chimed repeatedly, and there was only one person who had that number; she'd sent him an encrypted message what was now certainly hours ago. As she flipped it open to read with one hand, she found what she'd wanted with the other. She checked the screen. She had asked about next orders, it seemed she'd received them.

EXTRICATE NOW. COVER ID HAS BEEN COMPROMISED.

RENDEZVOUS SMITH'S POINT 0300.

ACKNOWLEDGE

ACKNOWLEDGE

ACKNOWLEDGE

ACKNOWLEDGE

ACKNOWLEDGE

ACKNOWLEDGE

Smith's Point. That was the Long Island safe house location, the place, she realized with a feeling that sank what had earlier risen in her throat, she had wanted to take Charli, where she'd also hoped she, they… She cursed herself fluently. Everything had changed; Romello had gone for and drawn first blood, and she knew she needed more information before she could plan next steps.

Another ping asking for acknowledgment came in, interrupting her musings as her fingers raised what they'd found. She held her prize up for inspection. It looked, she thought, a bit like a chewed wad of gum, a light translucent blue. Paraffin. Cooper had shot her with a wax bullet, but he hadn't acted like a man who'd known it wouldn't be a killing shot. She'd seen the fire that had lit his face for a moment before his expression froze, had seen his lips move, his eyes close, in the half instant before he'd fired and she'd dove. It was the quick observation, she concluded, that had probably convinced the lizard part of her brain that cares for nothing but survival to try.

And she'd seen John Romello. *Fucking brilliant, he's fucking brilliant*, she thought. He must have known what sort of load the weapon held, had to have been the one to give it to Cooper, and Cooper now believed he'd killed a federal agent. What amazing leverage. That he hadn't killed an agent, that Romello had left her alive after seeing him? That was his way of saying "fuck you" to the CIA. The same hubris that led him to rob his own country now had him thumbing his nose at one of its most elite investigative services and he—

Charli. A strange numbness scratched and crawled across her belly. Where was Charli?

She gave herself a quick evaluating shake before she stood. Too fast, she'd stood too fast and the accompanying wave of dizziness nearly dumped her back down. *Okay, all right, a little slower, then*, she told herself and she was a bit more careful this time, making sure she was steady before she surveyed her surroundings. The front door was closed, and other than the uninterrupted chirp from her phone, there was only the tone that invaded a place when it was empty, a specific ringing silence that told her she was definitely alone. A glimpse of white against the coffee-colored carpet caught her eye, replaying a memory of a flutter she'd seen when Cooper had drawn.

She glanced down at herself as she walked to the door—blood. A few drops of blood had already dried on the faded red sweatshirt Charli had lent her.

This was completely surreal, the lines she'd concerned herself about intersecting were now completely inextricably meshed, she admitted to herself as she picked up the scrap of paper and examined it.

She took stock as she stood in Charli's apartment, surrounded by the scent of her. She still felt the visceral reality of her, of Charli, warm and soft and glowing, suffusing her body with a throb of aching satisfaction that wanted more, deep in her groin and in the hardness of her nipples, while the rest of her was still so sensitive, so attuned, that she didn't even have to close her eyes to once more feel Charli, beautiful, vibrant, alive against her own skin, skin that now felt empty and cold without her.

She'd just been shot at and was alive only because the shooter didn't know he'd had wax bullets, and her own agency, while able to warn her that her cover ID had been implicated, would not extract her directly.

In being alive, she was now a direct witness, able to link Cooper to Romello, able to prove that it was in fact Romello at the helm, and not some new player, some unnamed and unknown foreign operative, as those in the Company sympathetic to Romello had theorized in their water cooler talks.

But now there was more than her testimony, not just for the Company, but also eventually for the Treas—she could completely clear Charli—she realized with a growing excitement and satisfaction as she read the torn scrap. Now she had hard evidence:

```
18:12:13 DsrtFx:   41°10'59"N, 72°11'25"W

18:12:14 DsrtFx:   13:00 Sunday. Get to Greenpoint

18:13:15 DsrtFx:   I'll escort the rest of way
```

Cooper had obviously taken a screen shot, then printed the information out. It was her good luck that he'd kept it in a pocket and even better luck that it had fallen just as he'd drawn. *Sometimes, a little luck is all it takes*, she told herself as she took hurried steps back over to the very same table she'd tripped over and knocked herself silly on earlier in the evening. She intended to boot up and use Charli's laptop—she had Charli's passwords, but access wouldn't have been a problem regardless. *This is one of those instances*, Anna thought, *that passwords simply don't matter.* It would do no good to use her system, the Treas used it to locate her and would know what she'd been looking for when they found it and tore it down in an attempt to learn what they could from it.

If the CIA was maintaining her cover, she wouldn't blow it, and she could in no way leave a hint to the Treas agents that would eventually show up as to where she—or her targets—might be headed.

There might be only one John Romello, but there were

thousands of opportunists, threats, agents willing to do harm to the government and to the country it ran; Romello might be the one currently in their crosshairs, and quite possibly the only one with his specific ideations, but she knew there was no way he'd be the last to threaten the civilian citizenry—and she respected the methods the Company employed. Their sole concern was the security of the nation, a security she was charged with safeguarding. *She* wouldn't be the one to threaten American safety, not if she could help it.

```
ACKNOWLEDGED. STAND BY FOR INTEL.
```

She typed that quickly into her cell and sent it off as she waited impatiently for the screen she wanted to come up on the booted system.

```
LOLA SURF SPOT FORECAST

Time Zone XXX Period XXX

Chart Center: Lat XXX Long XXX

Forecast Center: Lat XXX Long XXX
```

She'd surfed for too long and in too many different places not to recognize the numbers on that slip of paper for what they were—coordinates—and quickly plugged them into LOLA, knowing the results wouldn't just display the weather, but also name the precise location.

The results tabulated in tenths of a second, and for the first time in the entire night, she felt something new. A night that began in frustration combined with concern, then became a focused fix on thousands of lines of code had evolved into a definite arousal coupled with a growing sense of something she wasn't certain she had the right word for yet but wanted to find out. The something that had suffused her and Charli both as they'd touched had been followed by tenderness joined to an onslaught of emotions when Charli had finally let go, let her in just the littlest bit, confided in her something so very… Anna didn't yet have an accurate description for it, but Charli had said it so matter-of-factly. She also knew she couldn't think about it right now, though at the moment she welcomed the same rush of pure rage with its protective, warming strength that had raced through her earlier, the same feeling that had led her to want to be very physically present when Charli answered the door for Cooper. That, finally, had led to a frustrated resignation that took over when she'd looked straight into his eyes, read their emotion and intent, and known she'd hit an end.

All those things, confusing, conflicting, calming, confirming, all of them and more she'd felt over the last few hours, but she hadn't expected the icicle crush in her stomach, nor the burning freeze that now gripped, clammy and close, about her neck and thickened her throat.

This was something different, something completely unexpected, her response to what she knew the results on the screen meant. *No way, absolutely no way!* part of her mind protested even as she absorbed the implications.

There was one and only one reason to pick that specific destination, and with that knowledge, she now knew more than anyone on the planet other than John Romello himself—and perhaps any of his trusted associates, assuming he had any—what his plans truly contained, and she felt something within her sink as she forced her mind to rid itself of the image of Charli's swaying body, Charli in this man's hands, a man accompanied and aided by an insane Cooper.

She had been right; it had never been about the money—it was about the acquisition. She studied the screen before her. The forecast called for snow and the coordinates said they were headed to an island off the northeast coast of Long Island: Plum Island.

Anna might have had no name for what she'd experienced earlier, but she knew what gripped her now. What she felt was fear.

❖

History records that on August 11, 1775, one General David Wooster dispatched one hundred and twenty soldiers to an island, then known as Plumb Island. Upon arrival, they were immediately fired upon by the British. After managing to fire a single return volley, the soldiers retreated back to Long Island. No casualties were reported, and this brief skirmish is believed by many to have been the first engagement between the Continental Army and the Redcoats during the Revolutionary War, the site of the war's first naval battle, and even perhaps the first amphibious assault by an American army.

The first lighthouse placed there was constructed by order of George Washington in 1789, to mark the location of turbulent tidal waters and shoals.

Partially purchased by the federal government during the Spanish-American War, the island was home to Fort Terry, a military installation. It was activated as an anti-submarine base during World War II, as well as a biological warfare research facility. Later, it became a Chemical Corps facility. The Department of Agriculture took over the island in 1954, establishing the Plum Island Animal Disease Center, dedicated to the study of—words and names flew through Charli's aching head. She heard questions asked—that was Ben's voice; the answers were returned in the deep stentorian tones of another man, one she didn't know.

She kept her eyes closed and tried to orient herself while the conversation flowed on around her, a discussion about hemorrhagic fevers, dengue, Marburg, Ebola, Hanta, Lassa fever, Crimean-Congo hemorrhagic fever, and the name Erich Traub repeated as well as something called Operation Paper Clip. "And now, with this new work, we'll use the CIA's *best* weapon against them," the same deep voice continued, "we'll create a tabula rasa—the blank slate—to set it all to rights."

Maybe she was dreaming, a strange dream where she'd opened her door to talk with Cooper about the server problems, a dream where a large man who seemed vaguely familiar had greeted her and then—had she fainted? Had she seen Coop draw a gun, heard a shot? Where was Anna? Hadn't they just—the dizzying spasm that wrenched through her, a pained burning up her chest and limbs, drew her almost upright and she found a paper cup of water in her hand and a strong arm around her shoulders, guiding her to drink, and as she swallowed and opened her eyes, she felt sick again.

None of it, not the good, not the bad, had been a dream.

She blinked, then focused before her and her sight found Ben. He stared at her, a surprisingly doleful expression in his eyes before he dropped his gaze to stare down at his hands. He folded them nervously.

"Well, Charli, now that you're with us, it's time for proper introductions," said the man who no longer sat next to her but instead now stood two feet away.

A coolness had descended over and through her, something she'd not felt for years, but very familiar all the same, and the chill that caressed her showed in Charli's gaze as she continued to examine Cooper.

"I'm John," the man continued.

Charli refused to look at him as she silently measured the distance between herself and Cooper, from him to the closed door, and let the information process through her. She was bound in no way, nor did she see any obvious display of weapons, implying that there was no concern about her successfully leaving, and she had her coat on, which meant someone had taken the time to retrieve it. She shifted her shoulders under the leather and shearling, glad for its heaviness and warmth. A deep quiet surrounded them, indicating that it was not only probably very late, but possibly also isolated as well and...even the most frozen of winters couldn't change or hide that scent: low tide.

Cooper began to fidget under the relentless visual probe and Charli began to piece together the information that she had: one, this was not a voluntary trip; two, the lack of screaming demand in her body for either food or bathroom meant it had been three hours maximum—and quite probably less; three, the foul taste in her mouth and nose as well as the crawling sick that slid up her throat indicated an inhaled substance; and four, the man she'd considered an odd and quirky character in the way some coders were but who was also a highly skilled and reliable employee had…

The cold turned to ice, frozen little chunks that slammed through and under her skin, each chill collision a bruise replacing a heartbeat. She felt nothing—no anger nor sorrow, not even fear for herself. Instead her mind burned clear and Cooper's dark eyes finally met hers.

"You shot Anna." The words were flat, uninflected, a cold observation of fact, as cold as the freeze that possessed her, and even as she watched him open his mouth to either protest or explain, the man who'd introduced himself as John entered and filled her field of vision.

"Dear Charli," he said as he took both her hands in his and she let him, unresisting. His voice, his expression, even his touch was warm, but the warmth ended at his eyes. Pale blue, she noted. Salt sprinkled through dark wavy hair. It curled just below his collar. Thick brows evenly spaced over a defined Roman nose.

"She would have hurt you—*betrayed* you." His eyes snapped and glowed almost feverishly, and that was what she paid attention to. "Why, did you know," he said conversationally as he dropped one of Charli's hands to wave Ben over, "that Anna was not her real name? That's right," he nodded at both of them, "a spy and a mole and a would-be traitor—to you, to me, to *all* of us."

Charli listened with the part of her mind not given over to analysis. John crouched to below her eye level—he wanted her trust. He took her hand—she let him, to see what it would tell her. The avuncular squeeze he gave her let her know he not only thought he had gained it—the trust he sought—but also that he thought he knew her, while the too-warm temperature of it betrayed excitement over something. It had to be something huge, she concluded, something he wasn't quite ready yet to reveal—and she was certain that he was the one with the answers.

The touch told her something else as well: he wanted something from her—it wasn't sexual, not really, she could tell that, but it carried the same sort of naked hunger, something desperate, and the expectation he held bled from his pores and over her skin, making it crawl. It charged the air that surrounded him.

"So you see, Charli," he said, returning his full attention to her, "Ben did nothing to Anna, because *Anna* does not exist." He smiled.

It was the smile, pleased and somehow smug, as if he shared a secret or an inside joke, that gave her another insight. This man, John, thought he knew everything, Charli thought. Quite likely, not everything, but enough to make it seem so. She listened to his tones. They bordered on patronizing, and his humor, well, it was intelligent, certainly, but it was weak, and considering how widely he smiled at his own jokes…it indicated how highly he thought of his own cleverness. And then, there was what he wanted…

A small crack appeared in her inner ice, and a familiar fear, the one she'd thought buried so long ago but risen up again recently, the source of which had so very recently been the briefest topic of conversation between her and the person John had just told her did not exist, had now come again. She knew why this time, though— because the part of her that remembered was reliving the past: a young girl, a trusted adult, a nondescript hotel room God-only-knew where.

But things were a lot different this time, Charli reminded herself grimly. The first difference was that she was not that young girl anymore; the second was that she trusted no one, and the neutrality with which she'd always regarded Cooper had given way to contempt, not just for what Charli already knew were his real reasons for holding a grudge against Anna, something she'd ignored because neither Anna nor Coop had made an issue of it at work (though it had been part of her decision to have his office located in the server room), but also for the fawning child's look on his face as he listened to John's words. It was that, more than anything else, that lost him whatever respect she'd previously had for him.

As for John, Charli gave him her full concentration. He was generous so long as he thought he was winning, Charli concluded, and considering everything else, including her own current position, he more than probably took insurance to make certain he did.

She had never been able to explain, not to herself, never mind anyone else, how she could know such a thing with the sort of definite certainty she had, but regardless of the mechanisms behind the "how," know she did, and that knowing led her to another conclusion: she now knew his weak spot. So long as he thought he was right, that he knew all the players and the parameters, he was in charge. But he'd already made one critical error, to her mind. Perhaps he had told the truth, perhaps an actual person named Anna did not exist, not as Charli had known and named her, but he was wrong, and Charli knew she held the proof of it. Anna, whether or not that was her name, *did* exist. Charli had held her, had looked into her eyes and her mind, had felt through her own body, her own skin, all the things Anna felt for her, as wordless as they might have been.

In the way Charli played the game with everything and everyone, there were tests: tests of trust, tests of reality, that had pass or fail options. Those responses opened or closed gates that allowed or forbade different levels of access. It was of almost desperate importance for her to know—always, in all ways—what cores lay beneath exteriors, whether it was the functionality of programs, rocks and reefs, rips and undertows beneath the waves, or the deceiving dichotomies of people.

So much of what she did, of who she was, of how she lived, depended on that information and because of that, there was no room in her life or her mind for false niceties or labels. Those solid-seeming surfaces had betrayed her once too often, and as a result she had learned quite early and well that they ultimately meant nothing.

What did have meaning for her, the truth she trusted and could work with, understood and made good use of, were the actions and reactions when stripped down to essence. That had been exactly what had happened between her and Anna—there had been that stripping away of layers until nothing but core was left. What she had seen and felt, what had been shared and exchanged...*that* she knew was real, more real than anything as trivial as a name.

Charli had already not only suspected, but also known with

an inner certainty there was something different about Anna—her records were too clean and there was a way she had sometimes, of standing, of making a turn…Charli had thought military, being so familiar with that thanks to her brother. If Anna—or whoever she was—chose not to talk about it, fine. Everyone had their secrets and Charli wouldn't push for those, not when she had so many herself. But this, John's revelation, it changed nothing.

The thought caught Charli abruptly, made all the slamming chunks crash into a dead stop with a crushing weight that made her face and chest grow numb: John had used past tense to discuss her, which meant she was more than likely dead.

Charli would deal with that later, when there was time to finally let herself feel and react, but for now… She narrowed her eyes slightly at Cooper, who drank in every word John issued as if they were pronouncements from an incarnate god, then peered at John, who either didn't notice or more than likely, she decided, expected it. It made her next choices easy, then. She'd listen, she'd play along, and then she'd figure a way out.

As far as Charli was concerned, John's first crucial mistake had been in telling her that the woman she'd last seen wearing her own sweatshirt wasn't real—nothing and no one had ever been more real to her, and that right there fed her what she considered to be critical information. However good John's source of intelligence was, he didn't really know her, how she thought, what she felt, or what had happened between her and…Anna. He knew some facts, perhaps many of them, but he didn't know the realities behind them or the engines that drove them. Ergo, he didn't know *her*. His attitude and tone led her to suspect that even if he did know those crucial pieces of intelligence, he still more than likely wouldn't understand either what had happened and why, or Charli herself, for that matter.

As for the second piece of the puzzle, it logically followed the first: he'd been wrong about Anna, he'd been wrong about her—and it would only be a matter of time before John was mistaken again.

She'd have to watch for it, and she wouldn't—couldn't, she corrected—let him know. The conversation she had heard as she came to told her there was machinery in motion that was much larger than whatever the mysterious actions on the computer system had been—and the implications were horrific. She could authentically confirm that Anna—or whoever—had been injured if not worse, and the fact that she herself was here in this place, wherever this was, without her own permission…it all added up to a danger she could only begin to appreciate—and not just to her, but to others as well.

If I can learn more, maybe I can find out exactly *what it is*, Charli decided, *maybe I can stop it from happening.* She knew what she had to do: act, not react, and *that* was something she excelled at. She took a breath, and with it turned an internal switch completely off. Game on.

"Well, now that we're all introduced, we've defined reality, and my stomach has stopped twisting, does anyone have coffee?" Charli asked.

"I'll go get some," Ben volunteered and stepped quickly out the door.

Charli played a hunch and took as much more control over the situation as she thought she could. It was time to start testing the boundaries. "After I use the bathroom, you can tell me what we're *really* doing here," Charli said to John, speaking to him directly for the first time as the door clicked shut. "I'm betting it has something to do with my system." She forced herself to smile at him as if he was any other member of her team and this was a normal code review.

John smiled back at her broadly in return. "Just this way," he told her, pointing to the door around the corner from the other bed.

She'd been right—he was expansive in his seeming triumph, and when Charli closed the door to the bathroom behind her, she quickly surveyed the windowless room. The sink sported neatly packaged and placed bars of soap, an ashtray, and a matchbook with the name of the hotel on the cover. Acting on impulse, she took the matches and put them in her pocket, along with the East Hampton brochure that had lain next to it. She didn't know precisely what she would do with them just yet, but she did know this: John had just made his next mistake.

❖

Charli was amazing, so much more than what Ben had told him about her, even more than what he'd hoped and deduced from his files and observations. Tough stuff, she was—no crying, no tears at all, no sentimentality. He should have predicted that—it was another mark of her breed.

All the preliminary testing as well as the theory he could find had said repeatedly that these subjects had something a little different, and very interesting, about their brain waves. They all ran an almost constant Beta wave—their minds were *never* at rest, and it was in this group that the discovery of Gamma waves had occurred: a subset of Beta waves, Gammas represented masses of neurons firing together, and this is what excited him. It was a hyperengagement of cognitive activity, was linked to the synchronization of both conscious and subliminal stimulus. The outward manifestation of that? A constant, cool, logic that arrived at answers in seemingly nonlinear ways.

And that logic…what a mind she had.

He began by discussing a little bit about genetics—without telling her of the experiment she was more than likely a result of, and he began with his theory of the improvements to human stock inadvertently begun during World War II. It was an opportunity to sound her out for himself, if she really would "believe" as Ben had put it, or argue him down.

"Hitler," he opened, "was a prisoner of his own inferiorities, and the mistakes of his culture. That's the problem with little brains," he said and smiled, "too small to crawl outside of their own holes. He wanted a Master Race—and he created one, out of the very people he tried to destroy."

The curious and inquiring glance she rewarded him with allowed him to continue with an enthusiasm he hadn't felt in a long time. A quick glance at Ben revealed his interest, and with his audience set, John continued.

"It's really quite simple," he told them. "By herding all those he considered undesirable into the horrible conditions he did—people already molded by generations of constantly being forced to adapt and overcome, people, thus, already a bit of an improvement over average—he weeded out the weakest of them. Think about it—it was only those with the strongest physiologies who survived the worst of conditions, only those with the ablest minds who escaped."

He paused and took another sip of his coffee. It was atrocious, but it was a civilized action, and he was a civilized man. Besides, it gave him a moment, the moment he needed to perfectly phrase the words he wanted to say, thoughts he hadn't shared with even his closest of associates. "Those that suffered, survived, and reproduced—Hitler's wrongheaded policies made the best even better."

He waited and watched them both for their reactions.

"That definitely has a certain…Darwinian…poetry to it," Charli said finally, seeming suitably impressed.

"Man, that's just…that's so…" Ben shook his head. He glanced up and met John's eyes with his.

"It *is*," John agreed. "Now imagine, just imagine, if that sort of breeding—selection for better stock, as it were—was done purposely and irrespective of cultural conditions."

Ben appeared stunned at the very thought, but not Charli. She jumped right on top of it. "What do you mean, purposely?"

The question made him smile—he didn't want to tell her, or Ben, or any of them, just yet. It was a special surprise and it needed the right moment to be sprung.

"The Nazis were not the only ones to play with genetics," he said solemnly, "and right now, there are other, more pertinent issues for us to discuss."

Charli sat back and cocked her head inquiringly. "Is this where you explain why you needed to hit a major investment system?" He studied her carefully. There was nothing in her tone to indicate anything other than a genuine curiosity, and the corner of her mouth quirked in a way that suggested that instead of upsetting her, it amused her.

"Ben deserves the credit for that, Charli." He could see that Ben was visibly anxious about the revelation, but what John wanted to see, what would be the "tell" to what she really thought and felt, was Charli's reaction. There were several that he expected, but to his great surprise, she laughed.

"Good thing your plans move now—or a few people would have ended up so fuckin' fired!"

That she could laugh and make a joke about it—he considered it a good sign; she was rapidly adjusting.

"You see, Charli, money changes value with time. In order for it to have roughly the same value a few years from now that it does today—in order for the variations to be moderate, rather than extreme—certain things must happen. Some industries must be allowed to dominate, and others to die. Governments, by playing with interest rates, by manipulating the economy, also play their parts. There must always, *always*," and he held up a finger for emphasis, "be a part of the population that's on the dole, always a segment unemployed, or these rates won't provide the returns investors require. Billions suffer—so millions can be made."

Charli nodded. "That makes mathematical sense."

Ben jumped in again. "It sure does," he said, nodding enthusiastically. "And anyone who's able to see it—" He drew his finger across his neck.

All in all, John felt the discussion and discovery had gone very well and now, while they refreshed and recharged, there were only a few steps left.

The situation at Plum was a unique one—the installation was government funded but no longer under the direct control of any single agency. This allowed for plausible deniability should any of their discoveries prove to result in something that was as tactically effective as napalm had been, as well as the same complete public relations nightmare.

The secrecy they enjoyed and operated under meant that they were able to hire outside contractors—several private firms—to handle aspects of security, research, and cleanup. This permitted another level of deniability should there be any aspects of research to violate federal law. The scientists could claim that as investigators, they were unfamiliar with certain particulars, or that the particulars didn't concern them since they were civilians, while the facility administration could claim they had no idea of what the research would involve.

However, they were officially and at least on paper *partially* government funded as well as recognized as a biosafety level 2 facility—which meant they could work with communicable agents that were generally transmissible via ingestion, mucous membrane exposure, or intradermal exposure, such as measles, salmonella, hepatitis B, things that had either an immunization or an antibiotic treatment available. Some protective gear, lab access restrictions, strict sanitation standards, and a double venting process for air were required.

But in actuality, despite its bio level 2 set and origin, Plum operated at bio level 3 and investigated agents that could also be spread via aerosol, like tuberculosis and encephalitis—a particular favorite which still had no real cure.

This was the true reason that the operation, which in reality was funded almost solely by tax dollars, had to pay outsiders to handle it properly. Plainly, that made sense. Only those who worked outside of national restrictions and military reporting conventions would have access to the information, to the materials, to the proper procedures required, since some of what was done on Plum was beyond the bounds of federal law. And if the government turned a blind eye to whatever was discovered, then it was able to pretend its collective hands were clean when it swooped in with an official "no, we don't condone that, but since it's here, we should be the ones to decide its proper use and disposal." It was hypocrisy at its absolute bald-faced best.

It made John laugh—he'd met so many of these researchers and scientists during the course of his investigations and operations, a natural by-product of his career path. He had literally worked with, owed, and was, more importantly, owed to by a select handful of these intelligent investigators and one of them...well, this particular one was quite special as well as useful.

Dr. Chul-Moo Seung was, thanks to a series of lucky meetings, his own personal determination, and some words in the right ears at the right time, the current director of research at Plum.

His chance at freedom and education he owed to John and they both knew it. That knowledge, combined with his cultural sense of pride and honor, meant he would have helped John anyway—of that, John was certain. Honor between men, the debts of loyalty for deeds and blood shed, bound them in ways inexplicable to those who had not experienced them.

It was those ties, combined with an almost blind drive to be the first to make heady inroads into the delicate research he performed and the offer of the money necessary to bring the station to the next level necessary to facilitate the research, that made the difference between promised word and accomplished deed nothing more than a matter of time. The deal was done, needing only the exchange of funds to complete it.

With Chul-Moo's knowledge, it was easy to find the right mix of bioagents that would provide exactly the solutions John needed—so much more efficient than the clumsy use of spraying lower-income neighborhoods with pesticides after disseminating the misinformation that they were all in danger from mosquitoes, of all things, that carried a disease heretofore unheard of in this region.

It was, as far as John was concerned, yet another perfect example of government inefficiency: not only had both the insects and the disease come from the very place the group was headed to, but the method was haphazard. It didn't differentiate between the worthy and the non. It also proved John's case as well as Ben's: even the air people breathed was being poisoned, all part of the plan for the prison planet.

Another ally delivered the appropriate badges, and it was almost an afterthought to create the situation that would effect the exchange. And in just a very little while, one click, one electronic transaction at the speed of light, would leave him in possession of the cure—the cure for mankind.

Technology was a wonderful thing. It meant Chul-Moo practically slept with his phone and his pager next to him. Waking him to modify plans by a dozen hours or so had therefore been easy. And as that plan changed, so had another.

Originally, John had planned to leave Charli on the boat, letting Ben handle the technical aspects, but now... It was Charli who had made the leap in logic that made the funding possible, Charli who cut through his arguments with lightning quickness and then synthesized theory and fact. It was Charli who'd withstood the shocks of the night like a trouper. He wasn't a monster, he rationalized; much of what she'd experienced over the last few hours was certainly out of her normal experience, and certainly there had to be some sort of adjustment process to be gone through. But even with that, she had fallen in with him and both his immediate and larger plans, had demonstrated that she understood everything perfectly, and *that* deserved a reward. Let her witness the important first step, the very thing that would be the beginning of the new world order.

The program is running. Exit anyway? (y or n)

SYNCHRONICITY

She knew, as she'd texted rapid-made plans with equipment requests, slung the pager on her belt, and searched for what she needed through the apartment, that there would never be enough time to scramble a team to get them out to Charli in time, or at least before they reached Plum Island, and she knew timing was everything. No field operative had clean hands for very long, and Romello had quite the kill list in addition to the rest of his accomplishments. Yes, technically she was no longer an active outside operative, but there was too much at stake here for her to sit idly by. After all, it wasn't as if she'd never been part of a recon or extraction team before—and she'd performed admirably, even if she did say so herself. Besides, weren't those successes the reason she'd been pulled into a different sector? She was grateful that her handler had agreed—because she knew she would have gone on her own.

Plum Island had some quirky security—she'd known she needed to be creative and had to go a little lo-tech, at least on the approach. She would have had to anyway; returning to her apartment was not an option, especially since she was aware that she had two hours or possibly less before the Treas was on her. When she considered how quickly Romello's operation with Charli had gone down, she'd also known there simply wasn't enough time to gear up at the Smith's Point safe house.

She'd gone through Charli's apartment. The wet suit, her surfboard, her PDA, her laptop. That had been enough to start. She paged her handler with the info she had, the plans she'd made, and the list of equipment she needed.

A car had been dropped off for her use fifteen minutes later, and it had what she'd expected: the tools she required, and more importantly, weapons.

Now, not quite two hours later, she was waiting at the shore off Greenpoint for the tide to turn, for the flow tide, the very beginning of the returning rush of water, that would help her get onto the island.

This particular spot of Long Island Sound had a nickname among those who depended on it: the Race. The mouth of the Sound had a vicious rip and current—it made for great kayaking, but dangerous surfing and even more dangerous swimming.

There was also the report she'd been forwarded, brief but thorough: radar, sonar, and cameras running offshore, but no infrared or motion on the perimeter. The reason listed was harbor seals; they made it their home, and there were other animals, including deer, left to roam wild on the rest of the island that had been left as a preserve.

Since this part of the Sound was actively commercially trafficked—mostly by tugs and barges, recreational kayakers, some braver surfers, and Jet Skiers—there were no water patrols for her to be concerned with.

A recent strike by both the security team as well as the contractors used for decon supposedly made their scheduled foot patrol a bit more erratic as the staff-reduced substitute crew adjusted to the needs of their client. *The good ol' Mark 1A Eyeball*, she smirked to herself, *accept no substitutes*. That was the least of her worries, the human eye. She was after all, a fully qualified and field proven Company operative. She was CIA—disappearing was what she did, and did well.

Her plan was simple, but there was no reason for it to be anything but what she wanted it to be: damn effective. She'd come in off the water, under the board if she had to. She was too small an object to show up on most detecting devices, especially since they'd be calibrated to ignore things like seals and deer, animals that could approximate a single human in size. The true concern at Plum was a water vehicle–based insertion, bearing a small but well-trained cadre. As for the interior itself, she had no concerns; that was the easy part. She knew too many ways to disable, disarm, or simply evade the majority of detecting devices, and she doubted very highly that Plum deployed a technology she hadn't yet met or been trained in.

She shivered, more from anticipation than from the predawn cold, then glanced back over her shoulder, back toward the dark rise that signaled the presence of Orient Point County Park, her point of departure.

The tide chart was what she had to rely on, and as soon as it shifted from low to high, she'd move, too. She was about to enter the Plum Gut, a spot that the waters of Long Island Sound rushed through during ebb tide at currents exceeding five knots. The whitecaps and riptides along the mile-wide passageway were challenging for even the most experienced mariners, for just beneath the water lay Oyster Pond Reef.

That had factored into her decision to use the board, combined with the distance: two thousand meters, or one and a quarter miles. She had planned her departure point carefully. The board would carry her right over the hidden reef, which was especially dangerous during low tide; the flow, the incoming rush, would bring her a bit south of the ferry dock on Plum itself.

Not too much longer, she told herself as she cast the quickest beam from her lens across the water. She observed the shoreline where the wavelets were coming in rapidly, then doused the light. She tucked it into the belt around her waist, then quickly checked the rest of her setup.

Satisfied, she decided there was no time like the present and quashed the human instinct to take a breath as she waded into the water—if she could ride the tide in, it would make her job that much easier. She felt the weight and swirl of the water pull at her calves as she stepped carefully over rocks, through frozen grasses and ice, registered the cold as cooling through the military-issue neoprene that hugged her from head to toe in sealed, seamless—well, it wasn't true warmth, but it was protection.

The slippery mix of ice, water, and slimed-over organic debris thinned a bit when she reached a mid-thigh depth. She held on to and balanced the board one-handed, pulled the small paddle she'd attached to the board with a bungee cord with the other, and began the work it would take to get her to the center channel. It was an easy enough plan: get to the shore off Orient County, then get to Plum. Once there, she'd attempt to isolate both Romello and Cooper, as well as obtain or contain whatever horror of science the target acquisition was.

Despite the go-ahead she'd been granted to attempt insertion, the orders she'd received had been explicit: she was not to take any of them—Romello, Cooper, and whoever might be helping them within Plum—down. Based on the intel she'd provided as well as her recommendations, a team had already been scrambled. They would arrive within two hours of her original request. Given their different methods of travel to the location, that more than likely meant she'd spend anywhere from five to seven minutes on her own once she'd penetrated the location. She glanced about again, and assessed the weather. *Feels a heck of a lot like snow. Maybe I should make that twenty minutes, just in case they get caught up and delayed in this.*

She set herself on the board, felt the first cold wet flakes hit her face, and blinked them out of her eyes. She pushed away from the shore. Free of the first few feet of the treacherous mix of water, slush, and ice, the board simply shot out onto smooth, black glass. Plum Island was a deeper black area in an almost unrelieved red-tinged darkness ahead of her. Snow fell in earnest now, accompanied by the almost silent splash of the oar. She checked her chronometer: she was on track.

Out in the distance, she saw a single point of light in the unrelieved black. *Probably a tugboat,* she assumed.

In the waterproof sack she'd attached under the board was a change of clothes, lightweight and warm, her communications device, and her conceal-carry device: a SIG 229—and while she carried a .40 SW, it was loaded with .357 SIG. She'd hesitated a single second before loading, the memory of Cooper's expression as he drew and fired a quick flash through her mind's eye, then shrugged as she slammed the cartridge home, the sting of it against her palm somehow very satisfying. Besides, she had rationalized, it had better accuracy under repeat firing, and while she hoped it didn't come to that, she wanted the advantage of superior power and accuracy if it did.

She paused in her review, let her mind go where it wanted to while it could, when all she had before her for approximately the next quarter of a mile was the monotonous pull of the paddle. *Charli.*

Charli wasn't far from her mind, her thoughts, or even, she admitted with an ache of surprise, her body. Even under the thick and heavy wet suit she wore, Charli was still a silken brush against her chest, a heated breath followed by a whisper of touch that tightened the muscles in her stomach, a taste in her mouth, a flavor on a tongue that still made room for hers. She could still feel the skim of Charli's fingers through her hair, the sensitive line behind her ear, and her palms still bore the warm memory of the shape of Charli's shoulders and the length of her spine under her hands. She allowed herself to recollect and reflect on the last real conversation they'd had, the one before Cooper's frantic pages, before the confirming revelation of not only who was responsible for the inside part of the job, but also of the outside operator.

She had been surprised. Usually after coming, especially a second time, sleep would more than likely be the first consideration. But as the tide rolled out, then rolled back in, desire had also quickened through her once more, and this time, she had full access to Charli—body and mind.

She remembered quite clearly what it had been that seemed to turn the key: she'd paused during the round of exploratory play, a response to the slight toss of Charli's head, the different way she kissed, when her hands had finally reached to claim Charli's secrets.

"Do you want this?" Anna asked, remembering something else from the first time those months ago. Charli had not let herself be touched then, not really, anyway. It was easy, Charli made it easy, to

get lost, overwhelmed, overloaded by the environment she created to not realize that she was in essence avoiding being touched herself.

"It's important to *you*," Charli answered, and followed her answer with a kiss and a touch that should have made her forget the question or to look deeper into the answer. Another time, an earlier time, perhaps it would have. But this wasn't their first time together, and Anna *still* wanted...she wanted to reach through, to leave Charli gasping and undone, to show through the raw power of touch that this, this between them, meant more to her than the amazing orgasms she'd experienced under the body that now lay beneath hers. She wanted to show Charli she not only desired but cared, she wanted to touch essence, and in that moment of touch plainly reveal and say something fundamentally truthful underneath all the lies she'd had to tell.

Anna could, in an objective way, understand why, perhaps, someone might not notice Charli's discomfort: she was hard, she was wet, and that was usually all the enticement anyone needed. And suddenly, it bothered Anna, bothered her greatly that perhaps others hadn't noticed the slight stiffening of Charli's body, the briefly visible set to her jaw, the not-so-subtle head shake that was in reality a *no*, that Charli redirected the focus to what was important to Anna. "Char...there's a thousand other things if you don't enjoy that," Anna told her, her voice measured and low even while she still gently played her fingers along Charli's body. "Tell me what you like."

To her surprise, Charli kissed her again, took her hand and held it in one of her own, then cupped her cheek with the other. "It's not that I don't like it," she said softly. "It's just..." Charli took a deep breath, let it out slowly, then set and squared her shoulders as she did. Her eyes were intent on Anna's and they searched through her before she answered. "I don't always feel it." Charli gave her a small grin as if to say *it's no big deal*, but it was, to Anna, it was.

"I don't...I don't want you to do something just because you think I want it," Anna told her.

"What...you didn't enjoy earlier?" Charli asked, her tone teasing.

"More than," Anna rejoined, then kissed her. "And I'd like—no, I'd *really* love," she corrected as she eased a leg between Charli's, "to do the same for you."

So much more made sense, not just earlier in the evening, but earlier in the year, from the last time when they'd been together and Charli had asked her to—it didn't matter, she knew what to do. She started over, her own needs more than well abated except for this one, the one that left her wanting to know even more, to share the experience she'd just had from a different point of view.

Anna decided she needed to take Charli out of and away from her head, away from the place where she measured and analyzed, and yet still have her be aware of and in control of what happened to her body.

"I don't always feel it," Charli had said, not *I never feel it*, and that made a difference, it meant there was a threshold that needed to be crossed first to get there, a threshold that—given what they had just shared—changed when Charli wasn't in absolute control. There was a shut-off switch somewhere, and Anna realized she needed to work with and around it in order not to trigger it. Whatever she did, it would have to be slow, both steady and progressive, a buildup of the sensual, creating the right envelope to carry them both where Anna wanted to take her—and with no pressure to get there, either. Besides, they had the whole weekend before them—they had the time.

What most more immediately enjoyed Charli didn't, what most ignored Charli exploited, and Anna took a lesson from that, paid attention to every response, every nuance of breath and tone. She would have anyway. She wanted to know, to touch, everything about Charli, before the opportunity was gone. Anna harbored no false hopes or illusions. She was certain that once Charli knew the truth, regaining her trust would be a long process at best, and nearly—perhaps actually—impossible at worst, not unless she had something truly powerful to counter it with, something unequivocal. This was her chance, perhaps the only one she'd get.

She began with a kiss, the kind of kiss *she* wanted to give, letting lips and tongue speak for her and receiving answers she understood.

The kiss and the discussion continued, expanded, became the taste along Charli's neck, the contour of muscle, skin, brushed by Anna's mouth, the glide of hands along long expanses and shorter, glancing strokes that were done for no other reason than to learn every inch and to make those inches feel vibrantly alive.

Anna learned all of it, and something else as well, discovered she understood something new: Charli did not want to be—would not allow herself to be—forced or commanded, not in any real way, not in any way that went deeper than skin. What Charli wanted— what Charli *needed*—was to be read, read and understood, and with that understanding, anticipated. It was that simple, and all it required was something even simpler: caring enough to pay attention, to listen and really, fully hear everything. If this, then that.

And once the threshold was reached and the barrier crossed, when she knew she had Charli in that place, in that space that crossed between control and permission, she didn't let go.

"Do you feel this?" Her heart beat with such force as Charli responded to her, the soft groans and sharp breaths exquisite sounds in her ear, and Anna felt almost dizzy with the headiness of it, the sharp flush of pure pleasure that flowed through her with it.

"Yes…I feel you." The words were whispered, breathless; the clutch and knead on Anna's hip, the sharp intake of air that drew past her face all combined with the feel of the body that moved then held beneath her, hot and slick and—oh she was close, so *close*—

"I can't…I can't *do* this…not without—" Charli seemed almost frantic, on the edge of sudden panic as she reached for Anna with hands that knew her intimately, beautifully—"not without you."

"Okay," Anna breathed in agreement against her lips, brushed her cheek along Charli's. "Okay." Those were the only words she could get out past the beat that pounded through her, knowing in that moment that this was the final bridge to cross. Her body was so fully alive, burning with crave for the now-familiar touch even as Charli sank within her once more, filled her body with the pulse and pull she felt on her own fingers, the primal sound of satisfaction that sounded out from lips she never wanted to stop kissing—all the confirmation Anna needed or wanted that this was the place she'd wanted to go, to bring Charli. There was no holding back, no further tests or hesitations, the envelope was perfect, *complete*, and together they were suspended within it.

Charli held Anna's head to her own with her free hand even as her body flexed with fluid grace and strength against hers, playing the rhythm she moved to in Anna, and Anna knew the moment she came, wrapped around and in her, the gulped and held breath a more powerful statement than any declaration. Anna had no words for the sensation or the emotion that seared through her, couldn't help but respond physically to what her heart recognized as something… *This,* she thought in the sudden delivery of a full understanding of what drove poets and artists, what musicians and sages tried to convey through their many mediums, a wordless eternal truth. It was a burst of clarity and light as the eternal moment held them fast. *This "us" that we're creating now, right* now*, this very moment—this* is *what beautiful is.*

They lay there together for a few seconds, quiet, spent, and Anna brushed her lips against Charli's temple. "How're you doing?" she asked with soft concern, gazing into eyes that seemed to glow, were overbright as they looked back at hers, unaware that hers shone in the same way. "Are you all right?"

"That…that was very special," Charli said quietly. She ran her fingertips up Anna's side, drew light patterns on her shoulder, before reaching to do the same on her face. "Very," she repeated, then drew her in for another kiss, this one so very different from any of the others before.

"It was beautiful, Char," Anna answered, the word, the insight, and the unnamed sensations it had left still roiling through her. *We are*, she thought as the kiss continued and in the next breath knew Charli felt the same. "*You* are beautiful," she whispered, "so very beautiful."

As their bodies once more fit and moved, adjusted and joined, Anna found herself overwhelmed by everything: the job, the pressure and timing of the investigation, and the emotions that churned through her for the woman she'd just made love with—

That stopped her short.

Oh Christ, oh shit, she thought, and a flutter rose through her chest and to her throat as the realization slammed home for her. Anna knew, knew it unequivocally, in a place she'd never really known or felt before, that was *exactly* what they'd just done. The knowledge made her want to be free, to be fully naked and fully seen, to begin to bridge the chasm Charli didn't know existed between them, she wanted to— "Char, I *have* to tell you something," she said finally in between kisses and caresses. "It's—"

Charli placed her fingers across her lips. "Before you tell me anything, I'd better tell *you* something." Sparks of gold in deep caramel eyes gleamed at Anna as she spoke. "I think...I think we like each other, right?"

Anna nodded and kissed the fingertips against her mouth. "I certainly hope so," she answered and smiled, still very much filled with the unnamed feeling that reigned over and through her.

"I think it's safe to say that we'll probably do this again— preferably sooner rather than later," Charli said and gave her a small smile in return, a smile that was quickly eclipsed by the somber expression that took over. "There are more choices to be made, Anna. And you need information to make those choices. I want to tell you something—you have to tell me if at any point you can't or don't want to hear it. I'll respect that—I'll respect whatever decision you make. But you have to know, first, okay?"

For the first time since seconds before the kiss on the sofa when she'd willfully shut it off, the Company part of Anna's mind turned back on. Whatever was about to be said would be critical to understanding Charli, to unlocking that final door that would let her in. And she would have to be extremely cautious; if Charli told her something she already knew, knew as part of her mission as opposed to part of their association... There was, Anna thought, something monstrously unfair about sharing this moment—one she'd wanted, one she'd worked toward for purely personal reasons, this thing that had now evolved into something else, something delicate—with her larger assignment.

She decided to take her own advice. *Fuck the job tonight,* she told herself. She didn't have to say anything, she realized, didn't have to tell anyone everything she knew, or even anything at all, not really, not if there was no compelling reason to, and since Charli *was* innocent, there was no reason to say anything about her at all.

She felt strangely comfortable with the thought and half a second later discovered it wasn't because she'd just made a choice, but because she had already decided earlier. For this little while, she could still be, she wanted to be, the Anna that Charli knew, whatever the consequences were. And Charli, aware of it or not, knew more about who she really was, really felt, really thought, than anyone.

"Anything you want to tell me, I want to hear," she said finally. She meant it, every word of it. She brushed the back of her finger along Charli's face, then cupped it in her hands. "You think right—I like you." She said it quietly with a smile she couldn't help. "I think I like you a lot and…" She kissed her softly, slowly. "And I *do* want to do this again…preferably sooner rather than later."

That elicited the smile she had hoped for. "And I…*I* don't think there's anything you can tell me that's going to change either the way or how much we like each other, so tell me," she concluded and kissed Charli again, briefly and reassuringly. What she had to say could wait in the face of the intensity Charli presented. "Tell me anything you want."

"I'll bet you're shocked to hear I was a bit of a tomboy as a kid," Charli began, and Anna could hear the humor in her tone.

"Yes. Shocked. Absolutely stunned," she told her with the same amusement as her fingers drifted of their own accord along the contour of Charli's shoulder, an unconscious seeking of the rises and hollows she'd floated over then anchored into earlier. Her thumb found and rubbed lightly against the marks her teeth had left then, too, and visceral memory sent an echo of replay thrilling through her.

"And I suppose you took ballet and dressed your Barbies carefully?" Charli teased in return. She stretched her body along Anna's once again, the weight welcome, familiar, her skin missed for those few seconds it had been gone, and Charli slipped her hands through hers, a sensual scrape across the pulse point of her wrists, then a scratch along her palms until Anna was caught once more and Charli's mouth was once again a whisper above hers. "Or did you make them…surf?"

The dynamic between them was slipping, changing, and Anna knew that this was another test, a more important one than any of the others. Charli wanted to tell her something important, something that carried enough weight for her that she was certain it would determine anything further between them. If Anna let the moment go, it would be forever lost. She knew that. She closed her fingers through Charli's and held her hands with equal firmness. "Surfing," she said, her voice deep, then kissed the lips above hers. "Lots and lots of…surfing." Anna drew their joined hands down and back, a move unprotested, unresisted, then shifted so that they once again could face each other. "So what was it for you—GI Joes? Baseball? Mud pies or mud wrestling?" She held one of Charli's hands against her own hip and waited.

"Soccer," Charli said succinctly. "That was my obsession—outside of class, I *lived* for that ball." She shook her head, and the small laugh she gave as she shook her head, then gazed at a point somewhere beyond Anna's shoulder said the laugh was directed at Charli herself.

"I thought I was *so* lucky—the luckiest kid in the entire world." The words were soft, almost swallowed, and Anna strained to hear them even in the silence of the room. "My aunt married a retired semi-pro player, and Uncle Ted was the high school coach—I was all set to become the best player in the world—I wanted so much to impress him." Charli shook her head slowly in an unmistakable gesture of self-reproach. "Stupid, I know," she shrugged, "but apparently I did—just not in the way I thought I would."

Anna had known—whether it was her own background or merely a good gut instinct she wasn't certain, and she had no desire to analyze it right then—that there was a reason, a source, behind Charli's mercurial affections, occasional icy reserve, and the desperate, desperate way she threw herself into the ocean.

"'You're old enough now, Charli,' that's what Uncle Ted told me, 'time to learn what being a girl's *really* all about.'"

Anna now knew, finally, what no amount of research had been able to disclose, the black hole of information, the mystery revealed and uncovered. But it was no mystery, it was much more akin to tragedy, and its revelation shed light on much more than she expected, so much more that her own reactions caught her unawares.

She heard the words as Charli said them, the only ones that held any emotion at all, repeated more than likely in the same tone they'd first been heard in.

She wondered at the control that allowed Charli to be so apparently calm, so outwardly unaffected, because the words told her clearly what was coming next, created a sinking numbness that scorched down her throat as the beginnings of a rage she didn't know she was capable of began a white tide burn that surged from her bones and flowed under her skin. The new insight made Anna afraid, afraid to hold Charli too tightly, too closely, afraid that her own anger—over something so long gone, so past recovering, so damned *unchangeable*—might bleed through, spilling white fire, then shatter the layers that Charli had built, that protected her.

Outwardly instead Anna was cool, she was calm, she was collected—she was a trained Company operative, for fuck's sake. And she knew that if she'd had a target in front of her right then, she would have taken it cleanly out. White tide wipe out.

It didn't matter whether or not she'd told Charli her name, her mission, it didn't matter that Anna hadn't shared the particulars: Charli's leap into the ocean of trust with Anna had gone beyond that, to heart, to core, to the place where nothing but the truth remained. And the truth? In reaching through, in really touching Charli, it was Charli who had broken through and under. This woman who had already been under Anna's skin had blown her cover more completely than any simple revelation of something as simple as a name or a job ever could.

"Charli," she said, the name soft and round and real in her mouth, as real as the body against hers, and the blood that had eased down to quietly eddy within. "Charli...thank you...for sharing that. I know you didn't have to."

"Yes, I did." Charli laughed lightly, almost under her breath, and once more gazed deeply into Anna. "I did because I owe you an apology—an explanation—for last night." Anna's breath caught when Charli stretched gentle fingers for her face. "I...I had to be sure—for me," she told her as she stroked her thumb against Anna's cheek. "Me...you—it had to be because it was something real, something I really wanted, not just...not just a fear reaction, or because I can't—I don't want to be *afraid*, Anna."

Anna knew Charli well enough to read the distress that rose in her eyes as she tried to explain. There'd been enough of that in her life, and Anna didn't want to add to it. She covered Charli's hand with her own. "I get it," Anna interrupted gently and told her, "I do." She did.

She'd known, because it was part of her job, one of the parts she was growing to despise, that Charli had gone to Kevin's apartment the night before. She'd forced herself not to think about it, of her, of him, together, of his arms around her, of what they might or might not have done. It was just a data point, a new bit of information, that's all it was. One new piece of information.

Anna had told herself that repeatedly over the minutes that stretched into hours as they passed, but she couldn't pretend to herself that it didn't matter to her personally, nor could she deny that she'd spent the rest of the night steeped in files and research, analyzing and compiling data—all with a focus that would have been admirable, had it not been occasionally intercut by her imagination and the heated rush that had raced up her chest to her neck, had made her ears burn whenever she couldn't help but wonder what and where Charli was. She didn't dare let her mind wander to what she might have been doing.

Anna had never wanted to kiss Franko before she'd gotten the page about the breach.

Combining what had happened between them only a little while ago with what Charli had just shared with her, she not only had the answer to her silent question of the night before, she now knew not only what had *not* happened between Charli and Kevin, but also what Charli telling her both the background and her own intent meant, for her, for Charli, for *them*. And Anna had no words, nothing more coherent than the inadequate-feeling "thank you" she'd given.

She didn't know whether to laugh or cry. Cry because she didn't want to *think* that someone so admired and loved and trusted by a child could so violate all of that, or because she couldn't stand the thought of Charli being hurt, left with a disconnect so deep, that the woman who could push code and body to the very limits was a semi-stranger in her own skin. Or laugh because Charli existed, she lived, dared, and succeeded anyway, and she had decided that despite all that, she was going to take a chance, a chance on—*with*—Anna.

And what Anna had to tell her...

She had no idea how to even begin, but she did know what to do, and she once more gathered Charli into her arms, pulled her close, settled them both back into the warmth and comfort of the bed. She kissed her head, her cheek, the tender skin of her neck, and the delicate sigh Charli floated against her throat confirmed for her she'd done the right thing. "You don't owe me any apologies," Anna whispered against the fine hair that lay across Charli's temple. She didn't know where the words she spoke next came from, but she was certain of them anyway. "And you don't have to be sure of anything right now. It's okay if you're not—I'm okay if you're not." They lay there in a simple quiet.

"So..." Charli finally spoke into the silence, "any questions?"

The tone was a bit too joking, too bright, and Anna realized she'd been holding her breath. "Yes," she answered, letting her tone remain light even as she tightened her hold on Charli, not wanting to let her slip away from the fragile "us" they'd just created, to ease into sleep or into her head, back and away to wherever it was she usually watched from, back to the place where Anna couldn't feel or reach or touch her. "Where'd you learn to surf?"

Charli laughed, a relieved and light sound in the warm near

dark as she returned the hold. "Virginia Beach—when, you know, after…after the whole thing. Everybody needed time. Surfing saved my life."

"I'm glad," Anna answered, and kissed her head again. As they drifted off together, all she knew was that she finally understood what it meant to be willing to give one's life for a cause, for an idea. She'd understood it in the abstract, had taken an oath, had signed papers that said she would, wanted, and was willing to. First for the Company, and again when she'd been placed within the Treasury.

Still, she had never actually felt it before nor known it, not with the same gut-level fullness she felt then, before the frantic pages that had woken them, before the dime had dropped and the world had spun on it. She'd known, understood intellectually, had made solemn promises based on that understanding, but she'd never before really known what it meant, to truly want—to *need*—to be the one who would shield and guard, to protect something or someone, *even if it meant making some sort of ultimate sacrifice to ensure it.*

She felt it now, a strong steady force that beat in time with her heart, the white fire wave that flooded through the muscles in her arms and chest, a churning heat that made it easy to disregard the cold and the snow on her face even as she heard the distant splash that told her she wasn't too far from the shore she aimed for and after checking her wrist to ensure she was still on track—a habit borne out of precaution rather than actual need—she once more dug her paddle into the black glass she floated on.

She knew, because it was obvious, that Charli was more than smart, and Charli could play very cool when necessary—and in most situations, she could probably take care of herself. But Charli didn't know Romello, and Anna knew something else Charli didn't: Cooper and Anna didn't merely not get along, they *hated* each other.

She breathed with the freedom of admitting that to herself, letting it float out with the breath she couldn't see into the night air.

She hated the way Cooper stood and spoke, hated the way he walked and gazed, the twitch of his hands, the quirk to his mouth, the furrow of his brow. The cock to his hip whenever he was near

Charli absolutely infuriated her, though rationally she knew he probably wasn't even aware of it. Lust and attraction, attraction and admiration she could and did understand, but there was something about the manner in which he did it—perhaps it was that she knew that Charli wouldn't welcome the intention or the desire and that he seemed to so willfully disregard that, couldn't be bothered to disguise it somehow, to keep his mental hands to himself—oh, she knew that didn't make sense and it didn't matter, anyway, because the only word that came to her mind was *unclean*, and even as she remembered it, she felt the crawl of it and the fury it engendered, fury she'd spent so much time muting, under her skin.

But the antagonism and hatred had not only been as mutual as it was unspoken, it had also been, due to their work focus, a contest between peers, despite the differences in their rank: work created a level playing field. Funny, she mused, how as much as they hated each other, they understood each other—to a degree anyway, at least when it came to if not their feelings, then at least their intentions toward Charli.

Now, though, Cooper had what he undoubtedly believed was his first kill under his belt, and not just anyone, but someone he'd actively perceived as a rival. Flush with the success of that, who knew where else that already unstable mind would go, or what he'd do to—no. She had to rethink this.

Romello was a wannabe demagogue, a potential terrorist, not a rapist, and by his own manifesto, fancied himself some sort of super-civilized human being. Cooper, she was forced to admit, other than his facial expressions and broadcasting body language—and that wasn't true evidence—had never said or done anything inappropriate, to Charli, anyway. There had been that bit of trouble with him and Eunae… She swore under her breath. If he touched Charli, if he so much as laid a finger on her—Anna quashed that avenue of speculation. It would do neither her nor Charli any good, she told herself firmly. She had to trust Charli to take care of herself, and she had to keep her own head clear and in the game. Anna paused in her thoughts and checked her surroundings.

The tug was lit up and she saw it before she heard it. She dug deep into the water, a short hard stroke that reversed her direction, and stopped herself in time, not much more than twenty feet away from the vessel. The low throb of it seemed to surround her, a thrum that echoed even under the snug fit of the hood, a cotton echo in her ears, while the wake lifted the board, forcing her to stroke just to maintain her pace.

Impatience surged through her while she waited and as soon as it passed—there, finally. A few strong strokes and she shot forward. It was all about time, she had to make good time. *C'mon, c'mon— you can do this, you* have *to do this*, she told herself as she crossed the wake, and she lifted her paddle once more. In the breath between one stroke and the next, instinct made her glance to her right just as the first ripple hit under the board. An absence in the blackness, the hole in the dark, loomed swiftly and silently toward her and she pulled, swift and hard, heart pounding with exertion and adrenaline, past the empty shadow that grew ever larger as it drew closer, she paddled with focused strength over and against the lethal pull of its draw through the water.

When the threat and the wake of it was no more than a gentle kick beneath her, she glanced back in time to see it as it silently passed, first the green starboard light, then finally, the amber on the stern of the barge. She'd gotten lucky—had the tug traveled any faster, she would have gotten caught on the line that ran from it to the barge it towed, or worse, crushed by the barge itself, sucked into the wake, then more than likely keelhauled beneath its length.

The near miss didn't scare her and she used the adrenaline kick of it to strengthen her resolve. She was determined: she would do anything, face anything, brave anything to prevent anyone from ever, *ever*, hurting Charli again.

Starting program: /hacking/$ ./SHELLCODE=.HIJACK

BINARY

Ben Cooper was confused, and that didn't bode well. He was quite used—or so he believed—to feeling only one thing at a time, at least since adolescence, anyway. It was, or so he thought, what made him so certain in his ideas and beliefs. Used to being in, presenting, and discovering situations that could be narrowed to only yes/no or on/off possibilities, he let logic dictate his answers and outcomes.

Did a classmate want to sit next to him? Yes. He made room for them to sit. Did they want to talk with him? No. Fuck 'em then. He ate in silence. There was a social event after work. Did anyone ask him directly? No. He didn't go. Did Eunae say his presence was required? Yes. He showed up. It was all quite simple, really. A situation, an object, an event, either was something, or it wasn't.

If he was snubbed, he got angry. If he was included, he was happy. If he was working, he was satisfied. If he wasn't, he was bored. Of course, there were subpaths, different possibilities that opened and closed depending on each situation, but still, the process was straightforward and didn't require what he considered useless emotional wastes of time.

The problem with Ben's self-assessment was that it left things out, such as the hope that had shot through him that day in the lunchroom, and the angry tears that had formed but didn't fall when he'd overheard the same tablemate make fun of him later the same day. In the same way it had already let go of the earlier events of the evening, it also conveniently forgot that when Eunae had asked him to attend that particular party, he'd decided that it meant she was interested in him and had acted accordingly. That had gotten him into a bit of trouble, but Charli had smoothed it all out—she understood him, or at least, he thought she did, usually.

At the moment, he didn't know whether to be pleased, concerned, or furious. John practically ignored him, Charli refused to speak to him, and he wasn't certain what to make of the attention John paid her or how she responded to it.

It hadn't bothered him, not at first, because he hadn't noticed. He had known Charli would understand, would *get* it, and Ben had to admit that he'd felt not only pleased, but also a distinct flush of pride when he'd returned with coffee not only for Charli but for all of them, and saw the serious and intent way that Charli listened to John.

He reviewed the events as best he could from when she'd woken. Yes, he'd been thrown for a bit, just a few seconds.

"You shot Anna," Charli stated. The flat tone, the frozen immobility of her eyes, her face—she radiated chill, a chill that had left him scattered when all he'd wanted to do was explain. John had probably explained it better than he could have even as he thought of what he would have, *should* have said. It wasn't murder, of that he was certain. If this was war, if this was revolution, then he was a front-line soldier. "Casualties," as his father used to say, "are to be expected."

His father had crawled, sweated, and bled through a jungle half a world away; now he, Ben, would do the same, only his jungle was made of concrete and wires, electric enemies that counted directly in dollars, ignoring the carnage they left behind. And this time—unlike Vietnam, free of bureaucratic mistakes driven by the military-industrial complex, the man who ruled the world—this time, this was a winnable war.

The hour they spent waiting in the roadside hotel—John had insisted they wait somewhere where they could rest for a bit because he wanted them to be as alert as possible in case contingencies arose, plus it gave them time to recharge their various electronica—had gone well, with John discussing and explaining to Charli the same eagle-eye clear view of the world he'd given Ben. But that was then.

There had been an intense exchange of questions and answers between Charli and John, but it was during the drive over to the boatslip, the almost silent ride over while John explained the roles they'd play once on the other side of the water, and then the careful but swift walk up the path, the entrance to the first building of the complex—that's when Ben had finally noticed that other than her direct initial statement, and then a quip about work that quasi involved him but was told to John, Charli had not said another word to him except for the briefest nod of thanks when he'd handed her the coffee he'd brought in its Styrofoam cup.

That stupid ugly cup. He could still feel the texture in his hands, almost as if its poison had leached through his skin and left a buried tactile memory. Ben hated Styrofoam and what it did to the environment—the damn synthetic stuff was a planet wrecker, what with it never degrading, mucking up the food chain, and releasing noxious toxins—but it was all the local store supplied. And the coffee…ugh. It probably wasn't even shade grown, sustainable growth stock, either, which made him unwillingly complicit in planetary rape. That would change soon, he reminded himself, that would all change very soon.

But still, now that he sat there, waiting instead of being there for the big moment, Ben felt the stirrings of resentment, unable to admit that what he really wanted was Charli to *see* him do it, to watch him bring the Man—or rather the military-industrial complex that was the force behind the global fall, the boot on the neck of the world—*down*, on their knees and begging for the same mercy they historically had withheld.

Him. It had been *his* idea, Ben's, to bring Charli in, his idea to use her code and modify it. None of this would be happening—could not *exist* as reality—had he not hacked and cracked the code, the servers, and the firewall, written an accompanying set of programs that made the final transactions unidentifiable, untraceable to any of them, and essentially victimless. He'd imagined himself a sort of techno Robin Hood as he'd done it.

John chose him, had needed him to set it up, to tap into his own network of associates, like-minded people that John culled through.

Ben wasn't certain what exactly he'd expected, but certainly not this, the coldness Charli emanated, the faint laughter that he thought John held in his eyes and in the corners of his mouth every time he and Charli glanced his way.

He knew how to recognize that, silent laughter. He'd endured it growing up when his classmates made fun of his father, called him a lazy pothead, an unemployed loser, and him his egghead son. It used to infuriate him, that they didn't care or understand that his father was a *hero*, had fought and lost a part of himself so they could enjoy their neon drinks and casual curses, but then one day he realized they didn't understand because they couldn't—they simply weren't capable of it.

Those sorts of beings were what made the world a miserable place, those were the ones who couldn't see beyond their noses and bellies unless it was to put down what they couldn't comprehend, or to take more of whatever would fill their enormous appetites.

Ben thanked the day he had discovered computers, and then the Internet. Through it he found others who thought and felt as he did, and from there, he'd found DsrtFx, the man who had found a solution, a solution that Ben himself had helped create, was an actual part of.

And now, at the most critical point, when the exchange was to actually be made, it was Charli who would do the technical piece, not him. Ben wasn't sure if he was supposed to be jealous or relieved.

Things had gone even more easily than he'd thought they would. He'd known, he'd simply known that Charli would understand about everything. Maybe it was no big deal at all that he wouldn't be there to witness the exchange. After all, John trusted him to ensure that they wouldn't be interrupted, that there would be no unwanted witnesses.

And so he waited, right in the door for the outer lab, the complex surprisingly quiet, all things considered. Ben had been honestly surprised. John had told them—him and Charli—all about the history and the current activities of the place, and as a result, Ben had imagined that they'd have to be much more cautious in their approach; he'd expected the place would be filled to bristling with military types and rigid academics in full pursuit of the micro mysteries of the universe, but it wasn't that at all. Instead, it was a laboratory and testing facility that ran with regular business hours, and it had a workforce that commuted back and forth via ferry every day. Now, after the strike, there was a less-than-skeleton staff on hand, and security, due to that same strike, while present, certainly seemed lax to his civilian eyes.

He examined his surroundings once more. The room he was in could have been a high school lab, if that chemistry lab had been well funded. Cream yellow and white tiles lined the walls to about two feet over his head, while neat and empty cages lined a back wall next to gated windows. The antiseptic smell was a faint burn in his nostrils despite the occasional swirl from the vents that hummed over his head.

There was nothing to do but watch and wait for John and Charli to return with the laptop and the vial—or whatever it was contained in—that would change the world, and Ben quickly grew overwarm and bored.

He wondered how it would happen—John hadn't told him specifics about that yet, and he wondered what kind of life they would come to lead, him, John, Charli, and the others they would help set free.

It wasn't complete yet, but still, they could live off the grid, he supposed, back at his place. He could easily picture the future, could easily see the center his home could become, his role in it, and Charli's. They'd live the way people were supposed to—in harmony with nature and their own multiple potentials. They'd have clean water and air, they'd hunt…that was it, he decided. That was the reason John had asked him to stand guard. He was a hunter, and weren't hunters really warriors that weren't at war?

The thought made him almost giddy with joy. He'd finally proven himself, to John, to the world, and he was a real man, a true warrior and—he grinned to himself with the realization—there was no way that Charli hadn't seen that for herself.

Charli…she needed time, he decided, time to get used to these new thoughts that he and John were already used to, to meet some of the other people online, to... What was that chirp? Probably crickets, he dismissed. Hadn't John told them they experimented on bugs as well as other animals there? It wasn't crickets, though, it was...ticks. That was right. Ticks.

He eyed the cages against the wall. Had to be more than ticks for those, too large for most rodents, he thought. Cats? Dogs? Monkeys? He stood, craning his head to see if he could find a tag on any of them.

His cell phone went off, an almost-mute vibration in the front pocket of his jeans that made him jump, thinking he'd been electrocuted or some such for half a second before he slammed his elbow into the tiled wall, sending another shock down his arm and he remembered. "Fuck," he muttered in soft surprise as he rubbed the bruised joint, then reached for his phone.

The worn and frayed denim edge was almost satin soft against his knuckles, and the pocket liner warm against his palm calmed him as he pulled out the precious piece of plastic. If he didn't have to worry about the Man anymore, then he wasn't going to wear his uniform either, he'd decided when John had contacted him.

COORDINATES CLEAR AS EXPECTED; SHIP AND LOCATION

SECURE FOR NEXT APPROX 20 MINUTES. ETA SAME?

Ben frowned down at the display, addressed to both him and John, from a user named IMcre8tor. The tag was familiar to him, although he was sure he hadn't met its owner yet. As John had explained to Ben—to all of them, he was certain—it simply wasn't safe. Ben also didn't know all the details of exactly what would happen next, but he trusted John—everything he'd said, everything he'd planned, had all worked out perfectly so far; Ben wouldn't be the one to jeopardize that by second-guessing now.

ALL IS COPACETIC. EXCHANGE SHOULD BE COMPLETE
SHORTLY.

He carefully typed in his reply, then pressed the button that
would send his answer winging its electronic way to both the sender
and John. He sat back down. His skin…he wasn't cold, he realized,
he itched, and as he rubbed his arm through his sleeve for some
relief, he wondered if it was poison from that damn cup—he was
normally much more vigilant about environmental toxins—or if
there were any ticks left crawling about the lab. What was it they
did with ticks, anyway? John had told him the experiments involved
using them as a disease vector, and the ones they'd most recently
worked with were now spread up the northeast coast, carrying with
them a debilitating disease that had heretofore been restricted to
some very distant part of the country. Ah…the country. It was going
to change, was about to start changing in just a very few minutes.

Ben returned to his musing, his hand warm in his pocket, his
cell phone warm in his palm while he created *his* perfect world in
his mind, where the air was clean and so was the water, where men
could be free and women—there was that sound again. He picked
his head up from the wall.

Did the door on the other end of the room move?

This waiting was making him nervous, he decided. How long
could it take them to move through a corridor, to perform one little
electronic exchange? Even given that they needed time for the
laptop to boot, for the link to engage…where *were* they? He got off
his stool and pulled the gun from its holster under his coat.

The weapon was warm and while he knew it was really from his
own body heat, he couldn't help but imagine he still smelled cordite
from when he'd drawn it earlier as he stepped carefully down the
aisle between the stone-covered stations.

He was halfway across, certain now that the door he'd thought completely closed had been cracked just the slightest bit open. There was nothing in the room, no sound either, just the faint whoosh of air through the vents, vents he suspected that given the nature of the research were more than likely isolated from one section to another. He could hear his own breathing as he reached for the brass knob and checked it.

Closed. The door hadn't moved at all, not since he'd seen it close behind John and Charli. His face twitched, a stiff movement of muscle, a jerk in his neck as he silently made fun of himself.

Too many stupid movies and too much caffeine are making you the stupid screamer girl who loses her dog in the basement and investigates in the dark only to get herself killed in her underwear, that's all that's going on, he told himself. *Hey, at least you've got a flashlight* and *a gun—and the lights are on.*

Armed with that reminder, he felt relief flood through him. There was nothing out of place, he was merely spooked by the hour, the place. It was easily explained—it was natural to feel some tension when so much was on the line. The skin at the nape of his neck crawled and crawled *hard*; hard enough to feel like a pinch, hard enough for him to speak out loud to the part of his brain that screamed at him to *turn around*. He grudgingly gave in to it. "There's nothing—" He choked on his words as he turned and saw what, or rather who, stood behind him.

"You—you're dead," he said dumbly, disbelieving what his eyes told him, knowing he sounded stupid, knowing what he saw was equally impossible. He gripped the pistol tightly as adrenaline, which had just started to ease down, came roaring back through him with a fury that made his still crawling skin tighten further. "I shot you dead-on," he continued, saying the only thing he could think, thoughts now words as he stared into eyes made brilliant chips of malachite—dark and hard—over the barrel of what he recognized as a service-standard issue SIG 229. He saw the bruise that covered her temple, and the scraped line of skin that disappeared into her hairline, and came to the only conclusion that made sense. "I missed?"

"You didn't," the woman he could now admit he despised and knew only as Anna Pendleton told him. "And the only reason you're not about to face a capital murder charge is because you didn't really check your weapon first. Did you know your gun's loaded with wax bullets?" she asked conversationally. "Trusts you a lot, Romello does. So you've been helping him, and you've been rewarded—a murder you didn't commit to hold over your head. Although you *did* draw and shoot with deadly intent. And now… Where's Charli? He took her with him, right?"

Ben popped the chamber with a fingertip and let the proof of her words drop into his palm. He checked the round in his hand, scratched the blue paraffin in its copper casing, and still in the hard grip of shock, stared at the crescent-moon indentation his nail had left in its otherwise smooth surface.

"Now drop it—and put your hands up."

He gaped back at her even as he nodded, not knowing what to say, to think, to do, except to follow orders. He raised his arms over his head. The useless weapon dangled from his finger even as he felt his wrist grabbed hard and his mind twisted with his body. The planet swirled and his chest hit the wall while his hands—weapon free—were locked together, wrist to wrist, behind him.

John had given him an almost useless weapon. There *had* to have been a good reason, he was a good man, a smart man, a man like his father, a man who valued freedom and true American values, a man who—a man who'd lied to him, Ben realized, or if not lied, then had left out some extremely vital and pertinent information.

Good reasons, there have to be good, sound reasons. Ben's mind raced. What was it his father used to say? Need to know—soldiers operated on a need-to-know basis. Information was withheld all the time so that larger aims could be accomplished without doubts or distractions, or the potential for leaking critical intelligence. Perhaps…perhaps it was something similar, and John's nondisclosure was to keep Ben safe, or maybe it was about something Ben, unaware of the aims it would serve in the larger picture, wouldn't immediately like or agree with.

For the first time in ages, maybe ever, with his skull full and pounding, a gun before it and a churn within it, Ben asked himself a truly deeper question: Did John have goals Ben wouldn't have concurred with? And if that was the case, then was withholding the *same* as lying? Was it actually deception? The answer came to him slowly. It was almost the same thing, he concluded.

She wasn't rough, merely efficient as she once more turned him so that he faced her, and Ben felt his knees give way when his back hit the wall, leaving him to slump against it.

He shook once more with the instant cold that seemed to invade the room. He seemed to have trouble breathing, and the sudden rush of the vents overhead pulled the air from his lungs. Something was very wrong. He knew it, had *known* it somehow and not wanted to face it. John had been too quick to agree about Charli, too quick to set up Anna, and right now John was with— Suddenly, Ben was clear again and an ugly suspicion raced through him.

He remembered the infuriating certainty that had raced through him scant hours ago in the moments before he'd drawn and pulled the trigger. But with the new idea that had just grown in his mind, it suddenly didn't matter that he hated the woman before him or that judging from the weapon pointed at him, the feeling was coldly returned. The one topic that divided them they could also agree on—she could help, she had to know.

"You have the right to remain silent. Anything—"

"Listen, Anna," he interrupted desperately, using the only name he had for her as he straightened against the wall to convey the strength of his inention, "John's with her—he's got—"

The concussive blast that shook the walls around them sent Anna flying past him and through the door he'd only moments ago inspected, and Ben fell back on his heels, unable to hear her footsteps as she ran to the source of the explosion. When the five members of the extraction team arrived almost half a minute after she'd gone in, one pulled him roughly to his feet and quick-marched him in the opposite direction, back to the place they'd come from. An alarm sounded, a klaxon call that bit through his skull and his thick jacket, made his ears hum and his chest burn while lights dimmed and flashed. Though he wondered where they were going and how they'd get there, he knew—as his heart beat like a frantic caged rat in time to the swirl of the lights, and his eyes stung—that his role in the revolution he'd wanted so much to be part of was over.

❖

"'We are just an advanced breed of monkeys on a minor planet of a very average star. But we can understand the Universe. That makes us something very special,'" Charli read aloud from a plaque on the wall as they walked through the darkened and quiet hallways as John halted momentarily to check his cell phone. Her peripheral vision caught the satisfied smile that crossed his face as he read it.

"Ah yes, Stephen Hawking, the most brilliant man of our age," John agreed, with what she assumed was his version of a gallant smile as he pocketed the tool, then took her arm. "Of course, the majority of human beings are nowhere near his status—more like hairless monkeys than advanced ones."

"Oh, I don't know," Charli countered. "I've tended to think that we're all about ninety-eight percent monkey and the rest is caffeine and food dye—probably yellow number five."

John stopped and let her go to face her directly. "Did you just make a joke?"

Charli dropped her serious mien, then smiled at him. "Well, what's a revolution without a little humor?" she asked him. "I mean, laughter *will* be allowed in the new world order, won't it?"

He stared another moment, then gave a laugh of his own. "You're priceless!" He chuckled. "Perfect and priceless. Come," he said, his tone both inviting and officious as he took her arm once more, "we're almost there."

This girl game she played, the careful line between almost-fawning admiration and "spunky independence" was wearing her thin, but based on his behavior, she felt she had no other choice, or rather, no other *safe* choice. Given his avuncular attitude coupled with the smug superiority that oozed from the air he breathed, it was the only thing she could think of that would truly work, gain his confidence. She was certain it was what had allowed her to have gotten this far. It was alarmingly simple, and the simplicity of it left her with a sour feeling—a cross of disgust for herself that she could do it and contempt for him because he so easily fell for it—that she didn't know what to do with.

All of them, young, old, smart, stupid, even the insane, as she considered John, all of them were the same: hold out even the vaguest, remotest potential that there was any sort of admiration for them, and they took that to mean "she wants me."

There were, Charli conceded as they bustled down the corridor, degrees of difference. For Ben, the "it" factor was as simple as breathing on the same planet, or even giving him anything beyond formal politeness—she knew that, had known it for a long time. John wasn't quite that easy, but not that much more difficult, either. John required agreement—not an easy, unreasoned acceptance, he wanted to share conviction, and to receive some sort of metaphorical applause for his conclusions, affirmation and validation of his abilities. While with Kevin, well, that had been her own mistake but still... He operated—perhaps more politely and with much more social awareness than Ben, but the underlying working had still been the same—with the conviction that if person A, meaning himself, had such strong feelings, then it was impossible that B didn't or couldn't return them to some degree, if not an equal one.

That assumption, the forcing of one's emotional state on another, had always infuriated her, as if one could be forced to feel a specific way for a specific person or place or idea, that one person's feelings overrode another's. That politeness, or even friendly kindness, implied some sort of deeper desire.

Still, though, it didn't matter, because in the end the results were the same, always the same, so damn easy, no challenge whatsoever and always the knowledge that underneath everything, they all *really* wanted the same thing: *touch my dick.* That was the gear that turned the world.

The promise of sex, no matter how distant, improbable, or even downright impossible, was the overriding factor, the true coin of the realm, the purely self-serving basic motive—the *true* motive— behind every single interaction, no matter how seemingly innocent. Sex was the promise, the desire, the underpinning wish and hope that drove everything; men and women were, in that respect, no different from one another—or such had been Charli's experience with everyone. Everyone wanted someone to get them off.

Not everyone, she corrected herself. There had been one exception, and that exception—Charlie muffled her sigh, forced the painful thud that shook her chest down and in, contained someplace she'd reach for later as another door hove into view.

John almost imperceptibly tightened his grip on her arm and the pace quickened.

It seemed to be the entrance to yet another lab, retrofitted for security purposes. The entire complex as they'd walked through it looked that way to her—old construction, with newer overlays. What was it John had said? They were able to operate as long as all the air vented out, and took extra precautions in addition to working at—was it Level Three? Whatever it was, Charli was pretty sure she knew what the money was going to: upgrading the facility—it surely needed it.

That didn't matter at the moment, she told herself impatiently as they approached. This was it, then, where the exchange for the substances she'd been told about earlier would happen unless she could delay or derail his plans. She racked her mind for anything she could remember from high school and the requisite classes she'd taken in college. Most labs were the same, weren't they? Had to have certain universal characteristics.

She saw the panel on the wall, the inset rectangle with its clear plexi cover and evenly spaced holes. One was green, which meant, if she remembered correctly, oxygen. The other was yellow—she got a quick glance at the plastic label between the openings. *Emergency valve shut-off,* she read.

There were gas lines in there, she realized as she self-consciously slipped her hand into her pants pocket. Her fingers found the brochure she'd jammed in there earlier, then curled comfortably around the matchbook beneath it. Something in that room—either in what she assumed would be the connection they'd hook into for the laptop John carried or in the surrounding structure itself—something would help her to at least create a delay. There had to be something—maybe something electrical, or perhaps an issue with the laptop John carried, or even the network hookup. Whatever it was, she'd either find it or create it. She had to.

❖

Ben had been left and set to stand a rear-guard action in the lab that preceded this hallway, and John knew, after countless hours of memorizing paths, halls, and schematic layouts, exactly where he was going. His contact, a working relationship developed over several decades and through multiple operations, was his key resource to setting off the cascade-chain of events he planned on unleashing.

To contain information, minimize both leakage and mistakes, John had spent several days working to create the strike that would reduce the number of security personnel on hand. He'd used one of his contacts who was a part of the crew to put that into motion, citing safety concerns for personnel over the adequacy of the bio level strictures that had been stretched to quite probably unsafe limits.

He didn't tell Chul-Moo how the strike started—it kept him clean, provided a layer of plausible deniability should the need arise, and also protected his man on the inside. But John *did* point out that it presented an excellent opportunity.

Dr. Seung, who waited for them in the next lab, quickly saw the benefit of the unique opportunity, and had used the strike as justification to reduce the on-hand research team and workers, citing safety and privacy concerns for his team. Ultimately, he was the director, so his word was law in his sterile-field world. Of course, there were very few who would protest the opportunity to have an unexpected, but paid, free day, a day relieved of the wait for the ferry, the security precautions, and the decontamination process some of them had to endure.

And if Dr. Seung had suspicions about the fortuitous timing, he kept them very much to himself. As far as John could see, his operation had so far gone so very well.

The schematic rose in his mind's eye as their feet made oddly muffled smacks along the waxed tiles of the corridor. He could see it—see the lab and its structure, the original lab that had been upgraded over the years and the floating room within a room. What was it Chul-Moo had said they'd nicknamed it? Ah yes, the tool shed. Not because it held tools per se but because it housed the weapon he needed, and he knew exactly how and on whom to use it. "Your contribution," Chul-Moo told him, "will bring this to the next level, and the tool shed will be more than a holding area—it'll become your private arsenal."

That was exactly what he needed: a custom arsenal. He hadn't told Ben or Charli his complete plans—not really, because there was no need, because it could endanger his entire operation. He had others in place, waiting for him, all waiting for the word to perform their parts and soon, oh so very, *very* soon, all the pieces would be in place.

"You know, Charli, jokes aside, the average person *is* a monkey, an unthinking idiot. UFOs—hah!" he said forcefully, then stopped and faced her. "They're not covering up UFOs, Charli, they *are* the cover. It's a nested lie—and the monkeys are too busy oohing and ahhing over the bright lights and shiny things to notice." He shook his head with the disgust he couldn't help but feel rise through him whenever he thought about it, the hordes of the dumb, who would soon become the damned and the dead.

"So…you're saying there really *are* men from Mars?"

"They're not from Mars," he said, shaking his head as he reached into his coat. "It's further and closer than that. They're from tomorrow, what we will become, if we're lucky, if we do things right, if the damn monkeys don't get us all killed first." Just as his fingers found the plastic key card they'd searched for, his cell phone began to vibrate again. "Well," he said softly, "that doesn't matter anymore, not really." The words comforted him, reassured and reminded him of his purpose as he removed both the key card and the phone, then once more flipped the case open.

PENDLETON—AKA AGENT ELAINE HARPER—HAS ORDERED AN EXTRACTION TEAM. ETA NOT PRECISE (WEATHER VAGARIES). YOU'VE APPROXIMATELY TEN MINUTES.

He nodded once as he read that, knowing he had everything he needed, including the necessary time, to make it happen.

"Tonight, in just a few moments"—he snapped the case closed and returned it to the same pocket from which he pulled the plastic key card. He pressed it to the reader—"we start to fix that—*all* of that."

He was close, so close his fingers itched the way they always did when he was on the cusp of gaining his objective. The indicator light on the reader flashed from red to green.

"By the way," he said, the words casual, the gesture an afterthought when he realized she would more than probably want to know. He opened the door, then waved Charli in before him. "Her *real* name was Harper—Elaine Harper."

Charli acknowledged his words with a quick glance and a lift to her brow, then walked in before him, and as John quickly slung the case with its laptop from his shoulder and followed, a growing sense of triumph crowded in his throat.

❖

Dr. Chul-Moo Seung was not a man who practiced patience as a natural virtue, nor was he gifted with genius. Certainly he was intelligent, capable of grasping and manipulating the abstract, but his true talent lay in engineering—but not in the more traditional ways, the building of physical structures, of bridges and balance, the defiance of gravity and conquering of elements. His skills lay in areas more modern and more arcane. He understood the science of the small, of the minuscule, from molecules to moments.

In the same way that one charged particle could change an entire equation, or an entire set of reactions, so too could statements, people, one small event.

Dr. Seung certainly wasn't a genius, not in the way that many would define it. What he had instead was a full measure of ambition combined with a very complete grasp of the politics of bureaucracy, and the conviction that his personal and preferred research would not only make him famous, but would also have the very welcome side effect of making him quite wealthy. And that wealth would be key to continuing even further developments, by both creating the requisite environment—since so few ever said no to cash in whatever their preferred denomination—and obtaining the materials and the workers he needed.

He'd known John for many years, first during the secret wars with Laos and then with the development and deployment of various experimental weapons during further Pacific Theater involvements. He would help John because John had helped him in Laos—first when Chul-Moo had been a very young man who helped the men and women of Air America smuggle food and medicines to the struggling Laotians, then by once again helping the Americans several years later during their next conflict.

He neither really knew nor really cared what John would do with his purchases, for ultimately they enabled Chul-Moo to pursue his own ends. The importance of politics as far as he saw it had nothing to do either with philosophical ideations or any sort of "good for the masses" rhetoric that all politicians sold. The most important thing to accomplish was to be on the winning side—that was all that mattered, was the only thing that guaranteed the potential for survival—and Chul-Moo had absorbed that lesson well as a child, first at the hands of his family as they fled the North Koreans, then again during their diaspora through Asia.

It was John who had first respected his mind and not just his street connections, who had enabled him to become so much more than the street leader he might otherwise have been, another street leader and then another dead thug. These issues of loyalty, of debt, these were the things that had meaning.

If John wanted to support or subvert a government, it mattered not. He had asked Chul-Moo for help and help he would receive, in return for which John would do what he had always done: enable him to continue pursuing his interests.

Dysentery, malaria, cholera, random nameless flus and fevers, maladies named after local rivers and animals and gods—Chul-Moo had witnessed the devastation they caused, and the part of his heart that had still believed in some sort of goodness had once yearned to be able to do something, something good, and helpful, and healing.

Those dreams had faded as his studies and later his research took him in related, but then-unexpected, directions. He shook his head and smiled with self-derision, mind swirling with the new discoveries he'd made, his most recent success, and the new possibilities that John brought to him.

Now, I am become Death, the destroyer of worlds, he thought, not realizing he whispered the words into the stillness of the lab, the words of a holy book from a religion he had long ago abandoned, the message of a god he had replaced with his own self-image. He did not know he echoed another man, another scientist, who had also discovered and unleashed a grand panorama of Death in minutiae.

Chul-Moo did not need to hear John's reasons, nor his plans. John was as clever as the fox he'd named himself for, and perhaps whatever he had in mind might work—for a little while, at least. No idea, good or bad, no matter how powerfully implemented, ever lasted for long when governments were involved, he thought. He did wish John luck, though, and in any case, if the winds of change were once again blowing, then at least he, Chul-Moo, knew in what direction they swirled.

And truly, Dr. Seung mused as he reviewed all the materials, the settings, double-checked one last time that all that had been requested was there, what place did politics or governments have in the relationships between men, in the ties and obligations forged of blood and debt and honor? None, he decided as he checked the tool shed one final time, then his watch. He ran his hands through his hair, straightened his lab coat. Any moment now, and he would begin to repay the debt he owed the man who helped him get his family to Hong Kong, who financed his education, and who, he was certain, had a hand in gaining him the "Plum," as so many in his field called this position.

The revamped ventilation system and the insulating layer built over the original wall prevented him from hearing steps in the hallway, but nothing short of total blindness would have stopped him from seeing the indicator lights over the door change from red to green. The time had come.

Starting program: /hacking/$ ./HIJACKHACK

HEX

If she'd had a moment to think about it, Charli would have considered it interesting the way she was able to function on so many different levels: the multiple inner ones—an emotional one that flayed icily through her, threatening to bury her in its frozen depths, the analytical one that took those same cold blocks and used them to build the final, outer one, protecting, or so she hoped, the rapid working within.

That wall gave her a freedom she would otherwise have not had, permitted her to fully examine the options available for her to work with in the framework she was currently limited to.

Her analysis told her this much: Cooper was useless—he practically drooled over every word John said and that, combined with his earlier behavior...he was dangerous, but he was on John's leash.

Alternately, however, Cooper was used to following directives from her, and Charli knew, because she'd worked with him, that the less and less direct attention he got from her as her captivity progressed would eat at him. He'd jumped through quite a set of hoops, she thought, to impress John. He'd broken the strictures of his bonding—the fingerprinted promise they'd all made when Whitestone had taken them on—not to use or modify proprietary technology, and while she still didn't know exactly what his program had done, she could guess, which meant he'd broken the law.

Despite his misanthropic behavior and dropout attitude, Coop followed the rules; even his new home, the one he was building to take off the grid, he'd spent weeks agonizing over finding the right engineers to make certain it not only fit his standards, but the county's—he'd had it built to code.

Once he'd understood what was considered proper and improper conduct when it came to interpersonal relationships on the job, he'd followed to the letter, even taking the time on occasion to ask her if what he'd said or done "was okay."

Ben Cooper, her employee, had a rebellious streak but ultimately, he obeyed the law—grudgingly sometimes, willingly others, but no matter that; the fact was, he complied, even down to trimming his beard and tying his hair back.

That he now followed John…and Charli was certain that, earlier in the evening, even as John had done whatever he'd done to ensure she was out of it, it was his voice she'd heard say, quite clearly, "Take the agent."

It was as apparent to her as Cooper's ill-hidden feelings toward her that this man's opinion meant very much, quite possibly everything, to Cooper.

But even with all of that, she suspected that it was that crush Coop had on her that was the reason she was there in the first place, and she had easily read the joy in his eyes as he'd watched her appear to go along with both him and his…keeper. This meant her opinion of him still carried weight, and she was gambling that just as he'd danced to John's tune to please him, he might very well do the same for her if he believed he'd lost her regard.

At the very least, the lack of attention should more than likely unsettle Cooper, and that uncertainty might break some of the hold John had over him; it could slow or perhaps even change his reactions. She knew she was taking a risk with someone who'd proven himself to be dangerous, but there were really no other options.

The man she knew only as John, however, operated under a completely different set of rules, and those rules were quite obviously his. It was equally evident that the power lay in John's hands—crack him, and Charli thought she might have a fighting chance. She didn't think personal escape was a true possibility on her horizon—John's casual disregard of Anna's probable fate had spelled that out to her quite clearly very early on, while the other, equally nonchalant discussion of deaths on a massive scale put the spelling in large, bold letters.

But if she couldn't get completely away, then she could hopefully partially sabotage, perhaps even completely stymie, the plans John so openly stated he had.

What she did immediately exploit was a weakness he didn't know he had, one it certainly appeared that most men who prided themselves on intellect thought they were immune to: a woman's smile and attention.

It wasn't a game she usually played, and in fact she had a scathing contempt that immediately dismissed those who relied solely on behavior of that sort to make their way through the world, but a dose of it was not only seemingly required here, but apparently quite effective. John didn't question what he saw, and more importantly, it appeared he truly believed what she wanted him to: she agreed with and even admired his theories.

And logical they were, in a way that twisted cynicism, paranoia, and theory to heights Charli had known were possible but had never really considered to be probable, nor had she ever thought that anyone would take action on them.

"I know all about you, Charli," he told her back in the nondescript "no-tell motel" when she'd returned from the bathroom with the matchbook and the brochure tucked deeply in her pocket, and Cooper still gone on his quest for coffee. His voice was deep and rich, the tones measured and precise, and with that exact same precision, he told her exactly what he knew about her, and why.

"I know who your parents are—Aaron and Helen. I know your brother Cole is in Angola *and* I can tell you what he's really doing there." He recited her own history—from grammar school through college to her jobs.

Charli managed to maintain a neutral expression—interested, but neutral. "You do seem to know quite a bit of my background— but most of that's a matter of public record." She said that merely to test him, to see his reaction to it. The fact was that Charli had been as thorough as the rest of her cohorts in expunging electronic traces of herself from the Web. To gather the knowledge John had—that required special access, a sign of actual investigation into records that were off-limits to most civilians. There were advantages, Charli mused, to having a brother who worked for the military and who had the clearances he did. For a moment, she wondered if her brother Cole knew or had ever heard of this man.

"Of course, there are those missing two years from high school," John continued through Charli's musing. "That's not on any record."

"I guess not," she commented blandly. If he didn't know, she wasn't going to tell him. Let him attempt to deduce it like so many had tried—and failed. It had come up too often recently, and as far as she was concerned, too many people already knew.

He accepted her silence before he continued. "I've been searching for *you*, Charli, for you and others like you. You don't know how special you really are. You, your brother more than likely, and others like you…"

John spoke of genetic manipulations performed on a mass scale on an unsuspecting populace. His logic was frighteningly compelling, and he backed the possibility and high probability of his argument by repeating the well-documented tale of the Tuskeegee sharecroppers—men infected with syphilis and experimented upon in the name of "science"—as well as the now-famous experiments on airborne disease carried out in the New York City subway system.

"It's more than a mere conspiracy," he said, waving a hand for emphasis. "It's a global program, run by a combined military-industrial complex," he insisted.

At some point during his lecture? didacticism? diatribe?—she was no longer certain of when, exactly—the door to the room had opened, announcing Cooper's return, and a cardboard tray with three lidded Styrofoam cups preceded him as a cool gust followed.

"It's no accident they're called captains of industry, Charli." The quick smile he gave her did nothing to soften the frost that filled his eyes, nor the anger that smoldered, evident and palpable, in his tone. "And I know the names—the faces and the names—of every single one of them."

Silence, broken only by the scuff of Ben's boots along the industrial carpet, filled the room.

"Coffee—best I could find at this hour," Ben said as he carefully passed first one, then the other along.

"Thanks, son. Good job," John said with a smile as he accepted it with a small flourish, then saluted Ben with it before taking a sip. He made a small contented sound after he swallowed, then focused once more on Charli.

"It's the feudal system," he explained, his voice soft, serious, "creation of the prison planet. Destroy the environment so you'll have to buy clean food, water, air—have everyone live, work, and die for the machine."

"That's who the Man *is*, Charli, the Man wants to ruin it for everyone, keep all the good shit for himself, make the rest of us slaves—for *them*," Ben broke in, his voice full of excitement and righteous anger, a tone Charli had heard from him before during his occasional workplace tirades. "It's *working*, Charli, they're destroying the planet, decimating its resources. The economy is for shit and getting worse every single year, we're being watched, we're being analyzed, *eliminated*, they're—"

John quieted him with a simple wave and returned his attention to Charli. "The thing of it is, we can *win*, Charli, we can fix it and make it right—we can start now, *right now*." He leaned forward, closer to her in his earnestness. "Reason, logic, the might of right, Charli, the dream of the ages—a world run, protected, *cared* for and shepherded, by those who were created to do exactly that and made intelligent enough to do so properly."

John was very clear: he wasn't, in his estimation, a racist—that was a biologically incorrect term, since race was a cultural construct. He merely believed in the power of intelligence, of right making might as he'd said.

She listened with an interest that was unfeigned, not because she believed or agreed with him, but because it became clearer and clearer to her he was quite likely the most dangerous sort of insane: someone not only fanatically convinced of his mission, of his vision, but also intelligent enough to disjoint arguments that ran counter to it, and what she considered most threatening, someone resourceful enough to bring it to some sort of fruition.

"We eliminate the obstacles, Charli, the living, breathing, monsters in charge of the whole ugly thing, and then?" John sat back, a large and satisfied smile on his face. He spread his hands wide to emphasize his words. They were large, Charli noted, yet his fingers—long, lean—had a strange, almost delicate look. They were, she decided, the hands of a man careful with small details.

"Then evolution takes over—and the reign of *homo logos* begins. It's the only way."

She nodded a dismissive thanks to Cooper as he handed her the coffee she'd requested, careful not to touch him as she took it from his hands, uncertain if the sudden rush of nausea that lurched into her throat was from his proximity or the scent that wafted up through the plastic lid. It was almost too hot as she held it, and the smell—like diesel fumes on a humid day—threatened to once more raise in her throat what she'd just forced herself to swallow down moments before. But at least, she thought, it gave her something to wrap her hands around, a focus, and as foul as it seemed, it was caffeinated and she needed to be as aware as possible. She forced herself to swallow before she returned her attention to John.

"How…and why?" she asked simply. She sipped again, her gaze fixed on the pale blue of his eyes as he answered.

There were phases and parts to his plan, and John painted a broad picture for her. For those who were guilty of nothing more than the accident of their birth, John had something relatively painless in mind.

"Saxitoxin—barely feel a thing," he'd said, "puts them into a calm, almost dreamlike state as the body shuts down." But for those who were responsible for creating what he called the slow holocaust—the destruction of the brightest and the best until only the idiot and therefore obedient zombie masses remained—his solution was ricin. It was deadly, it was quick, an amount no larger than a pinhead was needed, and it was, as he put it, "rather unpleasant."

And the only way, he believed, to make this ideal come true was to eliminate those incapable of thinking, of creating—after all, wasn't it the ignorant, through inferior brain capacity and the breeding capability of rats, that made up the majority? And weren't they the ones after all ultimately responsible for the horror show that had been human history? "It's time, finally," he told her. "Technology and the times—the special people like you, Charli—it's all caught up now, all possible. It's the next phase, natural, inevitable—the revolution of evolution. We will forcibly replace what has come before, and correct the mistakes of the past."

She could see Cooper's head bob in perfect agreement somewhere off to her side, and then John glanced at his watch.

She noticed it because it was different, large, and he removed it to adjust buttons on the satin-brushed steel as he read it.

"It's time," he repeated, only this time it was an announcement, as he stood. "Let's not keep the world waiting any longer than it's already had to." He snapped the steel band back on his wrist and the hasp caught her eye—it was an incongruous flat black, a stark contrast against the shinier links. He'd covered it with his sleeve and she walked—was escorted, really—between him and Ben to the car.

The very air was quiet, filled with a heavy expectancy, and the first flakes of snow fell against her cheeks through the reddened black sky. She took a deep breath as she stared up into the downfall.

"Ah, the fresh air of freedom," John said and smiled as he held the door for her. She forced one in return as she tucked herself in and the door swung shut, sweeping a solid wall of cold air before it. She knew it was cold only because she could see her breath, *not because she felt it.*

Now, a minute, an hour, however much later it was, Charli had no idea how she'd been able to make a joke, smile, act as if this was all just the normal part of another day and come up with questions as well as arguments that dug for further information without seeming to counter him too much. She had cleared herself, rid herself, of almost every feeling or reaction, the absolute shut-off allowing her to rely solely on her wits to provide the next steps.

Still, every now and again, she was aware that her heart had yet to stop racing, the sharp report that had gone off so close to her ears echoed in cruel replay, and whenever she took a deep breath, she still smelled the faint sick smell of the cloth that had covered her mouth and robbed her of consciousness, however temporarily.

"By the way," John told her as she watched the indicator light shine green and he opened the door to wave her in before him. "Her *real* name was Harper—Elaine Harper."

Another quick wave of nausea threatened to swamp her senses. *There's got to be* some *residual effect*, she thought as she swallowed the potentially disorienting discomfort down. *Now* that *could be key, maybe I can use that somehow*. She considered the possibilities with absorbed interest as they passed through the next door into the lab to meet the tall and slender man John called Dr. Seung who waited for them just inside.

If Dr. Seung was surprised to be introduced to Charli, it didn't show, and neither did the rapid absorption of information he gave away and she took in as they shook.

There was knowledge to be gained in the quick and light grasp, not only its style but also its temperature and texture. She observed the shadows that further darkened his eyes when she angled her head to study his serious face, noted his expression was broken only by a quick polite smile, and just as quickly caught that it was more reflex twitch at social nicety than genuine expression, the same as his handshake. His thick hair, graying at the temples, was somewhat unkempt although his white coat appeared pristine, the red stitching that bore his name almost shocking in its stark contrast. Charli wondered what exactly went through his mind; Dr. Seung certainly did not have the air of someone who had the same expectations that John did. She surreptitiously inspected the rest of the room.

Despite the newer construction that included carefully masqueraded electric lines run through squared conduits along the walls to create additional power sources that were, in turn, layered under paint that from both the residual smell and soft sheen made her suspect might have been only a few months old, age, decay, and the hint of obsolescence clung to the architecture.

This room was large, even larger than the one Cooper had been told to wait and stand guard in, and as she cautiously peered about, she recognized the usual lab trophies—specimens preserved in alcohol—set on different low shelves that divided the sides of the stone-covered lab tables from one another. Each one had a small metal wastebasket next to it. She also recognized the gas lines she'd seen the shut-off valves for just outside the room: oxygen and propane.

Farther into the room, set within against the back of it, in fact, was a smaller steel housing. She eyed the dials and the door set on it. It looked, she thought, for all the world like a meat locker or a freezer. For a moment, she wondered if what Romello sought was in there, and then decided it really didn't matter. Time was growing short, she could *feel* it, a soapy film that covered her hands, creeped up her arms, breathed in her ear, foul-scented, hot, and wet. It was vital that she develop some sort of action plan, and quickly—it couldn't be long before—

"Let's do this, shall we?" John asked them both and he handed her the laptop.

Time's almost up, she told herself as she hefted the plastic case. She found a clear spot along one of the workstations and set the laptop between two stainless steel valves, each with a colored button on its face—one green, the other yellow. She began the booting sequence. "Are you wireless in here?" she asked, noting the icon on the lower right hand corner of the screen that announced it was still searching for a signal.

"No," Dr. Seung answered as he approached, a length of cable in hand. Charli noticed the wide end hookup. Ethernet, then. "You can patch directly through our network—you'll bypass the fireline or whatever it's called."

"*Kamsa hamnida*," she said unthinkingly as she took the cable end.

"You speak Korean?" he asked in obvious surprise.

"No," and to her own surprise, she felt herself blush, not because she was embarrassed, but because she had slipped. His soft accent, the musical lilt to his words so similar to that of some of the coders she'd worked with, such as her shift head, Eunae, had told her, and she'd responded without even thinking.

Get your head back in the game, she ordered herself firmly. She had to think and think fast, because the crux was almost upon them. She slipped the connector into the port. "Some of my workmates have taught me enough to be polite—and to count all the way to ten," she said nonchalantly. "Beyond that, it might as well be Greek to me." She gave him a brief smile and focused on the screen. She typed in the network request.

"Well, *that's* all geek to me," he said and pointed to the screen.

"I'm very used to that," she said politely. The link was in and another icon blinked in the same lower corner, alerting her to its available status.

This, in a few moments, would be it, the final payment, and she would hit the network to make it happen, and once it did—game over. For everyone.

"Charli—the exchange link, it's the eagle icon on the desktop. It'll bring you right into the account. There's a menu to choose from, then just enter the password."

"I see it," she informed him and nodded, eyes focused on the stylized icon as she clicked on it. "It's opening." A tune she didn't recognize played as the program started.

She had to be quick, and it had to not only look like an accident, it had to be unnoticeable. She could stall, since with an outbound signal, there were several things she could do, but there really wasn't enough time; she couldn't stop the exchange, not really. As she tapped through the setup screens, she brought up another small one that bypassed the surface operating system and a few quick key commands enabled her to learn several important things: her link was directly in the heart of their network, the computer she was on was completely outside of the firewall, and she had unlimited access—to everything.

There were, she concluded as she closed the session and paid careful attention to her surroundings, the fume hood, the gas lines, and the air vents overhead that had just turned off, a few things she could do, and she knew exactly what they were. Dr. Seung's "all geek to me" had given her a piece of it.

Only one of her options was a calculated risk, no different than tackling and taming the waves, finding and riding the line of best probability. If she rode it right... *Johnny can't code*, Charli reminded herself as she brought up yet another small screen and typed in the commands.

```
To: redbetta@zenchat.com; lpendowski@whitestone.com;
cole.a.riven@msc.navy.mil
```

```
Laura: attached going straight to your and my work
server folders. 2 data dumps: one "Fox" and the
other "Plum." My password: dbl-ovrhang2go. Send
this to Eric ASAP.
Cole: Use this—find something. My fave surfboard is
in the office—take care of it. And thanks for the
rubbers.
```

```
C
```

She thought about it for half a second, then added one more address—the one she had for Anna, or Agent whatever it was John had said. If he'd told the truth, and like it or not, Charli had so far no reason to think he hadn't, then someone had to be monitoring Anna's e-mail accounts. Someone, somewhere, would know what to do with the data dump she sent—it just needed enough time to send.

Charli mentally took a deep breath; she knew what she had to do and she had to do it—*Now*, she told herself. She turned up the volume on the laptop, then feigned dizziness, letting the temporary loss of balance bring her toward the shelf set just above the counter, where her elbow hit and loosened but didn't open the oxygen gas cock and her hand slapped against and knocked over a quart jar that held a preserved specimen.

The quiet atmosphere shattered with the glass as it hit the stone counter, drawing all eyes toward her. Hers found and focused on a dead frog with an extra set of flippers right above the front pair as it floated along the stream of alcohol it had sat within for who knew how long, and a pungent scent filled the air.

John was—as Charli had expected—instantly solicitous, placing a hand beneath her elbow. The too-warm and wanting touch of it now carried an additional eagerness, all of it still very palpable to her through the layers she wore. It was enough to almost make the feigned-ill feeling real. Almost. "Are you all right?"

Charli gave what she hoped was a wan smile and waved him away, using the opportunity to let her elbow hit the valve. She felt the "give" of it, which meant she'd managed to open it slightly. She straightened and shoved the laptop against the stone backstop of the counter, away from the puddle she'd just created, and used the screen to quietly nudge the other valve, too. "I'm fine—nerves, I suppose. Just want things to go smoothly."

He nodded, seemingly satisfied with the answer, and Charli ignored the clouded eyes of the mutant frog as it lay on its side, no more than five inches away from the laptop. It stared at her, gap-mouthed and white-tongued as she once more placed her hands on the keyboard. She sighted, then clicked the program icon she needed. She was grateful for the strange melody that played as it ran since it hid the hiss of gas, while the alcohol, still strong in the air, hid the propane. The first part had gone well enough. It was almost time for phase two of her plan.

She watched the indicator in the corner that told her how strong the signal the system received was. It was fine, but she had wiggle room, she could play with it a bit, buy herself a few precious seconds. "The system's a little slow," she said to no one in particular. The icon next to it blinked steadily, downloading data across the ether.

Already, it was at fifty percent. Charli risked a quick glance at her companions.

It was a funny thing, she observed. As expert as people were in their fields, as competent as they could be with certain software, they were happy to ignore someone working on or with something they considered unknown, rather in the same way people ignored repairmen or mechanics, and true to form, both John and Dr. Seung ignored her as they sank once more into conversation.

That played perfectly to the plan she'd now formed, and she used it to her advantage. Charli shifted the black plastic, sliding it between the gas cocks, tapping one, then the other again, increasing the amount of gas that escaped and gathered in the room as she half heard John and Dr. Seung discussing both precautions and delivery methods. She watched them in her peripheral vision. "Just like *Air America*," Dr. Seung said with a slight chuckle as he handed a flat package to John and the right screen came up.

Seventy percent complete, the blinking notice told her, and she knew she had only about thirty seconds as she typed in the password that would allow the exchange. She didn't even have to ask. Everything John said and did had already told her: *tabula rasa*. Had the situation not been so dire, she would have considered it a good hack.

Charli casually slid a hand into her pants pocket, then found the matches and the crumpled brochure beneath it. Carefully, she untucked the cover from its fold, then eased one of the matches out from under it. She bent it back with painstaking slowness to avoid detection, flexing the thick cardboard until the head touched the striker on the back. There simply wasn't enough time for anything else. Between the alcohol vapors, the extra oxygen, and the propane now mixing in the air... *I hope this works—I hope it's quick.* She fought to keep her breath steady.

John neared as Charli hit the Enter key with one hand and pulled the matches from her pocket with the other just as a screen message popped up showing both a new status bar for the transaction in process and another one reading "100% Complete. Message sent."

"Done," she stated while she hurriedly closed the window, and as she palmed the matches once more, then turned to face the man who peered over her shoulder, she hoped she'd been fast enough, that he hadn't seen the Sent message. She held the matchbook in her hand, the unglazed interior a stutter-slip under her fingers.

John glanced at her, then to the screen that showed the almost-complete status of the exchange, then quickly looked at her again. She could actually see his mind work through his eyes as he took it all in. He waved his head slowly from side to side. "Charli…what are you doing?" he asked in the tone one would use with a child, the disappointed voice of a beloved parent, and his eyes seemed sad as they gazed into hers.

That tone, she decided, really pissed her off. Charli flicked her thumb against the match head, forcing it against the striker. Nothing happened.

"Charli," John said quietly, "it won't work. And if it does, you'll die. That would be an unfortunate waste of good genetic material."

"I'm just a monkey, John," Charli answered him evenly as she flicked again, harder. This time she was rewarded when the sharp burn of sulfur stung the pad of her finger. She calculated the time, she calculated the risk. There were barely seconds left. *Wanna lead? Gotta bleed—and this is* really *gonna hurt.* She knew she had to do this.

"Never," Charli said grimly, her eyes fixed on his, "trust a monkey with matches and dynamite." She tossed the matchbook into the puddle that still lay on the stone table. Once again, for the space of one full breath, four heartbeats, and just enough time for that same heart to sink, nothing happened.

She stared, startled when the whole book suddenly caught, sending a blue flame leaping up and racing along the shiny wet contours of the frog's last home.

The room seemed to gather, tighten, as if it held its breath, taking it from her own lungs, and the sudden light was almost blinding, the very air seeming to ignite around her. It had been quicker than she'd expected.

She felt two things almost simultaneously, the sharp impact

just under her shoulder blade and the push against the small of her back that sent her tumbling off balance with the same give and drop of the wave when it let her go.

Every wave hits the shore, she thought just before the flare took over with a sound that seemed to ribbon the ground beneath her even as it painfully invaded her head through her ears, quashed the air from her chest, and then every part of her squeezed before it all went blank.

$ /hacking/cleared_stack test

TURTLES ALL THE WAY DOWN

The decision had been made behind closed doors at some higher level of Olympus Elaine was not privy to. Dr. Seung had been found near Charli and was being held, but he had special status and would either be repatriated somewhere after he'd been pumped for information, or more than likely, be put to work in a government-funded lab in exchange for his "freedom." She shouldn't have been surprised, not really. After all, Dr. Seung was a true leader in his field and he, like others who had once worked for enemy regimes, was considered an asset—an unfriendly one, but still valuable.

The official approach to him was, in fact, no different than it had been to many other such enemy experts including—and Elaine shook her head at the irony of it all—Erich Traub, the man who had been head of germ warfare research under the Nazi regime, reporting directly to Heinrich Himmler, Hitler's second in command. After the war, he had been recruited to become what he would later be called: the father of biological research at Plum Island.

It was funny in a way that didn't make her laugh at all as she weighed the implications, what the interests of National Security—words that had been a touchstone for her for so long—could do to one's sense of ethics, and how those ethics seemed so malleable when applied by the people she worked for.

Right and wrong worked on a completely different scale, measured different values, and suddenly, she wasn't certain that she understood, or that she wanted to. Disappointed, she realized, that's what she was. Disappointed with herself, with what it all seemed to mean, for the nagging sense of dissatisfaction she couldn't seem to shake.

It had been so very simple for such a long time, her whole life, really: there were good guys, and there were bad guys. Dr. Seung, who would have definitely been in her estimation a bad guy, complete with all sorts of evidence to prove that, was to be, in essence, rewarded. Charli, who the Treas had originally thought despite evidence to the contrary was a bad guy, not only wasn't, but had put herself on the line, ignorant perhaps of the larger ramifications of Romello's plan but willing to try to stop him anyway. That definitely made her a good guy. Her reward, though, was to be forced... The thickness that grew in Elaine's throat forced her to think of something else, and since her last few hours had involved a convoluted discussion of her career, she focused on that, instead.

She had not only done her job, but done it exceptionally well, yet as compensation she was to be temporarily pulled from the job she was so damned good at while brass cleared her name with the Treas. The officers and agents she had trained with there would never trust her again, or so she'd been told. She'd sworn the same oaths, held the same loyalties, had done what any single one of them would have done, and sure, there'd be some grudging admiration for her from others among her rank set, but still...it made her skin feel like it had twisted on her frame.

To add to the discomfiture, she, who had gotten close enough to Romello to be moments shy of actually apprehending him—oh, she'd been asked repeatedly to explain her methods, her deductive reasoning, had even tried to demonstrate on a whiteboard schematically the path she'd taken to arrive at her conclusions, but what was to her a single clear straight line, an easily read path from one point to another was, given the repeated requests for clarification, a route apparent only to her.

"Enough, Harper," her handler said, halting her with a firm wave as she drew her dotted line from one found fact to a deduction. He, the attending clerk, and two officers she did not know exchanged brief glances. "Please sit."

No one spoke again until she'd settled, and it was the officer with the heavier braid that crossed his head cover—scrambled eggs, as the gold insignia was commonly and sometimes derisively referred to—that told her their plans. "You've done great work, but you're compromised in the field for now. You're good with this technology crap—so six months in techno-wonderland. We need someone with skills like yours to figure out the chatter."

"This is a great position for you," her handler leaned forward and said, cutting through the heavy silence that had settled around the table. "It's an opportunity for you to"—he coughed delicately—"reacquaint."

He cleared his throat under the steely gaze the brass gave him and silence weighed heavy in the small conference room. Moments later, outside the door after they'd all exited, he was neither delicate nor careful as he motioned her aside.

"Listen, Harper," he began, "you fucked up. This could have wrapped differently—you had the opportunity to give the Treas a rock-solid alibi on Riven or you could have let her sink with it. Instead, you let whatever your personal issues are—issues you didn't have a few months ago—interfere. Okay, fine. You didn't want to do that, no problem. But—"

The blatant untruth of the statement burned through her and Elaine shocked herself with her own temerity, unable to stop the words that scorched their way from her mind to her lips. "But *nothing*," she interrupted vehemently. "Someone internal dropped the dime on me and you *know* that. That alibi wouldn't have mattered—and face it, I got you rock-solid evidence, *and* I got you someone who actually might know more about what Romello's future plans could be." She breathed hard a moment and felt heat rise through her ears.

"I fucked up? *I* did?" she asked with sarcastic incredulity as she stared into eyes the color of a winter sky and she voiced the suspicion that had settled, a dark and malignant seed, in her mind. "Whose ass are you covering for, anyway?" Right then and there she knew she'd gone too far, but she also found she didn't care even as she watched his face set into hard lines.

"Enough, Harper," he snapped coldly. "Don't think you know more than you do—you're on need-to-know only status like everyone else. You spend the next six months the right way. Refamiliarize and reimmerse yourself in our internal protocols, or find yourself another line of work—I'm sure *that* would make your parents, make your father, really proud."

Frustration roiled silently through her as he turned on his heel and left her there in the corridor. She visualized what her future would be. Six months chained to a desk, not even working in analytics or communications but in pure cryptology. It wasn't that it was hard work, not at all. It merely bored her to the point of depression.

Elaine was startled to realize that the job change and the way it had been handled, the patently false why of it, infuriated her.

This, she thought with a burst of insight, *this is what happened to Romello, what turned him.* Not one event, but many, compounded, confusing, and something in his mind had...broken, snapped, then restructured things in a way that made the world make sense for him again. *The difference between him and me, though*, she decided, pausing for a moment in her progress, *is I'm not a total nut-burger.*

His plans were hopefully in ruins for now, though, and as for himself... Romello had seemingly disappeared, neither body nor parts found—only a final token: the watch he'd been given for his twenty-fifth year of service had been found by the cleanup crew, not far from remains of the laptop, the hands set at two minutes to midnight, and otherwise pristine aside from the fact that it had stopped there.

She couldn't shake the suspicion that someone on the team had helped him, and she was certain there were good reasons for thinking so—nothing quite as concrete as actual evidence, just a chain of events and circumstances leading to specific conclusions.

It couldn't have been too hard, Elaine thought as she walked with quick, efficient steps across the compound and reviewed what she knew.

A successful recovery or attack was made of three distinct and essential parts: surprise, speed, and violence of action.

The team had arrived what felt like hours later although it had only been scant moments behind her. It wasn't hard to figure out where to go—as solid as the surrounding structure was, it wasn't soundproof, nor was it airtight. She followed her ears and her nose, the scent of gas drawing her onward. Light flared from the small space beneath the door even as it flashed through the steel mesh reinforced window, and she saw the panel on the wall, the inset with its plexi cover, and ripped it off, then yanked on the wire hoops that secured the shut-off valves to give them each a hard and vicious twist. The petal-like knobs dug into her palms even through the flexible gloves Elaine wore, but she didn't notice.

An alarm went off, sending a series of lights flashing in the hall, a swirl of amber and shadow as they spun in their fixtures.

The door was already too hot and as she spied about for a fire extinguisher, a heavy thud sounded, sending something caroming off the door from the interior. The extraction crew swept in while Elaine forced herself to not think about what might be happening in there while two operatives set up the "gate crasher"—basically a modified Alford strip. Speed.

She had several Alford strips herself—narrow and hollow tubes filled with an explosive resin and set into a water-filled frame, directing the blast in a specific direction. The gate crasher was the same, only larger, about the size of a boogie board. It blasted out an entrance about two and a half feet wide by four feet tall—without any burning debris to contend with for the entering team. *Doors,* she found herself mentally repeating from a long-ago training session as she assumed a position with the team, *we don't need no stinkin' doors.*

The fuse was quickly set and the device detonated with a strangely muffled burst, blowing through the wall. Surprise.

Even as water and bits of the plastic rained down, she and the team members rushed through the opening and into the lab. Violence of action—very well accomplished.

Without a true source of fuel to burn other than the gas, the only fire that remained was that on the shelves, the paint of the ceiling, and the paperwork, and even that smoldered to a fizzled mess under the antiquated sprinkler system that had automatically gone off—too late to prevent anything but the lab's annihilation. The six separate workstations appeared almost untouched, the stone impervious to it all—the fire, the foam, the people that moved carefully between.

Glassware continued to snap and pop and one member picked up a shredded piece of metal from the floor, about the size of his hand.

"Nitrogen tank," he said quietly as they approached the center of the room, and had it been possible, their faces appeared even grimmer as they realized immediately what it meant: the remnant had once been part of a steel container that had more than likely held liquid nitrogen. The heat of the fire had also raised the temperature of the steel, which in turn affected whatever it had contained. That had resulted in rapid sublimation of the contents—the almost instantaneous change from liquid to gas state—and it was the pressure of the expanding gas that had burst and shredded the container.

"We have casualties!" the front person called and waved them forward.

It was at that point that whatever control Elaine had possessed, the calm process that had allowed her to plan and execute step by step, shattered as fully as the glass that littered the slippery tiles they walked on.

She recognized the charred coat, the still frame it covered, and she'd frozen for what seemed like forever—pain and fear mixed to make something cold, something that jabbed icy fingers into her ribs to grab and crush what was beneath them. Unreal, she felt unreal, a witness even as she participated. Dr. Seung, or so his lab coat labeled him, moaned as one person bent over him and someone else reached before she could to find a pulse in Charli's neck.

"We need to evacuate them immediately—everything we need's on the chopper," one said to the other.

There was no time to be careful about anything but the most life-threatening of injuries to the two—*they're* not *bodies*, Elaine told herself sharply as she watched them—they'd recovered, and this time the team walked out the remains of the door. Elaine followed behind them automatically.

She smirked to herself, a half-laugh under her breath. She understood now what Charli had meant when she'd told her earlier about feeling nothing, because nothing was exactly what Elaine felt.

Her eyes caught the remains of the laptop, the twisted pieces, only the motherboard somewhat intact under the melted frame, then caught the glint of the watch on the floor.

This was something she could hold on to, make sense of, and she stopped. "Where's Romello?" she asked, casting about. "We should have another casualty here."

Another operative took her arm. "Down the rabbit hole," she said and pointed to the far wall. That had to have been the source of one of the sounds they'd heard—probably the concussive blast, Elaine concluded as she unthinkingly walked toward the blasted section of wall that opened into an air duct.

"Agent," the operative called, and once more caught her arm. "Agent Harper, someone's already investigating, and the sweep team will be here in"—she glanced down at her wrist—"seconds. Go with the first chopper—get debriefed."

Elaine was about to protest—she didn't really know why, force of habit perhaps, or simply the only thing that she could recognize. "But—"

"I'm Agent Fowler—go with the team, go with Charli, she's going to need you."

Elaine felt her internal temperature flip from cold to hot, an instant sublimation as dark eyes shone intently at hers. *They know*, she thought. For half a second she tried again to hold on to what she knew, what she understood, her job, her cover, who she had been. And in the next half second, she gratefully gave in to who she now was. "Thanks, Fowler," she said quickly, then took off after the retreating team. She barely acknowledged the sweepers she passed as she raced back along her previous route, nor the escort team which she knew in the back of her mind was composed of Navy SEALS—once upon a time, not more than a year or so ago, her father would have been among them—as she went back into the cold night air.

Elaine could barely see, though she could clearly hear the Black Hawk that had brought them about a dozen yards away, just behind the silhouette of the MH-47. Light spilled from the gaping entrance ramp, and the sparks that occasionally burst from the twin structures beneath the rear rotor made it appear like the gaping hungry mouth of an angry fish. Snow swirled and gleamed around them, a blizzard of wind and white and wet, a white tide wipe-out on land. It echoed the vortex that spun through her chest *as she caught up with the team and boarded.*

❖

He couldn't quite put his finger on where it had all gone so damned wrong, but reality hadn't quite sunk in yet for Ben. His shoulders hurt, and he hadn't expected the pigs to be as efficient as they were in handling him—not that they were excessively gentle, either, he snorted as he was led to what he recognized as a modified Chinook. Both rotors spun with purpose as they approached, and no one made eye contact with him as he was led up the ramp and into the vehicle proper.

The noise level almost hurt his head and he could hear nothing until the pig put his mouth next to his ear.

"Right here—sit down," the government stooge ordered, the words felt more than heard, and Ben complied. A chain was applied to the center of his cuffs and affixed to a D-ring along a track that ran between the steel of the floor and the wall behind him. So much for comfort. They wouldn't get shit out of him, absofuckinglutely nothing, he determined. They could play all the mind games they wanted: his was better, and he knew it. He didn't realize how cold he'd been until he began to warm and the tang of oil and electronics filled his nose.

Disgusting. He snorted and shook his head heartily in a fruitless attempt to clear the smell. The petrochemicals were going to give him cancer, he was sure of it, as he looked around. Snow thundered past the ramp they'd entered from to his right, and the vibrations of the craft—what was it his father had said? "My first time in a helo? Felt like I'd shit all my guts out my ass."

Ben completely understood what his father had meant while

his own eyes watered and he felt the jelly that filled them vibrate. Still, he tried to see what he could. Farther to his left and several feet away was a compartment—a med bay, he realized from the insignia on the clear window, beyond which had to be the cockpit itself. This was no regular transport, and he quickly assembled the facts. Modified Chinook, seating for almost a dozen along both walls with room, and a med bay…this was a CSAR, Combat Search and Rescue, vehicle. That meant they expected—

"Stand by for injuries." The announcement came from a speaker several feet above his head, harsh and metallic over and through the whine of the rotors, the words etching into the vibration of the craft, his elbows bouncing with it.

Ben looked curiously down the length he'd just frog-marched to watch the pigs scramble. His eye line went no higher than mid thigh as jumpsuited crew with helmets and insignia he could barely see raced out from what he could now confirm was their med bay as he caught glimpses of the interior. He wondered for a moment if it was Anna or whatever her name was, but didn't recognize the first person carried past him. *Serves the fuckers right*, he thought. *Fuck the Man!*

Even if his mission hadn't been completely successful, at least they *got* one of them! It filled him with a satisfied smugness as he shifted his shoulder and leaned back against the curved wall behind him to release some of the ache in the tendons.

There was a rush to and from the med bay door to receive the next casualty, and booted feet raced quickly past him, exchanging terse words, words he wouldn't have heard or understood anyway as he recognized Charli's jacket—he'd pulled it from the front closet before they'd left her apartment what seemed forever ago—on the limp form they loaded in.

"She's dead!" Cooper yelped from his perch as first the med bay door slammed shut, then the outer ramp closed. "That's not what's supposed to happen," he said, not even realizing he spoke or that someone approached and knelt next to him as he stared at the closed interior doors. The pain and discomfort were now nothing but background annoyances as he strained against his restraints to catch a better glimpse, but he could see only a pair of heads moving through the window. "That's not the plan."

"And what exactly *was* the plan?" Even though it was a barely heard shout, again more felt than heard despite the breath that warmed his ear, he knew that voice and he twisted with renewed surprise to gaze up past the black of her clothes and the length of her hair pushed to the side of her neck where the tendons stood in sharp relief, to once more see the woman he'd known as Anna Pendleton focused on him. His pale face was a study in confused shock, eyes darting between her and the gloved fingers wrapped around the SIG aimed right at his temple as the whine of the rotors overhead increased.

"All hands secure for take off in five," a male voice echoed over the rumble and thunder, and she nodded in automatic response. "If Charli's hurt—or worse," and her words spoken almost directly against his ear chilled him through the increased shake of the frame he sat against, "you're more than just an accessory to murder, Cooper. *You've* killed her. You."

In seconds she sat directly across from him, her focus and aim unwavering even through the lurch of liftoff.

He tried to stare her down, the enemy he mistakenly thought he'd defeated, but the bruise on her forehead stared back at him with purple reproach.

"You don't hit girls, son," his father had told him when he was a young boy. It was one of the days before his mother had left. His parents had yelled—screamed, really—for what seemed like hours, and afterward the door had truly and finally slammed shut, she on one side, he and his father on the other. Blood streamed down the side of his father's head, and bits of porcelain littered the ground by his feet.

"Why not, Daddy? She hit you first." He'd watched as his father wiped the blood from his face with the faded blue bandana that was almost a part of his jeans.

"Because you don't, son," his father had answered him with a heavy sigh. "You just don't."

It was in the gaze that accompanied the strange silence that Ben first noticed, really noticed, his father's eyes. "You don't hurt things that aren't as strong as you," he said while Ben stared into the muddled mix of green and brown, the whites that surrounded them a cloudy red. "Promise me you won't, Ben—not ever—I want you to be a *good* man."

Ben gave his word, the most solemn little-boy promise he could muster, and the words echoed back at him down through time as he stared at an accusing bruise. The color stood out in sharp relief to the pale skin that surrounded it, wasn't hidden by the tendrils of hair that drifted over it.

Suddenly Ben noticed, perhaps for the first time, perhaps since the initial few weeks when they'd first met, or perhaps it was simply that he finally remembered that the person who sat across from him was a woman and—it bothered him to admit it, made strange sensations crawl through his stomach and up his thighs that not even the vibrations of the helo could mute—a beautiful one at that.

He didn't know it was possible for the craft to shake even harder, but it did, and in his mind, her words—their lack of inflection, the flatness despite the shout of her voice—replayed over and over, while the darkened hardness and simple accusation of her eyes upon him sank in, created a unified message. And quite suddenly, he got it.

She'd held power over him, but hadn't abused it or him—not now nor in the past—and he was able to admit that Charli aside, shooting her with deadly intent was some very obvious provocation. Meanwhile, he…he'd broken his promise, the solemn vow he'd made to his father, that good man, to be a good man himself. Shame rose through his gut even as the full meaning of his long-ago promise, manifest and apparent, stared back at him, and he understood one more thing as he dropped his eyes from that unflinching gaze: she no longer cared whether he lived or died. And in that instant, buried in the ruins of broken promises and plans, his mission failed and his dream dying, neither did he.

❖

Cole Riven wasn't a man given to many idle fancies, but he'd always prided himself on having a certain amount of imagination, a bit of creativity, a special spark of something, he brought to his command, assumed it was the reason behind the good work he got from his crews. As a result of this thinking, it had been more than a mere shock for him to read the last psych eval he'd received. "Intelligent, but lacks creativity," he'd read, then read the bold black letters over again, realizing his feelings were actually hurt. "Old man, you don't *know* me," had been his first incredulous thought as he repeatedly reread those words. He had shared the results with his sister during their next conversation.

"Dude—they don't *know* you—that's just a whole bunch of crap," she'd said and reassured by the echo of his own thoughts, he laughed with her about it before they spoke of other things. Cole was a marine engineer and a Navy officer, but he was old school—"haze gray and away," as they said—a true sailor who went to sea, not a career administrator who kissed scrambled-egg ass on land.

Like any true sailor, when he was at sea, he dreamed of being on land, and when he was on land, he dreamed of being at sea. And then there were the nightmares that all true sailors shared: drowning and death, destruction of their ships. A Scheherazade of a dark and dripping doom sang in their dreams, every night, for a thousand and more. These were the fantasies and phantasms of sea men, of true mariners.

Yet these men and women who dreamed of death still answered the siren call of the sea, answered with an obsessive love unrivaled by any, wooed and loved her with a romantic intensity displayed in songs and sweat, imaginative feats of daring, a love that could and would one day be equaled and returned to these stalwart lovers by the only possible reward: her final salty embrace.

So when Cole woke before the alarm clock went off at 0600 local time on his "free" day with dreams of a fire in his head and his sister flashing through his mind, this man of reported small creativity paid attention. It left him with a nagging sense of unease, set him to showering and dressing quickly, determined to stop by his office to log onto his system and check in at home.

Besides, he hadn't heard from Charli in a couple of weeks, so when he entered his office, he sent mental greetings to pictures he'd taped to his screen, pictures of his parents, a snapshot his sister had sent him from a beach party she'd attended. "My kind of work function," she'd said in the e-mail that had accompanied the group shot.

He booted his computer, and despite the tingle of warning that haunted his head, he grinned back at the open smile she wore, the surfboard she leaned against on one side, and the woman whose hand rested on her waist on the other. He couldn't remember the name offhand—Andrea? Anna? Ada?—but Cole liked the way her eyes rested on his sister. He wondered idly if Charli had started dating her by now—it wasn't so much that he'd disliked Raven per se, it was simply that he thought her too shallow and somehow failing in some fundamental way to truly suit his sister.

That train of thought derailed as he typed in his passwords, and when his mail system opened, he was pleased but not too surprised, the nagging sense of concern momentarily dismissed, when he saw Charli's e-mail address pop up in his inbox. To his way of thinking, he'd thought of her so strongly because she'd thought of him. A strange thought to many, perhaps, but not to Cole, for in his experience, such happenings were common and more importantly, accurate.

He settled into his seat, filled with the happy anticipation of the friendly and fun exchange he'd have with his sister, and he smiled again at the picture taped to his screen as the message downloaded. The smile disappeared as he read, and he'd already picked up the phone before he hit the last line.

"I need Commander Ridgeway in Intelligence, and I need to arrange for an immediate transport back to the United States—I have a family emergency."

In that moment, Charli's gamble had paid off.

❖

URGENT: EYES ONLY

To: The Secretary
From: CLASSIFIED
Date: XX/XX/XXXX
Topic: FOX HUNT

Word has just been received that he has escaped the noose. Civilians and non-coms have been involved, as well as several Naval officers and one retired Army officer as follows:

Commander Cole Riven; Commander Earl Ridgeway; Civilian Charlotte Riven; Civilian Laura Pendowski; Lieutenant Eric Lundenman, Retired.

Injured have been brought to fourth level medical wing,

Need immediate approvals for investigations and testing after debriefing—internal housekeeping a probability. Please advise asap.

Sandy Corcorran

 # grep –n –A 12 "void.*send_reset"

TABULA RASA

It was warm, it was dark, and many things hurt. She didn't realize she'd made a small sound, but in the instant just before she did, a voice soothed her and a smooth hand gripped hers. "Shh…it's okay, you're okay. Sleep if you can."

Yes, she knew that voice, that touch. It was Anna's voice and Anna's touch. She remembered, because she'd fallen asleep to it earlier.

"Anna," she said, her throat tight and sore, her own voice no more than a strangely painful whisper she wasn't certain she heard herself as it burned through her neck. "I had the strangest dream…" She drifted, and images, disjointed, unreal, floated through her mind. There was the water, there was a fire. There was softness and warmth, there was a man and a gunshot—for a moment she struggled to breathe and she held the hand in hers tighter. The imperative that drove her turned to desperation. She wanted to sit, to open her eyes, and fueled by adrenaline, for the space of a few heartbeats, she did. "I dreamt you died, Anna—Coop, Ben Cooper, he—"

She didn't notice the IV lines that ran into her arm, and she registered the oxygen mask she wore only as an uncomfortable pressure across the bridge of her nose, overwhelmed as she was by the pain that tore through her chest, a heavy bruising pressure where there had only been ice before, the ache timed to her pulse. Although she felt their sting, she didn't recognize the tears that filled her eyes and made everything she saw waver further.

"It's okay, Charli, baby, I'm okay—I'm right here."

The humanoid shadow moving in her peripheral vision meant nothing to her as she reached for that voice, the only thing she could focus on, the only thing that mattered. "You're okay," she repeated as she grasped Anna's hand, and her face, the face Charli had been certain she'd never see again, her jade eyes large and luminous, swam into focus. She held on tightly, suddenly both convinced and terrified the sight would simply disappear if she let go. "You're okay."

If that was true, and the full green eyes before her, the touch of lips against her fingertips and the sense that flowed from them said it was, then there was something Charli had to tell Anna. It was big, super way big, and she had to tell Anna, she *had* to know, and Charli's mind grasped at the most familiar thing first. "I sent everything—the server, Cole, he—" Despite the panic that drove her, a heaviness held her down and warm softness invaded her again, weighed her eyes, set her back against the pillows.

"It's okay, Charli, I'm okay, it's all been taken care of."

Partially satisfied, Charli nodded against the softness that held her, that drew her back to dreams. Still, though, there was something…something more, something other…one more thing she had to say, much more important than anything else. She couldn't *think*, couldn't find the right words, she was sinking, everything was just so heavy, and all she had left floated up in a whisper—primal, childlike, nakedly honest in its simplicity. "Anna…don't go."

The familiar and welcome touch gentled along the back of her hand, against her fingers, and she barely felt the kiss that was again laid on them. "I'm not going anywhere, Charli. Go back to sleep. I'll be right here."

Soothed, comforted, Charli slid back into a dreamless sleep.

❖

Elaine sat there for hours, watching, waiting, for what she didn't know, and as she sat there, Charli's hand curled tighter in hers, her breathing aided by whatever voodoo it was that the medical people applied. Sedation, upped when Charli had come to briefly just a short while ago, very obviously confused, upset and panicked, still ran through her veins. As far as Elaine could understand, the intent was pain management so that the broken rib Charli had sustained, and the worst of the burns and the inhalation damage from the fire, would neither hurt nor disturb her.

It was frightening in ways Elaine could barely explain to herself, how still, how pale, how absolutely silent Charli was at that moment, when normally, Charli always seemed so much larger than life. Elaine could see her in her mind in a thousand different ways, a thousand different moments, the way Charli focused on her screen or on the shore, the energy that seemed barely contained when she walked, the fierce welcome in her eyes when challenged by work or waves.

She stroked Charli's hand, fit their fingers together, remembered how they'd played over her and how they felt stroking against her cheek, her chest, how they had so fully mapped her, drawn her entire body to vibrant life, then fit so beautifully within her.

Even in their most naked, most vulnerable moments together, Charli had never seemed fragile, not the way she did now. And the tears in her eyes when she'd woken for those brief moments… Elaine knew those tears were for Anna, and they had pierced through her with a force that made her breath catch and break, created an answering smart she couldn't and didn't try to stop. She realized she had never, not once, ever *really* seen Charli cry before, not so openly, not like this, the searing, tearing pain of it an actual physical presence, not even when—

Their last conversation once more played through Elaine's head as monitors hissed and beeped in the low light of the ward.

She stroked the shoulder under her fingertips, still afraid of reacting, of saying or asking too much, of breaking the fragile trust Charli had finally returned.

"How…" She swallowed and tried again. "How old were you?" She was proud of the careful neutrality she heard in her voice, the successful containment of the flood that swirled through her.

Charli shifted, a restive twitch to her shoulder, and Elaine released her, sensing that she needed the bit of distance. Still, though, their bodies connected along their lengths, Charli's thigh resting just over hers, and she neither pulled away nor protested when Elaine reached once more for her hand. She heard the breath Charli took as she curled her fingers through Elaine's.

"Seven, I think, just about eight when the whole thing started, nothing major, just some stupid touching shit, you know, no big deal, but that...it was the summer after my freshman year of high school," Charli told her, her tone very matter of fact. "*That* was on the overnight back from soccer camp. I, uh, I kinda ran away when Uncle Ted fell asleep, walked about a mile or so to some supermarket and found some nice mom-like lady to ask for a ride—"

"Jesus, Charli—you could've gotten hurt!" Elaine hadn't meant to say it, hadn't thought it consciously, but the words were out past the power of recall, past her determination to remain neutral, nonreactive.

She caught the wry grin Charli tossed at her. "I didn't think at the time it could have gotten too much worse, and I got home just fine."

In possession of herself once again, Elaine was grateful for the training that allowed her to place her emotions on the side as she absorbed information. She wondered what it cost Charli, who had certainly not been similarly trained to repeat the tale in such calm tones, so matter-of-factly, almost as if it had happened to someone else, as if it didn't matter. But it did, it *did*, it mattered a lot.

"I'm glad you did."

"You see, Anna, you have to understand..." Charli stopped and turned her head, shifting as she did so that instead of connect, they barely touched. She did not let go of Elaine's hand and Elaine gave her the lightest of encouraging returns of pressure, the physical reminder that she was there and listening—*hearing*—that she cared.

"He showed up at my parents' house, before they sent me to Virginia. He stood right at the door—he was drunk, he was *screaming*. He'd lost his job, my aunt divorced him. He said..." Charli took a deep breath and gazed down, staring fixedly at the space between them.

Elaine let the silence continue for the space of a few more

heartbeats before she sat up, then stretched careful fingers for Charli's face. She ached, ached with a fullness that threatened to burst through her ribs and swamp her beneath it.

"What, Char?" she asked, once more catching the amber glow of Charli's eyes with her own. "What did he say?"

Charli stared deeply into her, and for the first time, Elaine saw a glimmer of something under, and perhaps even outside of, the rigid façade of control, as Charli set her jaw. "He said he was trying to save me, save me from being a total dyke."

The lift of her chin, the slight squaring of her shoulders, the wall that Elaine could now really see rise in her eyes, half up and ready to close, she understood. The best defense was a good offense, and Charli was ready to go either way: let her in and stay there, or shut her out forever.

"I see," Elaine said with a small nod, accepting both the statement and the challenge. "What did your parents say to that?"

Charli withdrew her hand from Elaine's to run it through her hair as she moved away to sit. "My mom, she told him, 'I don't think you've done us any favors,' and a few days later, I was in Virginia Beach with my dad's brother and his family."

Away. They'd sent their daughter, hurt, injured, confused, away from her school, her friends, away from the family she needed probably then more than ever. Elaine thought of her own family, her parents and her siblings, what they would have said or done. Death, she was certain, would have swiftly visited anyone who'd dared to touch her that way, and since her father wasn't merely career Navy, but Naval Intelligence—Navy SEAL—she was also especially certain it would have been something creatively painful. Her sibs would have settled for a simple "take 'im out back and shoot 'im" solution, and to be completely honest, she knew that if it were her decision to make for any of them, she'd feel the same. But she also knew that under no circumstances would either he or her mother have sent her away—to anyone. They'd moved all over the country and, indeed, the world during her childhood, but unlike other military brats who she knew were parked with relatives, she and her sibs had been raised at home. Her parents were very clear on that: home wasn't a fixed address, it was wherever the family was, together.

Elaine allowed herself to once more visually measure the stress and strain in the way Charli held her arms, the strength in the angle of her neck, her shoulders, then finally, the soft vulnerability of her lips, the unflinching return of her eyes. Elaine finally saw what she had never seen, and never really understood before, not with the same cold and crystalline clarity: Charli was alone.

It made her want to pull Charli into her arms and hold her until it simply went away. She didn't know who she wanted to tell more—Charli or herself—that in some fundamental way she wasn't alone, not anymore.

Elaine didn't realize she sighed as she reached for Charli. Something intrinsic—a part of her own base foundation—had permanently changed. "Babe, you've got to be cold," she said quietly as she drew Charli in, felt the slide of skin on skin, the fierce pulse against her chest so hard she couldn't tell who it belonged to. She felt the shiver that raced through Charli's frame before she settled comfortably, and the whisper of lips against her own neck.

"I'm not—not right now." The warm breath that dusted across her throat made her close her eyes *as she filled her arms as much as she could.*

The light sound of foot tread brought her back to the present and as a nurse came in to check on her patient, Elaine once more kissed Charli's hand and hoped that somehow, in some way, Charli knew she was still there.

❖

BB84 Secure Session - - Loss 0

```
04:00 tRstN01:    ChknMn interrogated,

04:01 tRstN01:    agents debriefed
```

```
04:02 tRstN01:    awaiting final report

04:03 tRstN01:    Orders?

04:04 tRstN01:

04:05 tRstN01:

04:06 DsrtFx:     what about the girl? Riven.

04:07 DsrtFx:

04:08 tRstN01:    Serious, but no longer critical.

04:09 tRstN01:    In med bay.

04:10 DsrtFx:     Alone?

04:11 DsrtFx:

04:12 tRstN01:    Harper is with her.

04:13 tRstN01:    Commander Riven to be flown in -

04:14 tRstN01:    standard family emergency protocol

04:15 DsrtFx:     Orders are as follows:

04:16 DsrtFx:     the plan still in effect

04:17 DsrtFx:     continue to Ground Zero

04:18 DsrtFx:     notify the others

04:19 tRstN01:    Done. Stand-by for info.

04:20 tRstN01:    New intel on I-team designation
```

BB84 Secure Session TERMINATED

John smiled to himself as the snow and salt air flew into his face while he leaned against the railing and reflected on the last bit of intel he'd received from another of his inside operatives. He stared at the sun as it rose above the curve of the Atlantic. That, he thought, could not have gone better. On the face of it, it might seem like a partial loss, but in fact, it had been in many ways a beautiful, and if he didn't mind saying himself, brilliant, success.

And really, why shouldn't it have been, considering who he himself had been modeled on. Like all men, or at least, all the boys who'd grown to men that he'd known and worked with—his peers— he had a deep fascination with the near-fully-global conflict that had not only changed the European map, but had also changed the way war was fought in general. World War II had other side effects: it had not only initiated the Cold War but had also jump-started the technological age the world would subsequently enter.

Those important things aside, though, John found himself particularly focused on the men who'd led the various countries and their campaigns: Eisenhower. MacArthur. Nimitz. Chester. Patton. These were the names of American men, American heroes. Then there were the Brits: Churchill, Chamberlain, Montgomery and his most famous opponent, the best mind, the soldier's soldier, a man of reputed honor and decency, the Desert Fox himself, Erwin Johannes Eugen Rommel.

He fascinated a young John whose name was so similar to his, and in his mind John wondered things that could not be proved. His own father's family was from Isonzo, Italy, and born in 1918… and John had learned that in 1917 Rommel had fought, then been a prisoner of war, in Isonzo. Of course, amazing as he was, Rommel escaped and returned to Germany in two weeks. It was possible, John thought when he'd learned that, it was within the realm of possibility that their name, the family surname… The thought, the "what if" tantalized him as a boy, even though his father refused to answer any of his questions about what had happened over there, and forbade him from asking his Nona, who spoke no English, any questions about any of it.

"Your grandfather was killed in the war, Johnny. You don't want to be making Nona cry about it," his parents told him whenever curiosity got the better of him.

Still, John felt no guilt over admiring the Nazi hero, because as Churchill himself had said upon learning of his death, "He also deserves our respect, because, although a loyal German soldier, he came to hate Hitler and all his works, and took part in the conspiracy to rescue Germany by displacing the maniac and tyrant. For this, he paid the forfeit of his life."

The combination of childhood wondering and actual history inspired him to be a better soldier, a better leader, and the supposed mystery of it lent itself further to things he noticed and heard as a man.

True or not, the conceit had brought him very far, and this operation had only confirmed for him that he was at the very least the spiritual, if not necessarily the physical, inheritor of the Desert Fox mantle.

Tonight, John had learned quite a bit that would make him even better prepared for the next step. Soon he'd know what the I designation was, and, hopefully even better, how many and to whom it had been applied. He already had his suspicions, and they had everything to do with the Company projects he'd uncovered.

He had what he needed: a goodly supply of saxitoxin, a side project that Chul-Moo had been working on. It was even better than the various infectious agents they'd originally discussed; there would be a certain poetry, a sense of justice, in employing it. Saxitoxin was a by-product of the red-tide algae bloom that was a result of the poisoned oceans, and found its way into the human food chain via mollusks and the fish that ate them. It was colorless and odorless, and temperature did nothing to affect its toxicity level, which gave it a huge range of applications.

As he had explained to Charli, it acted quickly, sometimes within minutes, and would leave its recipients in an aware but mellow state as their bodies shut down. It wasn't really their fault they were born, they didn't need to suffer while they were erased.

The erasing of mistakes... He shook his head and chuckled under his breath as he made his way along the starboard side of the deck, past the anterior cabin and through the door that would lead to his berth below deck. In another hour the ship would arrive at predesignated coordinates and he'd switch to another ship, a commercial vessel that would take him to Santos, in São Paulo, Brazil. He wasn't starting over, no, not at all. He was merely continuing…somewhat differently. The only thing that had changed from the original plan was that he no longer had the company he thought he would.

Cooper had ultimately broken—John had expected that, although he did not yet know how deep the break had gone; the silence surrounding what John was certain had been a preliminary but thorough interrogation was, for the moment, absolute. It didn't matter: Cooper had been taken care of, and the second report John received confirmed that bit of intelligence along with the other information it gave. Harper had performed her expected role admirably—perhaps not from a Company perspective, but certainly from his. He'd expected her to come for Charli, to not merely sit back and let the teams take over—and she had.

Whether she actively knew it or not, she'd earned herself a higher ranking among her peers and even some of her superiors; she'd been the only one on her team to get so close to him, and the way she had accomplished it—he shook his head. That…that had taken not only a large degree of creativity, but quite some internal fortitude.

He'd been more than merely impressed by the way she'd handled her access to the island when he'd learned of it; it was not a route most would have considered in her position; many would prefer to either go wait everything out at a predesignated safe site or to simply accompany the extraction team, and it gave him a sense of satisfaction to confirm still further that his deduction of her feelings for Charli had been accurate. The last line of his report told him that as soon as Harper had been permitted, she'd fled her debriefing to be with Charli, who was under close observation in a medical unit. He wondered if any of Charli's family had been notified, then decided that more than likely her brother would have been informed immediately.

He shook his head as he once more removed his coat, placing it carefully on the foot of the bunk. Charli, oh that Charli…she'd played him brilliantly, he admitted as he inspected his firearm, set the safety, then placed it securely into an ankle holster. He hadn't suspected a thing until she'd already pulled the matchbook from her pocket.

She'd done exactly what she should have: she hacked, then she cracked his brain. And in doing so, she had proven once and for all that the experiment had been a roaring success. She had read him, then anticipated him. She had one of the final markers, the ability to deduce another's mental state, and quite probably, the ability to project the one she wanted to. He, who was schooled and well practiced in reading body language, tone, posture, had been completely taken in.

He wondered which, if any, of the other abilities she had. It was paramount, now, that he once again recover her into his custody—not to control her, but to protect her. She was even now in the belly of the beast that ruled the world, and if the Company ever had even the slightest clue…he knew how ruthlessly she'd be exploited.

He was glad now that he'd followed his own instincts, had literally shoved her over Chul-Moo and into the tool shed before he'd ducked behind another bench and made good his own escape. Not for nothing that he'd memorized not only the path he needed but the substructure. He knew where the newer wall had been built over the old ventilation system. In the confusion, and with the assistance he expected, no one would notice until he'd already crawled down it—and they hadn't.

It had worked perfectly, and as he reviewed how the operation had played out, he was pleased with how unexpectedly well—all things considered—it had gone. He had no concerns for Chul-Moo, his friend would be fine; his knowledge and abilities were crucial to national security interests, and even if he was forced to work under more direct supervision, he'd be given the budget as well as the resources he needed to continue. They'd use intermediaries to get in touch again—nothing any different than the majority of their past communications.

But now that he was absolutely certain about Charli—that in of itself was a prize that made the small losses of the evening pale into virtual insignificance. It meant there were others, it meant the experiment had been—still was—a success, and most importantly, it meant he was *right*. He was still on track, and Charli, not just her records, but also her abilities as he'd witnessed them, proved it once and for all. She would be the standard by which he could evaluate the rest, and that alone meant she was important to his plans; John knew that as surely as he knew the strength and speed of his firearms, the formidability of his mind, and the facts he'd spent years researching.

Harper was with Charli... He considered rapidly. It was obvious her cover with the Treas had been compromised beyond repair and it was possible, and more than likely probable, that her emotional connection to Charli had ruined her for further deep-cover work. As to what Charli might feel for her in return—that didn't matter, he realized, and his eyes widened as it all fell into place for him. Charli had proven that she was at heart an altruist, willing to sacrifice herself for the unworthy, the so-called *people*, out of a misguided sense of ethics and a misplaced compassion. Those were creatures she didn't even know.

He smiled into the dim light of his cabin. If that was what she was willing to do for strangers, then it was easy to imagine what she might sacrifice for those she knew—no matter what she might or might not feel for them. John, the Desert Fox, knew exactly what he needed to do next, and knew he didn't have to risk his operation to accomplish it, either. The smile on his face invaded his chest, made it swell with satisfaction.

He was the Desert Fox, and he would *make* her come to him, fully aware, and very willing. She would come, because she would feel she had to: he would have Harper.

char *create_memory()

GLASS ONION

It was no more than a few days before Charli was fully alert for more than a few moments at a time, and Elaine wasn't certain if it was luck or not that she was not the first person Charli consciously saw. She'd certainly wanted to be there.

There had been interviews and reviews, briefings and debriefings. Cooper had been sitting in a cell, a cozy one, to be certain. His information and his skills would contribute greatly to future investigations, but first, he was to show and then correct the modifications he'd performed at Whitestone.

Elaine would never forget the way she had felt as she stared down past the barrel and at the spot, right dead-center, of Cooper's brow. It would have been easy, so damn easy…and Cooper had committed treason. The calm she had felt as she contemplated putting a bullet into another human being at point-blank range was something she had never felt before, she'd never felt so detached from action and outcome…it simply didn't matter. There was only one thing that mattered, and as soon as her debriefing was over, that was where she'd fled, ignoring the glances—curious, sympathetic, or merely observant—when she'd made her hasty escape.

Elaine sighed and shook her head as she crossed the corridor to the elevator that would take her down to the level she wanted to visit.

Before any of Cooper's information could be used in a beneficial way, the official story was that some idiot had neglected to mandate a twenty-four-hour watch and—she couldn't help the shiver that shook her shoulders—it had been gruesome.

The report said that Cooper had sawed through his own carotid artery with the zipper of his jeans after scrawling "Die Free" on the wall, probably with the first bit of blood he'd drawn. They'd found him slumped over on the floor of the cell, blood still warm on the floor and flowing down his neck. The team had done everything they could, but he'd already lost too much blood and the jagged tear he'd opened in his flesh couldn't be closed in time. She didn't know what they would do with the body. She didn't care, either.

The fact that it had happened at two minutes to midnight, the same time Romello's watch had been set to—she knew that was not a coincidence.

Whitestone's Eric Lundenman had been flown in. He had in essence lost three mission-critical employees. Discussions were underway and Elaine suspected they involved asking Whitestone to voluntarily participate as part of a watchdog system.

Charli was going to be given what were supposed to be choices—either work directly for the Company within analytics and cryptology as a civilian, or work for the new DC division of Whitestone, and report to the Company. If she refused, they would use her brother as leverage since his ratings and clearances depended upon, among other things, the reliability, loyalty, and patriotism of his friends and family. Elaine's mind took a cynical turn—she knew what they would do. If those facts didn't impress Charli in the right way, all they had to do was simply imply that her choices might affect his deployments—and one never knew for certain where a sniper might hide.

Elaine had met the young commander.

"I want to meet the agent who got my sister out of there," she heard him say as he approached the sick bay. She was reluctant to stand, to let go of Charli's hand, protocols and formalities be damned. She wouldn't. "Your brother's here, baby," she whispered against the fingertips that barely stirred within hers.

"How is she?" he asked, his voice hushed, his steps quiet as he entered.

"She'll be all right," Elaine answered before she touched her lips to Charli's hand. She let it go reluctantly as she stood to face him as he neared. "A broken rib, some superficial burns. It was the heat and inhalation that really did the damage," she told him, realizing he probably already knew even as she spoke. "The light sedation's more for pain management than anything else. You must be Commander Cole Riven," she said, not needing to read the nameplate below the proud ribbons as she took in the broad uniformed shoulders, the eyes so like his sister's that creased under the brim of his hat as he stared at the bed, or the lips that quirked the same way Charli's did.

"And you're Agent Harper?" he asked as they shook hands, his eyes fixed upon the still form of his sister. "Thank you," he said quietly. "I just..." He stared at her finally, a frown of concentration creating a deep line in his brow. "I'm sorry—have we met before?"

Elaine quickly reviewed the official possibilities, then the unofficial ones. "No, I don't believe so," she told him, even as a likely scenario occurred to her. "I'll leave you to your visit, Commander," she said quietly, and walked to the door.

"You're her coworker, aren't you," he stated more than asked as she grasped the handle. Her back stiffened as she realized he knew. "You're the one in that picture, the surfer she's friends with. Ann. Anna something, right?"

Well, at least she had guessed the right scenario. She turned back to face him and instead saw that he sat carefully on the foot of the bed, his body between her and Charli. She wondered if he was aware that his body language screamed that he was shielding his sister even as he delicately stroked the hair from her brow before reaching for her hand, then decided that conscious of it or not, it was his absolute right and his oath-sworn duty as Charli's brother, as an officer.

She took a breath, then let it out slowly. "Yes," she answered simply. There was nothing else to say, and she waited for his response.

"Does she know?" The words were soft, almost a whisper, as he reached again to smooth the hair that lay raggedly across Charli's brow.

"I'm not—I don't know," she admitted as she stepped back in. "I don't think so."

She watched as Commander Riven removed his officer's cap and placed it on his knee, then ran a hand through the short scrub of hair that was the same color and texture as his sister's before he twisted his head to see her directly.

"I'm not a stupid man, Agent. As grateful as I am for what you've done, you may well have wrecked your career, but instead of kissing brass ass and glad-handing all over Washington," he shared a brief grin with her, "you're *here*. So," he said as he shifted slightly, "let me try again. Does she *know*?" His eyes were unblinking as they stared into hers.

Elaine stared back at him, not fully certain if he meant her cover or something else entirely. His eyes, eyes just like Charli's, did what hers did, conveyed hints of secret knowledge, searched deeply for answers with an assurance they'd be found.

"Commander Riven, I'm not certain I know what you—"

"It's Cole," he interrupted, "and please," he gestured with his free hand to the seat she'd left, "stay. If the gov hasn't chased you away, I won't, either."

She crossed the last few steps. "Thanks," she told him as she sat once more, and not caring what his opinion was or what he thought he knew, she again curled her fingers through Charli's.

Their eyes met and Cole gave her the briefest shadow of a grin before returning his gaze to the still form they both watched. Elaine and Cole sat together in concerned companionship the rest of the night, *before their respective duties forced them to leave.*

This was her first truly free moment since that time, and when she stood in the doorway, she found Charli standing by the false window, staring into the light that simulated a hazy day. Body language told her that Charli was aware of her presence, but she made no gesture of greeting.

"Where exactly are we?" she asked Elaine flatly. The burns on her face and hands had healed nicely, and she no longer needed the medications nor the monitoring she'd been under. In fact, other than the broken rib she'd suffered from flying debris, Charli was, thankfully, physically fine and would be moved to another section of the complex until her job decision was made.

Elaine didn't know what Charli had been told, but she knew she herself would never lie to her again—there'd be no more equivocation.

"DC—Washington, DC," Elaine said quietly as she fully entered the room.

"That's not real sunlight, is it." It wasn't a question, it was just another flat statement of fact.

Elaine sighed quietly. Charli refused to look at her. She hated it, but she understood it. "No. It's not."

"So where are we?"

She sat carefully on the chair near the bed, the same chair she'd spent those rare free moments in, the same chair she'd held Charli's hand from, had watched her sleep, had spoken to her and, occasionally, to her brother, during the frighteningly chill silence that Charli had been shrouded within during that critical time after their arrival.

Elaine let her breath out slowly. "We're four levels belowground—in the Pentagon med bay. All the rooms in this wing are lit that way because it supposedly aids in recovery by maintaining normal circadian rhythms."

She watched as Charli nodded and absorbed the information. "Below this is what they call techno-wonderland— where you've been offered the position with analytics and cryptology." She didn't know why she added that, but she did. "I'll more than likely be working there, too, listening to and decrypting the chatter."

She saw rather than heard the breath Charli took before she finally turned away from the false daylight and faced her. "Back in Virginia, then," she said with a small shake of her head. Charli leaned back against the sill, rested her hands along the ledge.

There was a lot implied in that statement, and Elaine now knew what some of it was. It hurt her to hear it, to know she'd been a part—even if it wasn't her fault, not really—of bringing Charli back to a place she hadn't wanted to return to, should never have had to go to in the first place.

The thought that filled Elaine's head began as an annoying insect hum through her brain before it became a burning roar that filled her, sent an unfamiliar scalding mix of anger and shame flowing down her neck, her arms.

The last time Charli had been in Virginia for any length of time had been after she'd been hurt, a core violated beyond seeming repair. This time, she was here, *again*, because other people had made decisions, had taken actions, that… Anger at the unfairness, anger with herself fired the flame that flowed under her skin.

She *had* fucked up—and not because Romello had not been caught, not because she hadn't maintained her cover with the Treas. Charli was here, in this place she didn't want to be, hurt in ways she shouldn't have been, because Elaine herself had not been brave enough to tell the Company to use another operative, nor strong enough to tell Charli the things she should have what now seemed like forever ago. She'd tried to play hero, but instead…

Once more, whether Elaine wanted to acknowledge it or not, and her brain insisted that she must, Charli had been betrayed by someone she trusted—and the person she had trusted was—

"And what do I call you?" The words were soft, low, and cut straight through Elaine's thoughts as she watched Charli. The person she'd gotten so close to, had held so tightly, had revealed the deepest parts of herself to, now held herself a thousand miles away, a distance and disconnect she felt as a cold breeze on her own skin. Elaine did her best to read what she could in what she saw.

The bruises, already made almost invisible by the light touch of makeup, would eventually fade even more, the burns were already more than partially healed, and somehow, Charli had managed to commandeer a haircut so that her hair hung in long spikes over her forehead and just past her eyes, shorter than ever at the sides in a way that further highlighted the angle of her cheeks, left on prominent display the sensual curve of her lips. She'd also had some of her things either sent, or more than likely replaced, and the shirt dress she wore fit her perfectly, open just far enough, but not too far, the rich deep hunter green hue of it a perfect contrast to the pale skin it rested against. Even the suede boots she wore, a rich and warm color that matched her eyes and hugged her calves, did nothing to hide her—this was Charli as Elaine had met her, Charli as she'd always known her, her façade intact, secrets once more well hidden. This was Charli as the world saw her: in charge.

"You can still call me Anna if you'd like," Elaine offered, her voice pitched to match. "It is…it was my grandmother's name, and Anna *is* actually my middle name."

The slightest of quirks lifted the corner of Charli's lips before it was gone. "It's really Elaine Harper—*Agent* Harper, though."

Elaine nodded again in agreement as tension grew in the room, grew between them, and Elaine stood, shrugging her shoulders, hoping some of the pressure of it would fall from them. It intensified instead.

"Charli, I swear I never…I tried to—" Elaine began as she stepped closer, but Charli interrupted her with a wave that warded her off.

"You tried to tell me, I know. I…I don't know what I thought, that maybe you didn't really want to, or to let you know it was okay, it could wait until you did or…" She shook her head, and Elaine followed her instinct and took her hand. Charli's eyes finally met hers for a moment when she did. "Or that it would end up like this." The words were low, quiet, barely more than a whisper, but in the clasp of hands the cold of her skin eased, and in that whisper Elaine heard something. She spoke to that.

"Charli," she began again and once more caught her gaze, "you have to know that you and I"—she held her hand even tighter, trying to communicate through her very skin—"that was *real*, Char. It was so beautiful, so very special," she said, repeating her own words and Charli's, hoping that in the repetition, Charli would not only know that she'd been truly heard, but also that Elaine had not forgotten. "Very special, and very, very real."

Charli stared down at their hands, lightly stroked Elaine's palm with her fingertips. She gazed back into Elaine's eyes. "I know that," she said quietly, "I just—"

The knock against the frame of the partially opened door and the throat clearing that accompanied it caught both their attention, and Charli gave Elaine's hand a final squeeze and a small sad smile that disappeared quickly. "I need a little time."

"Hey there, Charli girl!"

"Cole!"

"I got here as soon as I could get away," she heard him say, the words but not the visible affection and concern muted as he wrapped his arms around his sister. "Never any halfways with you, are there?" he said against her temple before he kissed it.

"Can we go surfing *now*?" Charli asked as she returned his hold, and Cole laughed, then said something quietly in her ear.

Elaine did not hear Charli's response, murmured as it was into the broad uniformed shoulder in their embrace. All she could hear was the deafening pound in her ears, the throb that accompanied the tearing within. Elaine was once more torn. She was happy for Charli, happy and relieved that in the midst of all the confusion, hurt, and things unfamiliar, that here was something, *someone*, not only familiar but comfortable for her, safe.

But Elaine hurt, too, a hurt that beat and pulsed with the same complete fullness she had worked and wanted, physically held and lo— It was, Elaine thought, a hell of a time to realize that she loved her. She couldn't tell Charli, not now when she herself had just figured it out, not now when the ghosts that haunted Charli's head had been brought to frightening life again, and were probably connected to—

"My apologies, Agent," Cole said as he straightened, partially releasing his sister, "I didn't realize—"

"That's quite unnecessary, Commander," she interrupted, suddenly fully aware that as much as she might know about him and about Charli, or even his easy acceptance of her when they'd first met, she had no real place here. "I quite understand your priorities."

"Thanks," he said as he reached for her hand. "I know you do." The firm handshake and grin were so like Charli's that she found herself at a loss for words, and she almost missed the quick wink he tossed at her.

Another knock sounded, this time accompanied by a voice and head that appeared past the frame. "Hi, I'm Jim Holloway, and I'm here to—" The young clerk's face flushed a deep red, highlighted by his sandy hair, when he saw everyone in the room.

Elaine was deaf to his stammered apologies for the interruption, nor did she hear the words spoken between him and Charli as she moved to the door.

She stood there, mute, watched as Charli peered over her shoulder to catch her eyes. Elaine stared into them for a long moment, a silent apology in her own until Charli broke the contact between them and turned away to take the arm her brother offered.

Cole, his relief a visible flash across his face once he had his sister safe on his arm, gave the agent the appropriate and required salute.

"Agent," he said, and his voice was deep and formal as his hand touched the brim of his cap.

"Commander," she acknowledged with a nod, then brother and sister followed the clerk out.

She stood alone a moment, the sounds of their footsteps in her ears even as they retreated. And as much as she hurt, hurt in ways she didn't know she could, Elaine understood, she really did. Old wounds had been touched on, new ones had been made, and Charli... She watched Charli walk away. *I need time*, she'd said, not *good-bye*. Elaine felt a growing sense of determination solidify in her chest. She'd gotten through to Charli, had touched the *X* once before; Elaine was certain she could do it again—she *had* to, she *needed* to, and when she did, this time? She wouldn't let go.

❖

URGENT: EYES ONLY

To: The Secretary
From: READ ONCE AND DESTROY
Date: XX/XX/XXXX
Topic: FOX HUNT

Leak of I-team intel accomplished. Pendowski's involvement minimal—continued surveillance for undetermined length; Charlotte Riven *must* become internal—Commander Riven's deployment can be used as leverage here. Both to be further investigated for I-Team use, Charlotte possibly Gate Team; recommend Harper for immediate Gate Team training subject to standard acclimatization protocol/timeline. Charlotte Riven still acquisition target for rogue agent. Can relationship to Agent Harper be leveraged to flush him out?

READ ONCE AND DESTROY

READ ONCE AND DESTROY

READ ONCE AND DESTROY

READ ONCE AND DESTROY

READ ONCE AND DESTROY

READ ONCE AND DESTROY

About the Author

JD Glass, author of Lambda Literary finalist *Punk Like Me*, *Punk and Zen*, Lambda Literary and Ben Franklin Award finalist *Red Light*, the well-received *American Goth*, and *X*, lives in the city of New York with her beloved partner.

When she's not writing or drawing, she's the lead singer (as well as alternately guitarist and bassist) in NY's Life Underwater (myspace.com/lifeunderwateronline and nimbitmusic.com/lifeunderwater), which also keeps her pretty busy.

If she's not creating something (she swears she's way too busy to ever be bored), she sleeps. Right.

Works in progress include the graphic presentation of *Sakura Gun* (trans: Cherry Blossom Warrior)—related to, yet separate from, both the Punk and the Goth series, beginning with *Sakura Gun* (London), a forty-page origin-story in the anthology *Yuri Monogatari 6*, the graphic novel *Sakura Gun*, and a couple o' few other things with ALC Publishing. Oh, and she's in the studio, recording a new album.

Further information can be found at www.myspace.com/jdglass, where she plays virtual DJ, shares blogs, and reviews of all sorts of fun things as well as showing the occasional flash of wit, while tunes can be heard and downloaded at nimbitmusic.com/lifeunderwater. And check out boldstrokesbooks.com and yuricon.org.

Books Available From Bold Strokes Books

Sistine Heresy by Justine Saracen. Adrianna Borgia, survivor of the Borgia court, presents Michelangelo with the greatest temptations of his life while struggling with soul-threatening desires for the painter Raphaela. (978-1-60282-051-7)

Radical Encounters by Radclyffe. An out-of-bounds, outside-the-lines collection of provocative, superheated erotica by award-winning romance and erotica author Radclyffe. (978-1-60282-050-0)

Thief of Always by Kim Baldwin & Xenia Alexiou. Stealing a diamond to save the world should be easy for Elite Operative Mishael Taylor, but she didn't figure on love getting in the way. (978-1-60282-049-4)

X by JD Glass. When X-hacker Charlie Riven is framed for a crime she didn't commit, she accepts help from an unlikely source—sexy Treasury Agent Elaine Harper. (978-1-60282-048-7)

The Middle of Somewhere by Clifford Henderson. Eadie T. Pratt sets out on a road trip in search of a new life and ends up in the middle of somewhere she never expected. (978-1-60282-047-0)

Paybacks by Gabrielle Goldsby. Cameron Howard wants to avoid her old nemesis Mackenzie Brandt but their high school reunion brings up more than just memories. (978-1-60282-046-3)

Uncross My Heart by Andrews & Austin. When a radio talk show diva sets out to interview a female priest, the two women end up at odds and neither heaven nor earth is safe from their feelings. (978-1-60282-045-6)

Fireside by Cate Culpepper. Mac, a therapist, and Abby, a nurse, fall in love against the backdrop of friendship, healing, and defending one's own within the Fireside shelter. (978-1-60282-044-9)

Green Eyed Monster by Gill McKnight. Mickey Rapowski believes her former boss has cheated her out of a small fortune, so she kidnaps the girlfriend and demands compensation—just a straightforward abduction that goes so wrong when Mickey falls for her captive. (978-1-60282-042-5)

Blind Faith by Diane and Jacob Anderson-Minshall. When private investigator Yoshi Yakamota and the Blind Eye Detective Agency are hired to find a woman's missing sister, the assignment seems fairly mundane—but in the detective business, the ordinary can quickly become deadly. (978-1-60282-041-8)

A Pirate's Heart by Catherine Friend. When rare book librarian Emma Boyd searches for a long-lost treasure map, she learns the hard way that pirates still exist in today's world—some modern pirates steal maps, others steal hearts. (978-1-60282-040-1)

Trails Merge by Rachel Spangler. Parker Riley escapes the high-powered world of politics to Campbell Carson's ski resort—and their mutual attraction produces anything but smooth running. (978-1-60282-039-5)

Dreams of Bali by C.J. Harte. Madison Barnes worships work, power, and success, and she's never allowed anyone to interfere—that is, until she runs into Karlie Henderson Stockard. Aeros EBook (978-1-60282-070-8)

The Limits of Justice by John Morgan Wilson. Benjamin Justice and reporter Alexandra Templeton search for a killer in a mysterious compound in the remote California desert. (978-1-60282-060-9)

Designed for Love by Erin Dutton. Jillian Sealy and Wil Johnson don't much like each other, but they do have to work together—and what they desire most is not what either of them had planned. (978-1-60282-038-8)

Calling the Dead by Ali Vali. Six months after Hurricane Katrina, NOLA Detective Sept Savoie is a cop who thinks making a relationship work is harder than catching a serial killer—but her current case may prove her wrong. (978-1-60282-037-1)

Shots Fired by MJ Williamz. Kyla and Echo seem to have the perfect relationship and the perfect life until someone shoots at Kyla—and Echo is the most likely suspect. (978-1-60282-035-7)